Ouha,
King of the Apes

Ouha,
King of the Apes

by
Félicien Champsaur

translated, annotated and introduced by
Brian Stableford

A Black Coat Press Book

Introduction

Ouha, roi des singes by Félicien Champsaur, here translated as *Ouha, King of the Apes*, was originally published in
Paris by Librairie Charpentier et Fasquelle in 1923. It thus
intermediate, in temporal terms, between the first publication
of Edgar Rice Burroughs' *Tarzan of the Apes* (1912) and the
release of the film *King Kong* (1933). It is also thematically
intermediate between the two, and might be regarded, if the
three texts are regarded as parts of an evolutionary sequence,
as the "missing link" between the two.

That thematic link might be more than merely coincidental. Although *Tarzan of the Apes* was not issued in French
translation until 1926, the first (silent) film version, released in
1918 would have been shown in Paris, and Champsaur would
almost certainly have been aware of the character and his bur-
geoning success in the U.S.A. Edgar Wallace, who wrote the
original script for the movie that became *King Kong*—
although illness and death prevented him from seeing the project through—spent a good deal of time in Paris and moved in
the same social circles as Champsaur; even if the two were not
acquainted, it is entirely possible that Wallace knew about the
existence of *Ouha*. Although the common reference of the last
lines of *Ouha* and *King Kong* could certainly be coincidental,
following logically from the inclination of the common elements of their underlying plots, but even if that is the case, it is
an intriguing echo.

Ouha was a new departure in Champsaur's career and
was written at a pivotal moment therein. He had been a highly
successful writer before the outbreak of the Great War, re-
nowned for mildly salacious novels about Parisian high society, simultaneously celebrating and lamenting its decadence.
The war interrupted his career decisively, although he was
able to resume publication in 1916, when the government decided that the publication of new novels might be good for

morale, provided that they were ideologically sound. After two propaganda pieces issued in 1916 Champsaur was able to augment a novel he was obviously written before the outbreak of the war, *Les Ailes de l'homme* (1917)[1], with a new section set during the war in order to adapt it as propaganda. Once the war was over, however, he immediately moved in a radically new direction, producing the six-volume "social epic" *L'Empereur des pauvres* (1920-22) (*The Emperor of the Poor*)—clearly an attempt to establish himself as a serious literary writer rather than a shallow entertainer. It had some success, and was filmed in 1922, but it probably made less money than his pre-war works, and cannot have done much to restore the erosion of his fortune by the effects of the war and the several years when he had not published anything.

In that context, *Ouha* seems like a blatant attempt to make some quick money. It is a slapdash novel, which obviously had no second draft and does not appear to have been proofread; characters' names change arbitrarily, and there are several breaks in the continuity of the plot, the most glaring of which could easily have been fixed with the aid of a blue pencil. If the novel really was a response to the success of the Tarzan movie, Ouha's relationship with Mabel Smith being intended as a parody of Tarzan's relationship with Jane Porter, the project might—given that *L'Empereur des pauvres* had just been filmed[2]—have been originally envisaged as a film, but there is also a possibility that it was imagined as a different kind of book. It is possible, too, that Champsaur might have written it to commission; the book's copyright notice is in the name of its publisher, Eugène Fasquelle. It advertises no less than three illustrators—Chimot, Jacquelux and Lorenzi—although there actually only four illustrations, confined to slick double endpapers, while the body of the text is printed on

---

[1] tr. as *The Human Arrow*, Black Coat Press, ISBN 978-1-61227-045-6.
[2] 1922, directed by René Leprince, starring Léon Mathot and Gina Relly.

much poorer paper—an oddity that suggests in itself that the original plan might have been more ambitious than the eventual product.

Champsaur and Fasquelle knew all three of the illustrators well; Jacquelux had illustrated several of Champsaur's previous books from the publisher, including two of his pre-war best-sellers, and had worked in collaboration with Lorenzi on books published by Fasquelle. Édouard Chimot was then just reaching the peak of a career that would eventually prove by far the most successful of the three, and was becoming more significant as an editor of illustrated books than as an illustrator. It is unlikely that Chimot actually drew any of the four illustrations, but his involvement suggests that the project might initially have been pitched—unsuccessfully—to publishers as a more lavishly illustrated book. The passages in the book that relate to the four illustrations are superfluous to the plot, and were probably written around the pictures, and there are several other gratuitous passages that might conceivably have been included to support projected illustrations.

If the illustrations had originally been intended to be more extensive and lavish, that inspiration could have been taken from either or both of *Ouha*'s most prestigious thematic predecessors in the French language: Léon Gozlan's classic *Les Émotions de Polydore Marasquin* (1856; tr. in various editions as *The Emotions of Polydore Marasquin*, *A Man Among the Monkeys* and *Monkey Island*), and Albert Robida's *Voyages très extraordinaires de Saturnin Farandoul* (1879)[3]. The former, which tells the story of a human cast away on an island in the Far East populated by various species of primates, who improvises a means of becoming their king for a while, was abundantly illustrated in volume form by various hands, including Gustave Doré; the second, whose first part, *Le Roi des singes* (tr. as "The Monkey King") tells the story of a castaway child raised by "orangutans" who becomes a kind

---

[3] tr. as *The Adventures of Saturnin Farandoul*, Black Coat Press, ISBN 978-1-934543-61-0.

of superman and eventually leads an army of apes on a Napoleonic conquest of Australia, was lavishly illustrated in its
part-work version by the author. Champsaur, Fasquelle and
Chimot were probably familiar with both works—*Ouha* re-
produces motifs found in both—and recognized them as significant, if entirely accidental, antecedents of Tarzan.

At any rate, the version of *Ouha* that was actually published was a more downmarket product than either of those
august predecessors; if it was intended as money-making exercise, however, it does seem to have achieved its object; the
list of the author's previous publications in *Nuit de fête* [Party
Night] (1926) records the current printing of *Ouha* as "nineti-
eth thousand," well in excess of all but two of his previous
works. After that, however, the novel seems to have faded
from view; it was never reprinted again and could not possibly
have been translated into English at the time because of the
flagrant obscenity of some of its passages. Indeed, while it
contains significant anticipatory echoes of *King Kong*, it contains no fewer anticipatory echoes, albeit in a somewhat more
caricaturish manner, of D. H. Lawrence's *Lady Chatterley's
Lover* (1928). Inevitably, the text has been largely judged on
the basis of its obscene element and its slapdash nature, and
dismissed in consequence as mere hackwork, but it is actually
more interesting than that, both in the context of the evolution
of Champsaur's own work[4] and the evolution of anthropological fantasies in general.

Champsaur's next publication after *Ouha* was a curious
philosophical novel, *Homo Deus, le satyre invisible* [Homo
Deus, the Invisible Satyr] (1924), on which he might well
have been working simultaneously (and of which I hope to
produce a translation in due course). Although it is much more
earnest in its narrative method, *Homo Deus* does have strong
thematic connections with the underlying argument of *Ouha*,

---

[4] A more detailed synoptic account of Champsaur's career can
be found in the introduction to the Black Coat Press edition of
The Human Arrow, q.v.

which imply that some aspects of the latter were meant more seriously than might seem to be the case. It is worth noting, too, that Champsaur had a long-term fascination with the relationship between apes and humans and the notion of transitions between the two; his earliest short stories, written in the mid-1880s while he was still a struggling member of the Club des Hydropathes on the periphery of the Decadent Movement, included a couplet entitled "Le Premier Homme" et "Le Dernier Homme" (translated in *The Human Arrow* as "The First Human" and "The Last Human"); both feature such transitions, as does his later novel *Nora, la guenon devenue femme* [Nora, the She-Ape Who Became a Woman] (1929), generally interpreted as a reference to Josephine Baker, in rank bad taste, although I can only rely on secondary sources in repeating that allegation.

An interest in ambiguous fictitious individuals sharing or exchanging the characteristics of animals and humans was, however, by no means a unique eccentricity on Champsaur's part, and *Ouha* fits, quite naturally and interestingly, into a whole series of fictions dealing hypothetically and symbolically with the relationship between humans and "apes." The last word warrants being put in inverted commas here because there is a vast difference between actual apes and literary apes, rooted in, but by no means confined to, confusions afflicting early taxonomical attempts to locate humans and the apparent kin within the "great chain of being." The question of human ancestry and filiation was, of course, very vexatious in the context of the long battle to establish the theory of evolution in the teeth of religious opposition.

It is perhaps worth noting, as a brief aside, that sharp differences between "literary biology" and actual natural history are commonplace, and not at all exceptional. Not only does literature routinely feature a great many imaginary creatures (dragons, unicorns, etc.) and "semi-imaginary" creatures (e.g., giant octopodes) but routinely makes and conserves such mistakes as imagining that it is female nightingales, rather than males, which sing, for entirely fictitious reasons. If ever there were creatures liable to facilitate such inventions, embellish-ments and calculated misunderstandings, it is the great apes, which remained utterly mysterious until the mid-nineteenth century, at the earliest, and yet demanded urgent philosophical consideration in the light of their evident similarities to hu-mankind.

The particular role played by the orangutan in the saga of literary apes, especially in France, is deeply confused, primari-ly because the first French popularizer of the term "ourang-outang," the great natural historian the Comte du Buffon, iden-tified two species under that heading whose description can now clearly be seen to be slightly fanciful accounts of chim-panzees. The volume of Buffon's epic natural history dealing with "ourang-outangs" appeared in the same year, 1766, as the volume of Carolus Linnaeus' epic taxonomy dealing with the higher mammals. Unlike Buffon, Linnaeus realized that the Bornean "ourang-outang" described in 1658 by the Dutch nat-uralist Jakob de Bondt was not the same species as the African apes nowadays known as chimpanzees, but that only made the task of classifying the mysterious creature—reported by de Bondt to be known locally as "the man of the woods"—more difficult.

Linnaeus, an evolutionist who dared not admit to it in print, took the bold step of suggesting that the orangutan might belong to the genus *Homo*, suggesting *Homo nocturnus* and *Homo silvestris* as potential appellations, but he was careful to hedge his bets by offering other generic alternatives. He said enough, however, to inspire the Scottish philosopher James Burnett, better known as Lord Monboddo, to speculate exten-sively about the nature of the relationship between orangutans and humans in his two six-volume treatises *Of the Origin and Progress of Language* (1773-1792) and *Ancient Metaphysics* (1779-1799). These speculations, in their turn, gave direct birth to the first significant literary orangutan, in the character of Sir Oran Haut-ton in Thomas Love Peacock's satire *Melincourt* (1817).

Sir Oran, introduced as a guest at Melincourt Castle by the naturalist Sylvan Forester, has been captured in infancy and brought up among humans, so profitably as eventually to earn a baronetcy. He is mute, but has learned to play the flute, and not only has perfect manners but a strong sense of gallantry, twice exerting his physical prowess to rescue the lovely Anthelia Melincourt—with whom the timid Forester is in love—from more brutally-inclined humans. The sections of the text featuring Sir Oran are abundantly footnoted with justificatory references to Lord Monboddo and various works quoted by the Scot, including Jean Delisle de Sales' *Philosophie de la Nature* (1778), but one of the most interesting observations in the story comes from Sir Telegraph Paxarett, who tells Forester that: "This wild man of yours will turn out some day to be the son of a king, lost in the woods, and suckled by a lioness:—'No waiter, but a knight templar':—no Oran, but a true prince."[5]

It is, of course, exceedingly unlikely that Edgar Rice Burroughs ever read *Melincourt*, but Sir Telegraph's approximate anticipation of the character of Tarzan is perhaps even more significant, given the number of other precursors of the idea of a feral child who becomes a kind of "noble savage." Rudyard Kipling might have read *Melincourt* before inventing Mowgli in the stories assembled in *The Jungle Book* (1894), just as Ronald Ross probably had before producing *The Child of Ocean* (1889), but they are very different developments of the theme. Burroughs is unlikely to have read either of those intermediaries, and, if he needed any prompting for his own invention other than the myth of Romulus and Remus, he is far more likely to have obtained it from H. Rider Haggard's *Allan's Wife* (1889), which features a female feral child of a

---

[5] Classic tales of ape-men including C.M. de Pougens' *Jocko* (1824), Emile Dodillon's *Hemo* (1886), Marcel Roland's *Almost A Man* (1905) and *The Missing Link* (1914) are included in the collection *The Missing Link*, Black Coat Press, ISBN 978-1-935558-14-9.

slightly more realistic sort. Given the importance of Jean-Jacques Rousseau as an influence on French Romanticism, however, it is not surprising that the French tradition of such fantasies, and their toying with the concept of uncorrupted primitivism, is even more adventurous than the English-language tradition, including, in addition to the work by Robida already cited, Jules Lermina's *To-Ho le tueur d'or* (1905)[6]. The most significant literary predecessors of the imaginary apes who rear Tarzan are those featured in Jules Verne's *Le Village aérien* (1901; tr. as *The Village in the Tree-Tops*) rather than Gozlan's.

Champsaur had, of course, sources much more recent than Lord Monboddo to draw upon in imagining his orangutan culture, but it is not obvious that he borrowed from anyone more recent that Buffon's most important successor, Georges Cuvier, who reclassified the primates in 1798 into "bimanes" and "quadrumanes," including the orangutan in the latter category and thus drawing a clearer line between the great apes and humans. It was, however, Robida who popularized the use of the term "quadrumanes" in the context of French anthropological fantasy, and it seems likely that Champsaur borrowed the term from *Saturnin Farandoul* rather than from any treatise on taxonomy. The character of Ouha definitely owes his origin and development to the literary tradition that branched off from the scholarly one in the late eighteenth century rather than to the march of science, and the physical anthropologist featured in the story, Dr. Abraham Goldry, seems to be a hundred years behind the development of his science.

Criticism of the story of Ouha on the grounds of its infidelity to known science is, however, largely irrelevant, because the narrative is a hypothetical exercise of a very different sort. If Rousseau would have found it amusing—as he surely would—so would Carl Jung, who would have recognized it as a attempt to delve into the depths of human psy-

---

[6] tr. as *Toho and the Gold Destroyers*, Black Coat Press, ISBN 978-1-935558-34-7.

chology rather than human evolution *per se*. There is an arche-typal quality to the character of Ouha, as there had been to Tarzan and would be to King Kong; if he is no more plausible as a guest in human society than Sir Oran Haut-ton, he is no less relevant as a specter at the feast of civilization and modern morality. He is, in essence, a player in an absurd melodrama, but his very absurdity raises questions about the sanity that rules him ridiculous, and the sheer extremism of the melodrama—especially its spectacularly overwrought climax—has a peculiar magnificence that transcends mere logic.

This translation is taken from a copy of the 1923 edition published by Charpentier and Fasquelle. I have unified the names of some of the characters, especially where minor errors seems to have been introduced by the typesetter, and have corrected a few obvious typos, but I have left most of the text's inconsistencies in place, adding footnotes where it seemed appropriate.

Brian Stableford

OUHA, KING OF THE APES

I. Ouha Will Interest You...

*Harry Smith Lauwer[7] to Dr. Abraham Goldry in Philadelphia
Borneo, Riddle-Temple, via Ambang*

My dear friend,

When I left Philadelphia on your specific orders, it was, for me, a question of life or death. Neurasthenia, arrived at its extreme point, would inevitably have driven me to suicide. While making an immense fortune by means of enormous overwork I had conceived such a disgust for humankind that we searched together for a country that civilization, or at least what we call by that name, had not yet penetrated, and one in which the great scenery of nature would offer my mind a new interest—in brief, an encouragement to live.

I yielded to your reasoning, my dear doctor, and left with my daughter Mabel, your goddaughter, for Borneo, the largest island in the Indo-Malaysian archipelago. The description of that island, two-thirds Dutch and English in the northern part, had not deceived me. On the coasts and in the towns proximal to the China Sea, and Java Sea and the Celebes Sea, rice and tobacco are grown, but the rest of Borneo is nothing but an immense forest of mangroves, coconut-palms, sago-palms, areca-palms, gum-trees, resin-trees and gigantic bamboos: a forest ideal for me, as a misanthrope, delightfully populated by orangutans, rhinoceroses and elephants.

As I tap the keyboard of my typewriter to write this epistle, I have a true contentment in my soul and at my fingertips. It's a salvation that you have wrought; you may consider it as

---

[7] The author subsequently abandons the "Lauwer" and is content to allow this character to be merely "Harry Smith."

one of the best of your medical career. Since we left—which is to say, in the last five and a half months, many changes have occurred. First of all, in spite of Major Bennett's very cordial hospitality, in need of more solitude, I found that of which I dreamed a few hundred miles away from him.

In the course of an excursion into the interior of Borneo, buried in the heart of the virgin forest, we discovered the ruins of a temple whose antiquity is lost in the night of time. The idea immediately struck me of restoring it and taking up residence there.

That whim, which cost me ten million dollars, saved me, because I have been occupied with that project for four months. I brought engineers and workers from India—the only ones capable of understanding the restoration—and had furniture, carpets and tapestries sent from Imbuk. Our friend Bennett has shown himself, on this occasion, the most devoted of friends. Bennett, my daughter, her governess and twenty carefully-chosen servants, who seem pleased with us, are sufficient for me. All that is lacking here, my dear doctor, is you—so I hope that you will soon find the opportunity to come and join us.

Mabel, in particular, needs you. She is generous enough not to be bored by me, but she is now 17 years-old and I am anticipating in terror the moment when she will require another companion. On that subject, please send us news of that Archibald Wilson, who began a flirtation with your goddaughter six months ago. He is, I believe, a friend of yours, and an appropriate suitor in all respects.

Here, my dear fellow, nature is splendid. Around Riddle-Temple I have cleared and ploughed up a few acres of land, but all around that is the forest, the virgin forest in all its virginity, wild and luxuriant.

From here we can hear monkeys chattering and tigers howling. To prevent accidents, I've encircled my temple with a strong fence, but beyond it is primitive life in all its beauty. Every so often, Mabel, myself and a few servants—good hunters—set off into the forest, and we have brought back some superb tiger skins and elephant tusks.

As for the orangutans, we have not yet made their acquaintance. Thus far, we have only encountered numerous varieties of monkeys. As one of the most ardent observers of our simian brethren, you could carry out studies here, for the forest is swarming with them. We already have ten of those forest-dwellers living inside the fence, who do not seem to regret the wilderness overmuch and are amusing companions for us. Moreover, you would find species of tropical vegetation that must be absolutely unknown in Europe.

Well, my dear doctor, that ought to tempt you: flowers, plants, monkeys and your friends.

Harry Smith Lauwer

Mabel Smith Lauwer to Abraham Goldry

Dear and beloved Godfather,

I have snatched the pen from Papa's hand in order to be the first to tell you our great news. We have captured an orangutan! A large, fine specimen; it seems that no one had ever seen one so big. He is taller than Papa, and you know that Papa is fairly tall—five foot nine. Personally, I think the orangutan is considerably more advanced than his fellows; he almost always walks upright and his arms only hang down to his knees. At the same time, his face has a Napoleonic expression and he sometimes moves his lips in a fashion that resembles a smile.

As you can imagine, we didn't take possession of the fellow without difficulty. It was a little native woman, of whom Papa recently made me a gift, who served as bait. I'd like to tell you that strange story, but it would take too long, and I'd rather wait until you're here. The main thing is the capture of the hairy giant.

Come to admire and study him, Godfather.

In your last letter you told us that my suitor, Archibald Wilson, was still inconsolable; tell him that he has a successor and that I have embarked on an original flirtation with a great lord who answers to the name of Ouha. My friend Ouha can pronounce that word quite clearly, and we have understood that in my ape's family (should I say ape?—he seems to me to be superior to many humans) Ouha must be his name, for he always answers to that appellation when one speaks to him, or pricks up his ears when anyone talks about him.

We have already had him for a month, and Papa is thinking of taking off his chains, for he seems totally inoffensive and does everything one wants him to do with extreme skill.

We're expecting you, my dear Godfather. Ouha will interest you. Come soon! Ouha! Ouha!

I love you dearly.

Mabel

II. The Enigmatic Ruins of a Buddhist Temple in Borneo

Major William Bennett was resident in Borneo in a concession granted as recompense for valiant conduct. Having taken successive engagements since he was old enough to be a soldier, first with the East India Company and then with the Dutch, he had become an associate of Colonel Werspick, justly known as the hero of Borneo, and had campaigned with him.

Pirates knows as "head-hunters"—because they took the heads of their enemies as trophies—made frequent landings in Java and the small islands subject to Dutch rule. In one of their recent expeditions, several Europeans who had fallen into their hands had been tortured atrociously. That action demanded vengeance. Colonel Werspick set off with two hundred European soldiers and four hundred coolies. The enemy, taking refuge in the heart of the island, protected by impenetrable woods and an insurmountable torrent, believed themselves to be sheltered from all danger.

For twenty-four days and twenty-four nights, the little column cleared a passage with hatchets through the virgin forest, with very little food, sustaining themselves with quinine, and without building a fire. Maintaining the most profound silence, they arrived at the pirates' camp and fell upon the unexpectedly. After a thirteen-hour battle, in spite of their numerical superiority, the twelve hundred pirates were utterly defeated.

After that, Major Bennett had bamboo rafts constructed, and embarked on the torrent with his small army and four hundred prisoners. In twenty-four hours they made the journey that had taken them twenty-four terrible days before, but the rafts, carried through rocks, rapids and cataracts covered the hundred leagues of the journey and all reached the sea, where they were picked up by the Dutch fleet.

It was in recompense for that exploit that Major William Bennett obtained a large concession some twenty miles from Imbuk. The location was a trifle hazardous, but the major had no fear of peril. Partly by virtue of his energy and partly by virtue of his spirit of justice and perfect honesty, he was able to overcome the fear of the natives and win their esteem. Soon, following his example, a few Europeans came to take up residence in the vicinity, and a sizeable colony was established on that island promontory. It was soon very prosperous.

The major married Meg Sulten, the sister of an Irish colonist, Patrick Sulten—his neighbor, forty miles away from White House, Bennett's home. From the viewpoint of administration and the direction of the plantation, his wife was a veritable pearl, but her character was exceedingly intractable. Always discontented with her husband and everything else, she never stopped grumbling, so she was feared by all the servants, her children—she gave the major two daughters and four sons—and the major himself, who gave in to all her caprices resignedly, for the sake of peace.

As much to get away from his wife as to distract his guest, William Bennett organized long excursions into the surroundings. In the course of one of these trips, he took Harry Smith Lauwer and his daughter—an astonishing masterpiece as a model of American maidenhood—to the ruins of the temple of Issager-Bong. Situated about four hundred miles from Imbuk, in the heart of the virgin forest, the ruins were one of the rare marvels of Oriental architecture.

Who had built the temple? To what worship was it devoted? No one knows. But the grandiose harmony of the sculptures and the minute detail in the majesty of the style testified to a surprising civilization many centuries in the past. Thousands of years had undoubtedly passed over that prodigious baobab of granite and multicolored marble, but such as the quality of the materials employed that they had resisted the action of time. Many of the floors and walls had been cracked by the pressure of an exuberant vegetation, but the stones had been loosened without breaking.

How could the presence of such a monument be explained in the heart of an island whose wild appearance and uncultivated land seemed to indicate a condition close to primitive savagery? The volcanic nature of the Malaysian archipelago suggested the possibility that in some very distant epoch, the region had been subject to an upheaval. Once no doubt, all the islands had formed a single vast continent. Was it united to India?[8] The Malaysian people, however, are not very similar to the Indian people; they seem rather to be a variety of the Indo-Chinese.

In any case, such as it appeared to the excursionists, the temple was a marvel. Its three terraces, formed as a pyramid truncated at the summit, were supported by alternating columns of marble and porphyry. The shafts, fluted in spiral fashion, were terminated by curiously-sculpted capitals, all dissimilar. Porticos overloaded with delicate ornamentation, like lacework of stone and sunlight, gave entry into immense halls whose mosaic tiling, reminiscent in its richness of that of St. Mark's Cathedral in Venice, was still in good condition. In some places, to be sure, the vegetation had invaded open galleries, but it was easy to see that restoration would not be difficult.

From the corner of his eye Major William Bennett followed the mounting enthusiasm in Harry Smith's face, which virtually transfigured the blasé and world-weary billionaire.

"What a pity," he said to Mabel, "that such a blossoming of magnificence remains buried in the forest."

"It would be an even greater pity," Mabel replied, "if the Vandals of Europe got their hands on it, to ornament their museums with its choice pieces. I remember the painful impression I had on seeing the fragments of the Parthenon in the

---

[8] The idea that there was once an advanced civilization in a hypothetical continent that connected the islands of the "East Indies" together prior to a prehistoric cataclysm, is commonplace in French adventure fiction, dating back at least as far as the works of Joseph Méry in the 1830s.

British Museum. What would have been admirable, as a whole, beneath the pure sky of Greece, was paltry in its effect, thus mutilated, in a hall that was darkened that day by the London fog."

"It would require a billionaire of considerable artistry to carry out the repair and maintenance of this monumental masterpiece."

"Me!" cried Harry Smith.

"You couldn't find a nobler employment for your fortune. That, my dear fellow, is an idea worthy of an American like you. Furthermore, you will find, in the activity and distraction of that enterprise, a powerful distraction from your neurasthenia."

III. Mabel's New Flirt

Six weeks after receiving Mabel's letter, Dr. Goldry made his appearance at Riddle-Temple. His first words were: "Where's the orangutan?"

"Have a little patience, my dear Godfather. First you're going to learn how we captured my hero. I've been saving up the pleasure of telling that tale—you shan't escape it.

"Go on—but hurry."

"I hope, Doctor, that you have no intention of leaving us again after ten days or so?"

"No, this time I'm free. I'm fifty-some years old. I've worked enough on behalf of others; now I want to live for my own pleasure. I've left an able and resourceful young man, Archibald Wilson, the task of liquidating my assets, and he'll bring me the final settlement. I'm sure that he'll do so diligently, and will be here soon."

"You don't say!" Mabel exclaimed. "Archibald was my last flirt."

"And I hope that he will be the last," muttered the doctor. "I don't approve of this changeability."

"You don't understand flirting at all—but leave Archibald to me. I'm determined to tell my tale, Doctor."

"I'm awaiting it with keen curiosity."

"Then I'll begin. Once upon a time there was a king, who had a daughter he adored. Her name was Princess Dilou."

"You're making fun of me, Mabel; I demand the story of the orangutan."

"If you interrupt me at every word, the story will last a long time. I'll start again. Once upon a time, there was an African king, who was captured, with a hundred of his subjects, by a neighboring petty king and sold by him to a slave-trader, who sold him on to Monsieur James Cernum in the American South. That unfortunate king was named Muni-Wali. As he was far from being stupid, he performed such valuable services for his master that James Cernum freed him during the War of Secession. Now, James Cernum had a son, Lloyd, for whom he bought an important concession in Borneo, and James Cernum's son brought King Muni-Wali—who was then about fifty years old—here with him. They both became neighbors, about fifty miles distant, of Major Bennett. Naturally, they became business associates and friends. Are you following me, Doctor?"

"Perfectly."

"Among the major's servants was a very pretty native of Sumatra, of whom the black monarch became enamored. He made his request, was gladly welcomed, and married the lovely Malay. They had two sons to begin with, and, five years later, a daughter—who, although as black as her father, became, like her mother, a very pretty girl. She's the one about whom I was going to talk to you, Doctor: Princess Dilou, now aged about twenty."

"I'm all ears, hanging on your lips."

"Lloyd Cernum's concession is, like Riddle-Temple, bordered by the virgin forest. Two years ago, on the advice of Muni-Wali, the colonist undertook the exploitation of timber and precious essences, which are abundant in these forests. There was, in consequence, a methodical deforestation, which promised handsome profits. Often, Princess Dilou went with her father and Lloyd Cernum to check up on the work in progress.

"One day, the young girl, who was tired, fell asleep on the moss at the foot of a superb tulip-tree. When the explorers came back, the girl had disappeared. The forest was searched, in vain, for a week. The months went by; two years elapsed. From that day on, Muni-Wali, who had been very vigorous until then, was gripped by a discouragement that turned into a wasting disease, of which he died."

"And afterwards, Mabel? What happened next?"

"Two months ago, we were on a excursion in the forest—Father, me and four of our hunters—when we heard screams: human screams. We launched ourselves in the direction from which the appeal as coming. Just in time! A superb tiger was stretching, while roaring, along the trunk of a coconut-tree in which a young black woman had taken refuge. I had the honor of firing the first shot, and hit the tiger in the ear, which fell dead. But then things took a different turn. Instead of coming toward us, the woman jumped down from her perch and ran away through the forest. Unfortunately for her, she hadn't seen our four servants, and she ran straight into their arms. 'Catch her!' I shouted. We didn't understand—we'd saved her life, but she was afraid of her rescuers. We had to tie her up in order to bring here. It was only after ten days that we succeeded in bringing her back somewhat to civilized life."

"I've guessed, Mabel—it was Dilou."

"She'd been brought up by orangutans and had lived with them for nearly two years. She'd forgotten her language and her family. It was only be reminding her of her history that Major Bennett, for whom we'd sent, was able to reawaken her memory.

"Now, Dilou had been with us for three days when one of the hunters who had accompanied us came to tell my father that a free man was prowling around the temple."

"A free man?"

"The Malays call the orangutans 'free men' because, according to legend, orangutans are human, like them, but much more intelligent. They could talk if they wanted to, but they pretend to be mute in order not to have to work."

"An amusing explanation."

"A number of us went out, and soon encountered a large ape—who, at the sight of us, took refuge in the forest. Later, when our protégée had, as I told you, recovered the memory of her past and was able to tell us about her sojourn among the anthropoids, we told her about the one that as always prowling around Riddle-Temple."

"'That's Ouha!' she exclaimed. 'That's Ouha! I want to see him. I want to go with him.'

"'Damn!' said my father. 'If we let her go, she'll be lost again—and I've written to Cernum's to inform her brothers.'

"'I've got a better idea,' said Bennett. 'Let's use her to attract the orangutan.'

"'Bravo! That way, we'll have a domesticated great ape.'

"We had some difficulty getting that idea into Dilou's head, but finally, she came to share our desire and followed our instructions. So she went out with us, and it wasn't long before we heard the calls of the orangutan, who risked showing himself in order to see Dilou. If the silly girl hadn't been restrained she'd certainly have run toward the orangutan, but she couldn't, and she called out in her turn...

"Hesitant at first, the terrible animal advanced, twirling an enormous club. But Dilou, entering into her role, set herself in front of us and made him understand that we were friends. Gradually, we beat a retreat toward Riddle-Temple, and the ape followed us...

"Finally, we arrived at the palisade and went in, leaving the gate open behind us. We'd set up a table a hundred meters away. We sat down there. Half an hour went by. We made Dilou sing, so that the ape, hearing her voice, decided to come closer and closer. Suddenly, we saw his head appear over the palisade, at the corner of the gate. We pretended not to pay any attention to him. He became bolder, and crossed the threshold of Riddle-Temple, attracted by the sight of the fruits with which the table was covered.

"Dilou picked up a banana and threw it to him, politely. He swallowed it immediately, then came further forward. Finally, after two hours, he was sitting a few meters away from us, eating all the fruits we gave him, one after another. From time to time he called out to Dilou, in an amorous plaint: 'Ouha! Ouha! Ouha! Ouha!' He seemed to have realized that she was with beings of the same species as herself, and, when we got up to go inside, he stood up too, apparently having momentarily had the idea of following us. Then he suddenly turned his back on us and fled back to the forest at top speed. We closed the gate behind him...

"The following day, the same scenes were repeated, but he came much closer. In order to reassure him, we had left our rifles behind and were only armed with revolvers, of which he had no suspicion. In brief, after five days, he came into Riddle-Temple, and since then..."

"What?" demanded Abraham, breathless with excitement.

Mabel rang a bell. "Johsa," she said, to the domestic who presented himself, "bring in Master Ouha."

A minute later, the Orang made a sensational entrance, dressed in a shirt and suit of white twill. He bowed, saluting with both arms forward, and walked over to Mabel, who offered him her hand. He took it, and raised it to his lips.

"My new flirt," said Mabel, turning to Dr. Goldry. "My new flirt, my dear."

IV. Ouha Flees and Abducts Dilou

In the two days that Abraham Goldry had been at Riddle-Temple, the doctor had only left his new friend, Ouha, in order to take the indispensable tour of the property with Smith and Mabel. The partly-restored temple—for the work was ongoing—had resumed its former appearance. The three stages of colonnades, cleared of parasitic plants, were now silhouetted against the transparent blue of the tropical sky in all their sculptural beauty.

Leaving in its original state the part doubtless consecrated to religious celebration, Harry Smith had had apartments installed in what must have been the priests' and servants' dwelling. Behind the truncated pyramid that formed the three stages of the temple extended an immense square with shady walkways, a oasis of coolness, surrounded by covered galleries supported by light pilasters, cut, carved and sculpted like precious jewels. On the far side of the square was a vast pool, dry now, but which the billionaire intended to return to its original purpose.

Then, to either side, were building in a marvelous millennial style, in harmony with the entirety of the edifice. It was there that Harry Smith had established his home: the section on the right for himself and his household, the one on the left for his future guests. Each of these wings must have lodged a thousand servants of the altars and the gods. Further away, behind the masters' roofs, were hangars, store-rooms and elephant-stables. To judge by the number of stalls, there ought to have been nearly a hundred pachyderms there.

After having visited all that with Mabel and her father, Dr. Goldry repeated the visit with his hairy friend Ouha, whose guide he became. In his turn, he explained the details of Riddle-Temple, sometimes forgetting and chatting with Ouha as with one of his colleagues in Philadelphia. At any rate, the ape appeared to be listening to him with interest, never showing any gesture of impatience.

From the temple, the conversation passed to natural history, and the doctor studied his companion, while making him party to the interest he inspired in him.

"Do you know, my dear Ouha, that as soon as I knew about your presence at Riddle, I no longer had any thought or desire except with your intention. I ought to tell you that I've been working for a long time on a major treatise on the anthropoids, the precursors of humankind on our globe. I've always followed with great care, from near or far, everything that might inform us as to our origins. Is there an important relationship between Dr. Goldry and prehistoric humans? I've always been jealous of the discoveries made in Europe, especially in France."

Taking the ape's arm, he continued: "Can you imagine, my dear friend, that in 1908 in France, in the département of Corrèze, near a place called Chapelle-aux-Saints, two French priests were lucky enough to discover, almost on their doorstep, in a cavern into which no one had ever stuck his nose, the almost complete skeleton of a fossil human, whose skull was quite similar to yours in terms of volume and facial angle? Would you permit me to feel your cranium?"

Ouha consented, and even appeared to take a certain pleasure in allowing his skull to be handled.

"Yes, certainly, there's a strong relationship. The more I look at you, the more astonished I am by your resemblance to our primitive ancestors. To begin with, there's your stature; you'd be a giant, even among men, if your stance was a little more perpendicular. Lift up your torso like me—make an effort. There, stand up straight. You see—you're a head taller than me now. Does that tire you, eh? Oh well, we'll bring you to that straightness gradually. I'll make you practice methodical gymnastics, and I'll make you entirely into a man, or my name's not Abraham Goldry. Then again, your face doesn't have the stupid appearance of the majority of great apes. Your eyes, although terrible, have expression and look—at the moment, you're smiling. Oh, what if it taught you to laugh? That's characteristic of humans, you know. Would you like to try?"

"Ah! Ah! Ah! Ouha!" Ouha gave voice to a sniggering groan, strung out like a rumble of thunder.

"My God! You mustn't laugh like thunder—you'll make it rain."

Amused by his joke, the doctor laughed frankly in Ouha's face—which appeared to displease the ape, for he grabbed the doctor by the collar, lifted him off the ground and shook him rudely. Then, doubtless understanding that he was not acting in a gentlemanly fashion, he put the scientist down and, bounding into an immense tamarind tree, disappeared into the foliage in the blink of an eye. The doctor readjusted his clothing, grumbling, after which he went back to his apartment.

He continued his monologue: "Make a note: laughter vexes the orangutan; he thinks he's being mocked. Damn! What a grip!"

If Doctor Goldry had been able to follow his favorite, he would have had many other notes to make. Scarcely had the doctor disappeared than the quadrumane descended from his perch. His twill garments had suffered somewhat during his ascent; he began by taking them off, and, finding himself more comfortable, cut a few capers. Then, moving on all fours in order to go more rapidly, he headed toward the palisade. He knew that he had to act rapidly; his new friends were not in the habit of letting him out of their sight for long.

Having reached he barrier he headed, without hesitation, toward an enormous boulder lying at the foot of the stout beams that formed the Americans' rampart. With an effort, he rolled the stone away and unmasked a hole deep enough to allow him to pass under the palisade. He leapt into the hole and made sure that it was easy enough to get out on the other side.

The sun was almost level with the horizon; in a few minutes, it would be dark. He left things as they were and went back to the habitation. On the way, he picked up his garments, which he put on dexterously. At that moment, the dinner-bell rang. He was just in time. For several days, Ouha had taken his place at table next to his friend Abraham, Dr. Goldry, who was teaching him to eat properly, in the European style. The orangutan had memorized the signal for meals quickly, and when the bell rang, they were sure of seeing him arrive. He was always welcomed by his masters like a spoiled child, especially by Mabel, who was full of attentions for her flirt—which annoyed Dr. Goldry.

The scientist said: "You're brutalizing my pupil, Miss."

Everyone took their places, and tucked into the evening meal cheerfully. In spite of the doctor's remonstrations, Ouha sometimes forgot good manners and, when he dropped something, he picked it up with his feet and put it in his mouth—to Goldry's great despair but the enthusiastic pleasure of Mabel and her father, who laughed wholeheartedly. The ape seemed astonished by these bursts of laughter, and looked at the diners with an irritated expression. The doctor told them about his adventure and the manner in which the ape had shaken him— which redoubled Mabel's delight.

"Oh," she said, "I can laugh. I'm convinced that my flirt won't hold it against me. Isn't that so, Ouha?" And she held out her hand.

Instead of kissing it, as he usually did, however, the ape pushed it away brutally.

Mabel frowned. "Did you see that vile beast? It seems that laughter displeases His Majesty Ouha. If gentleness doesn't succeed with him, we'll resort to the whip."

"Come, come, my dear child—don't get annoyed about such a little thing," said Harry Smith. "You've been spoiled by human beings; don't forget that you're dealing with an ape, and that we haven't had him long. With time, he'll get used to our laughter, and won't believe as Abraham says, that we're mocking him. Isn't that so, Ouha, old chap? You'll forgive us, won't you?"

Ouha was definitely in a bad mood. He ground his teeth and, standing up to his full height, beat his breast with his sovereign fists.

"He's furious!" cried the doctor, in despair. "Be careful—we're unarmed. He could kill us all."

In that attitude, Ouha was superb, but terrifying. His eyes were aflame. With one hand, he had seized the heavy stool that served him as a seat and began whirling it around his body. The two men had thrown themselves in front of Mabel, and were covering her with their bodies. It was a brief moment, but it seemed like hours to both of them. The ape seemed to be hesitating over the choice of his victim.

Meanwhile, Dilou had stood up. With her arms extended, the black princess implored the orangutan, shouting: "Ouha! Ouha! Ouha!"

That appeal halted the quadrumane's gesture. He turned toward the woman and his fury appeared to calm down. With an imperious gesture, he summoned the young woman, who came to him obediently. He took her gently by the hand; then, facing up to the two men, he walked backwards to the doorway, went through it and closed the door behind him, leading Dilou, who seemed to be following him gladly.

The two friends looked at one another.

"Fortunately, the gates are closed. We'll settle the matter by means of a torchlight search. This time, we'll lock the fellow up more solidly until he's more fully domesticated."

"That's all right," said the doctor. "I had a real scare. What a bad idea it was, Miss, to burst out laughing! It was going so well. We'd been chatting like two good friends. Anyway, let's hope that he calms down. Thanks to Dilou, we've got away clean."

"Poor girl. She thought she'd been liberated from her tyrant."

"Hmm!" said the doctor. "Tyrants are loved."

"Let's call our men and start searching for Ouha. Perhaps he's simply gone back to his room."

Precipitate footsteps were heard. The domestics came in tumultuously. They were all armed.

"Allah be praised!" cried the butler. "Your Excellencies are safe."

The waiters at the dinner had seen the orang and the woman flee. Two of them had tried to oppose their passage, but the ape, seizing them by the throat, had banged their heads together, fracturing their skulls. The others had run away, sounding the alarm, and everyone had raced to help their masters. Immediately, Harry organized the search. They were equipped with torches and ropes, for the two Europeans intended to capture the orang alive—which caused the Malays to murmur at first, although the promise of a generous reward caused them to change their opinion.

They began by visiting the residential quarters; then, certain that the orang must be within the enclosure, they all organized themselves into a single line equipped with torches, in order not to leave any space unexplored, the most distant going along the fence.

"Halt!" cried Tu Wang, the butler.[9] "The hunt is over; they prey has gone through the fence."

They all gathered at the location of the passage hollowed out by the wily quadrumane. Shreds of twill garment were lying in the hole.

The doctor leapt into the excavation and came out on the other side. Everything in the forest was silent.

"Ouha!" shouted the doctor. "Ouha! Come back!"

Far away, from the treetops, a cry replied to him, ironic and threatening: "Ouha! Ouha! Ouha!"

"Come back in, my friend," Harry Smith ordered. "A pursuit by night would be pure folly. Come back in and let's discuss the matter."

---

[9] This character is never mentioned again, but his name is recycled, a slight variant of it being attached to a different character.

The hole was covered up again with the rock displaced by the orangutan, which three men had difficulty putting back in place.

Everyone went into the drawing-room, where Mabel Smith was waiting in company with Betty Symian, her lady companion.

"Well, what's become of your friend Ouha?" Mabel asked the doctor, who seemed consternated.

"We arrived too late, alas. The fellow had prepared his escape—and that plan denotes an almost human intellect on his behalf. I've been too confident of his docility. I think, in sum, that he was only waiting for an opportunity to give us the slip."

"Yes, and to get his woman back."

"The annoying thing is that I was in too much of a hurry to write to Dilou's brothers. They'll come to find her, and we won't be able to hand her over."

"Why? Have you given up on taking possession of Ouha again?"

"It's easy to see that you've never penetrated very far into the mystery and dangers of the savage thousand-year-old forests of Borneo."

"Well, for my part, I, Dr. Abraham Goldry, swear that I won't leave Borneo without Ouha or one of his peers, if it costs me my life."

"In that case, we'll have you here for a long time."

"After all," said Mabel, "Do you intend to imprison yourselves in Riddle-Temple? Why not hunt the orangutan as one hunts tigers and elephants?"

"We don't have to go far to find elephants and tigers, while these great apes can draw us all the way to the Devil."

"Well, I'll go to the Devil if I have to," exclaimed Goldry, "and I'll make the expedition at my own expense. Tomorrow, I'll go have a chat with Bennett."

V. Preparations for War

The next day, as he had promised the previous evening, Abraham Goldry set off for White House in order to consult Major Bennett about the projected expedition.

As soon as the latter understood, he pulled a face. "My dear friend," he said, "on due reflection, this isn't a campaign to undertake lightly. I don't think the hunt is possible with our mean alone. It requires men accustomed to that kind of sport, and they're rare. Nevertheless, if you're utterly determined..."

"I am," said the doctor, coldly. "The short time I've spent with Ouha didn't permit me to study him in depth. It's precisely his escape the makes me so keen to recapture him, for it denotes an intelligence well above that of his peers, and I'm convinced that with a little education, I could bring that anthropoid close to our own humanity."

"Do you think that would be an advantage for him?"

"Don't joke about it!"

"All right! I'll organize the expedition—but I warn you that I expect to be part of it."

A domestic handed a card to the major. As soon as he had cast a glance at it he said: "Send them in. Here's rein-forcements arriving—Dilou's brothers."

Two young men appeared. The major made the introduc-tions: "Joshua and Jacob Muni-Wali, the brothers of the wom-an abducted by Ouha; the famous Dr. Abraham Goldry of Philadelphia. Gentlemen, we have bad news to give you. After a sojourn of a month in the home of my friend Harry Smith, your sister has fallen back into the power of her abductor. Dr. Goldry will tell you about the whole adventure while he takes you to Riddle-Temple, if you want to go to the theater where the events took place."

"And I assure you, gentlemen," Goldry put in, "that I in-tend to devote myself, body and soul, to the recapture of the abductor of your sister Dilou."

35

"I thank you on behalf of myself and my brother," said Joshua, "and we too will take part in that enterprise. With Mr. Cernum, we devote ourselves to the exploitation of precious wood, and we've already driven ten miles into the forest; in the course of our work we've had dealings with troops of great apes. That's to tell you that we're trained in that kind of hunting, and that our collaboration, augmented by fifty of our woodcutters, will be appreciable."

"Bravo!" said Bennett. "We'll contribute twenty Malay hunters. In addition, I'll appeal to a few of my friends. I think that, all being well-armed, we'll arrive at a successful result. In the meantime, gentlemen, you're my guests. Be welcome."

Meg—Mrs. Bennett—having been informed, came in angrily, as was her habit.

"So you're going off adventuring again, as always? I told you that these Smiths would cause us all kinds of trouble. And hasn't this Dr. Goldry buried enough Christians? Now he has to occupy himself with apes. He'd do better to go live with the animals—he wouldn't have far to go to become as stupid as them."

Nevertheless, having complained, that Xantippe made haste to ensure that her guests did not lack anything. Besides which, the two brothers immediately won her sympathy. Meg was not insensitive to physical beauty, and the sons of the former negro king were magnificent specimens of the mixture of African and Asiatic blood. Both were gigantic in stature and built like Antinous; only the faces left a little to be desired, having nothing of the Classical type of Apollo. Their education, quite complete, combined with a keen natural intelligence, rendered their conversation interesting.

Both brothers were married, to two Irish sisters who had come to Borneo with their parents, political refugees. For years, the MacGregors had been leaders of the revolutionary party and hereditary enemies of old England. On coming to Brunei for the ale and consignment of wood, Jacob Muni-Wali had made the acquaintance of Paddy MacGregor, who took him home. There he had met Mary and Betty. He fell in love with the former, judged that the latter would be to his brother's taste, and negotiated the two marriages. MacGregor, delighted to find a god match for his two eldest daughters at the same time—he had eight in all—accepted immediately. Jacob wrote to his brother, and a fortnight later, they were married, and had returned to Bha-rang-si, the Cernum residence.

On learning that her guests were married to two of her compatriots, Meg was transported by pleasure; immediately, the two Muni-Wali brothers, Joshua and Jacob, were considered members of the family.

After that, the expedition was rapidly organized. Bennett left for the island of Meng, where he knew that he would find the elite of Malay hunters, former pirates for the most part, but men of unlimited courage and endurance. The two brothers went back to Bha-rang-si to confer with their former masters, James and Lloyd Cernum, who were now their associates, with regard to the number of men that they could have at their disposal.

It was agreed that the general rendezvous would be at Riddle-Temple. Just as Abraham Goldry was about to go back, a new guest arrived at White House in the person of Archibald Wilson, who arrived with a leather briefcase under his arm in order settle up with the doctor for the liquidation of his medical practice in Philadelphia. Goldry thus learned that he was the possessor of a hundred and thirty thousand dollars, which Archibald was carrying in his briefcase.

Having approved the liquidation, Abraham took his business manager to Riddle-Temple, informing him on the way of all the events of the last few days. Archibald was particularly anxious to know whether Mabel Smith was well disposed in his favor, and whether she sometimes thought about her former flirt—to which the doctor replied that the young billionairess's more recent flirt interested him more than the old one, but that, until Ouha returned, Archibald might perhaps have some success, for he was almost as good as the anthropoid.

In that, the doctor was showing too much partiality to his friend the ape, for Archibald as a very handsome young man, who probably seemed too healthy to a Romantic spirit, but who was a superb specimen of modern beauty, vigorous, robust and accomplished in all sports. Undoubtedly, he lacked a little imagination, being primarily positive and practically-minded, but his gentle and obliging nature had once made him the slave of the spoiled child that Mabel Smith was.

VI. The Rivals: John Bull and Uncle Sam

When Archibald Wilson arrived at Riddle-Temple, he found a competitor there: a British resident of the island of Borneo, Sir Silven Gorden, a prosperous planter from the west coast. He had come as a neighbor to pay his respects to the new owner of Riddle-Temple, whom he was curious to visit. Harry Smith and his daughter, flattered in their vanity as artistic Maecenases, had given the visitor a good welcome.

The resident certainly admired the restored temple, but he was even more impressed by the beauty of the young American woman. Thus, Mabel, who no longer had an admirer since Ouha's escape, welcomed the Englishman with pleasure. When Goldry and Archibald arrived that evening, therefore, they found the new arrival installed and flirting with Mabel.

At that sight, Wilson frowned, but Mabel, happy to see her former worshipper and already foreseeing, in the rivalry of the two young men, all sorts of scenes that would be amusing from her viewpoint, welcomed him with her most gracious smile. She struck up a conversation with him, from which Silven Gorden was necessarily excluded, because it was a matter of obtaining news of all her old friends in Philadelphia and society events that had taken place since the Smiths' departure. Finally, when the young woman was satisfied, the conversation became generalized. Everyone, naturally, returned to the events of the day.

"In the case," Mabel joked, "it's a veritable army that you're raising against poor Ouha? Do you really think he's so redoubtable?"

"You ought to know, having seen him angry—and the two victims he claimed provided a demonstration of what our own fate have might been."

"The Muni-Wali brothers, who have pushed quite a long way into the virgin forest, say that the number of orangutans might be considerable and that it would be more than imprudent to venture there without being numerous and well-armed. Then again, remember that we don't have any intention of fighting before having rescued Dilou. Her brothers consider that her life would be imperiled if the orangs were attacked violently. It will be bad enough to have to make the return journey under their pursuit."

"I'd like to get one of them in my power," said Archibald. "I'm curious to know whether it could hold its own against this arm." Proudly, Wilson made his biceps stand out. He was not reluctant to exhibit his strength in front of Gorden, the tall and slim British resident, who seemed by comparison only half a man.

The Englishman smiled mockingly. "It's vexing for humankind," he said, "but I strongly doubt that you'd succeed. I even doubt that you'd prevail against certain gentlemen of my acquaintance."

Wilson burst out laughing. "I haven't found my master in America."

"You'd have found him in England," said Gorden, dryly.

Archibald Wilson displayed a pink, slightly sanguine face, framed by ardent blond hair, with gray-blue eyes the color of steel, a straight nose rounded at the tip, a square chin: a truly Anglo-Saxon face, which American generations extended over two centuries had begun to harden. The short and sturdy neck was mounted on broad, square, athletic shoulders. He seemed energetic and gentle; he shook his head without saying anything, like a child who knew that the reprimand was merited.

Silven Gorden, therefore, contrasted with the American. Tall and thin, he was all bone and muscle, pale blond, his bronzed complexion making the faded color of his hair stand out even more, with a long hooked nose. When he smiled, the thin lips of the sons of Albion allowed a glimpse of teeth that might break iron. His sloping shoulders supported long arms terminated by long, slender hands. Although he did not have the athletic appearance of his rival, he must, all the same, have been a sturdy companion. His mind, more alert and caustic than that of the phlegmatic Archibald, rendered his conversation more attractive and picturesque. If Archibald had the beating of him for physical beauty, Gorden could battle advantageously in terms of intelligence.

VII. Mabel Smith

Between those robust men—for Goldry and Harry Smith were also solid fellows—Mabel, slender and radiantly blonde, exquisite in a light Cashmere dress tightened at the waist by a pale green ribbon, came and went lightly, playing her role as mistress of the house, seconded by Betty Symian, serving tea or liqueurs, according to the taste of her guests. In truth, Mabel was reminiscent of a dainty fairy plying her artifices, all grace and beauty, between giant admirers.

That elegant maiden, however, accustomed to all sports, hid muscles and nerves of steel beneath her delicate appearance. She was tall and slender, with an improbably thin waist, a stem to the blossoming of her superb bosom, with firm and full lines, in which the twin cups of her breasts could be divined beneath the symmetrical folds of the corsage. Her neck was slim and graceful, a colonnette of immaculate flesh supporting the delicate oval of her face, her forehead narrow and rather high, framed by the soft diadem of her hair. Her darker eyebrows, broadly arched, shaded superb eyes with pale violet irises and a straight nose with pink nostrils, parted at the base., along with the small, delicately-curved mouth with strong lips, testified to curiosity and sensuality, as the gaze advertised dreams, and the forehead and the definite arc of the chin a firm and tenacious will, especially in its caprices.

VIII. The Spoiled Child

"So you believe, doctor," queried Silven Gorden, "that your search in the forest will be successful?"

"Certainly," Goldry replied. "We'll be numerous, and we'll have Malays with us who have already hunted great apes."

"Will you be joining the expedition, Mr. Smith, my dear neighbor?"

"I had every intention of doing so, at first, but I can't leave my daughter here alone."

"What are you saying, Papa? I have no intention of remaining at Riddle-Temple; I'm going with the expedition."

"Do you think that's wise, Miss Mabel?" exclaimed Gorden. "These forests are almost inaccessible to seasoned men."

"This time, Mabel, I can't give in to your desire," said Harry Smith, authoritatively. "It would be madness, and your presence among the hunters would be a hindrance rather than a help."

"You're joking, Papa dear. In what respect aren't I worth as much as the doctor? Is my godfather seasoned? And yet he wouldn't surrender his place for an empire."

"Your father's right," Archibald put in. "You know that I appreciate your performance in all sporting exercises better than anyone, but this isn't a matter of one day of fatigue. The pursuit might last for weeks, and that requires too much endurance."

Betty Symian thought she ought to intervene. "Your father and Archibald are right. It's not an exercise for a young woman."

Pale with anger, Mabel retorted; "For a start, you can wait to give your opinion until someone asks you for it."

"Mabel, Mabel!" said Smith severely.

"You're all annoying me. Truly, do you think that I'm going to stay here weaving a tapestry, like Penelope, while men are in peril? No matter what the dangers are, I want to run them."

"Bravo!" cried Gorden. "An Amazon couldn't put it better. What the hell, gentlemen—we'll be sufficiently numerous to capture an ape and protect a woman. For myself, I admire and approve of Miss Smith."

Archibald frowned; his rival was supporting Mabel in order to advance in her esteem. "If you're going to take that tone," he said, "I approve too. I didn't know that Gorden was going to be part of the expedition."

"I hadn't decided yet, Miss Smith's attitude has made me understand that it would be shameful not to do so."

"Miss Mabel," Betty risked saying again, "there are perils greater than you seem to believe. The forests of Borneo are full of the unexpected. You're going in order to capture an orangutan, but there are also tigers, wild elephants, snakes..."

"Oh, Miss Mabel is a woman," Gorden put in, "and since our mother Eve, her pretty descendants have had no fear of the serpent."

"This is no time for joking, sir," said the governess, severely. "It's not only ferocious animals; those are the least dangerous. There are, above all, apes that are as wicked as men. Remember Dilou."

"That's true," confessed the Englishman. "Orangutans adore women. Not a month passes among our neighboring islanders, without a Malaysian woman being carried off by apes. But I won't go back on my opinion. There will be enough of us to protect Miss Smith."

"Oh!" said Mabel. "You think that Dilou...?"

"It's certain," said Smith. "Without that, would she have had so much power over Ouha? Besides, she went with him of her own free will."

"All that's just tales to frighten little girls. You're all bad boys to oppose me like this. What I've resolved to do, I'm sticking to."

44

"Oh, Miss Mabel, the orang will carry you off and keep you. You'll be his wife! The mere idea doesn't frighten you?"

"You're going a little crazy, my dear. Know that Ouha never looked at me lustfully. He sought to please me, and that's all."

"I've never forbidden you anything, Mabel," Smith put in, "and you've always been free to make your own decisions—but who will look after Riddle-Temple? If you're going, I'm going too."

"Leave the house in the care of Mistress Symian. If we don't come back, she'll inherit it, which will cause her to forgive her wayward pupil everything."

"Oh, Miss," stammered the governess, "you know very well that when I oppose your whims, it's for your own good."

"I know that, my dear Betty, and I beg your pardon for my harsh words. I won't do it again." She embraced the old lady, coquettishly, and then said: "Well, then, when are we leaving?"

"That depends on Major Bennett. As soon as he arrives with his Malay hunters."

"In that case," said Gorden, "I'll have time to go home and come back with my continent of volunteers. I think I can bring fifty, as many Europeans as indigenous servants."

"Good, good!" exclaimed Mabel, sketching a few dance steps. "Ouha and the orangutans have only to hold still."

"My word," said Gorden, "it will be an opportunity to purge the island. These great apes, which are scarcely found anywhere but Borneo, are too dangerous!"

Mabel smiled. "No more so than humans."

IX. Ouha! Ouha! Ouha!

From then on there was feverish activity. Harry Smith and Archibald were continually shuttling between Riddle-Temple and White House, to which Major Bennett had returned from Sumatra. He had hired twenty Malays, who, to the great satisfaction of his shrewish wife Meg, had no right to set foot in the house and were camping in huts they had built for themselves in a matter of hours.

The Malays certainly had the appearance of true pirates, a profession that their ancestors had followed, and which they had replaced with that of hunting, the only one suited to their savage nature. Small and wiry, their noses flattened over broad mouths that opened like dark gulfs, their teeth were rendered jet-black by the use of an abominable drug composed of betel and chalk, which also made their gums bleed.

Their leader, To Wang, after a few skirmishes with Dutch justice, had escaped and taken refuge in the forests of the heartland. By means of his courage and skill, he had rapidly built a reputation, and that petty celebrity had put him at the head of the caste of "the Damned," a pirate band of the Malaysian islands, the bane of the civilized population. Thanks to his authority over the Damned, To Wang had several times averted revolts by those unfortunates, moved by famine to the pillage of plantations; in gratitude for his services, the Dutch government had forgotten the terrible pirate's former conduct and left him at liberty. Major Bennett had had occasion to use the good offices of the Malay himself, and, knowing him to be capable of great utility, had engaged him as captain and charged him with the recruitment of the little troop.

Two of the hunters, Sing Mah and Ehhi Facu, had brought their wives, and one of the youngest, Eg Merh, his sister Rava, who, extraordinarily, was relatively pretty. Thus, Rava was the queen of the encampment, the other hunters all having the hope of pleasing her.

The animation at White House was soon increased by numerous convoys bringing the necessary food, weapons and tools. Harry Smith had telegraphed America to order sticks of dynamite and various items of apparatus for frightening the apes—powerful batteries, for instance, designed to activate projectors—not to mention two machine-guns with their murderous chaplets. All of that arrived quite rapidly. Nevertheless, the expedition could not get under way before two months, at least—which is to say, two months after Ouha's escape.

As time went by, Bennett sent the men and the equipment to Riddle-Temple, with the exception of the Damned, who were not to leave until the last day, in order that they should not come into contact with the other Malays, who considered them to be impure. Fortunately, there was no lack of room at Riddle-Temple, but—oh, what profanation!—they were obliged to lodge men and equipment in the temple itself. Finally, a troop of three hundred coolies arrived from Java, who would fulfill the function of beasts of burden in the forest.

The contingents of the small army were thus enumerated as follows: three hundred coolie porters; twenty-three Malay hunters, three of them women; fifty woodcutters brought by the Muni-Wali brothers; fifty Europeans recruited by Silven Gorden, belonging to twenty nations, adventurers having traveled just about everywhere, all sturdy and capable of any kind of work provided that they were well-paid; and, finally, fifteen domestics from Riddle-Temple, brought by Smith to serve him and his daughter.

On the day fixed for the departure, the major, the two Muni-Wali brothers and Silven Gorden summoned To Wang, and the five men held a council. That was the fourteenth of April. Two days later, Bennett, the Muni-Walis, Gorden and To Wang carried out an inspection of all the equipment, which they divided up between the porters. Each coolie received a load of thirty kilos; there was, therefore, a total of nine thousand kilos, eight thousand of which were food—rice, biscuits and various canned goods—and alcohol, including palm-wine.

In addition, there were twenty kilos of quinine. The materiel comprised weapons, ammunition, hatchets, pickaxes, spades, rope and string. The quantity of foodstuffs was mediocre, scarcely twenty kilos per man, but they hoped to find fresh meat on the journey, for game was abundant—at least, it was around Riddle-Temple.

After having carefully discussed the column's marching orders, the leaders would set off on campaign. To Wang would head the march with his men, and the Muni-Wali brothers would follow him with their woodcutters, to clear the route. Then would come Gorden and his adventurers; then the group of amateurs, Harry Smith, his daughter, Archibald, Dr. Abraham Goldry and the master's servants; and finally, the coolie porters.

The Malays, charged with finding traces of orangutans, were the expedition's true guides. They were to precede the bulk of the army by a day and mark out the passage that the woodcutters would clear. In case of emergency, the two bodies would concentrate at the center and organize a defense. Major Bennett had judged that it was as well to anticipate an attack, and the brothers Joshua and Jacob were of the same opinion. Every time the caravan would be constrained to camp, in order to rest or hunt for provisions, a broad area around the tents would be cleared in order to avoid surprises.

Everything having been agreed and organized, Harry Smith wanted to bring everyone together on the eve of the departure for a magnificent meal, by way of a stirrup-cup. For that feast, the masters were installed on one of the terraces of the temple, and all the others in the central courtyard. Only the Malays refused, preferring to eat and drink in their huts. The men of impure caste were voluntarily placing themselves outside the society. Dr. Abraham Goldry, dreaming of equality even with the apes, made every effort to persuade them to join in with the communal joy, but it was a waste of his eloquence.

After the copious feast, replete with gaiety, Harry Smith thought he ought to make a speech to his gusts, and, leaning both hands on the stone balustrade, after coughing and spitting, he said:

"Companions, the American flag has been insulted in my person by…" (he hesitated) "…by a man of the woods. Ought I, isolated in this scarcely-civilized land, submit to this insult by ignoring it? Perhaps, it had only been words, I would have excused it and not sought any reparation. But my guest and friend, Dr. Abraham Goldry, citizen of the United States, has been insulted like me, and my daughter, who had offered a hand to that man of the woods, has also been maltreated. Furthermore, a young black princess whom I had welcomed and was to return to her family has been abducted and carried off by that…by that…by that individual. Thus, two honorable families have been challenged. For myself, as I've said, I would have forgiven the insult, the Divine Master having said…having said…that…having said…"

Harry Smith clapped his friend Dr. Abraham on the back—who, having drunk a little too much punch, like his friend, nodded approvingly.

"What the Devil did he say, the Divine Master?" demanded the billionaire, a trifle drunk.

Abraham Goldry shrugged his shoulders and said: "Have a round of punch distributed. That'll remind you."

But Harry collected himself, sticking to his idea. "The Divine Master said…raise your glasses and drink to peace… There, ladies and gentlemen. We leave tomorrow, the sixteenth of April, at sunrise. Go to bed."

That brilliant discourse was acclaimed by those who understood any of it, who were not very numerous, but the others, carried away by good cheer and drink, applauded confidently.

Everyone followed the billionaire's advice and retired to the tents. Soon, sleep came, bringing well-earned rest to all. In the Malay's huts, calm had reigned for some time; they were to depart in the middle of the night. Indeed, shortly after the feast, the Damned hunters slipped silently into the forest and plunged into it like shadows, after the fashion of apes.

The Malays only set foot on the ground when means of advancing through the branches and creepers were lacking. Thick darkness reigned in the ocean of foliage, but the hunters were like wild beasts. They could see well enough to navigate, and they were careful, while advancing, to leave traces of their passage—broken branches, torn-up creepers, tree-trunks marked with a cut. The three women kept company with their brother and husbands. Among the natives of the Malaysian islands, sex is only distinguished by coiffure, the costume being the same for both sexes.

Without a word, the little troop marched all night. At sunrise, it had covered about two miles without any incident. They had heard tigers roaring, snakes hissing and hectic pursuits beneath their feet, but no attack had taken place. At daybreak the little troop halted and gathered in the low branches of an enormous tulip-tree. The women prepared an uncomplicated meal—a handful of rice, a few bananas and a draught of palm-wine.

Suddenly, To Wang raised his hand and made a sign bidding them to listen. Mastication ceased. A clear silvery noise was audible, in a continuous fashion.

"Spring," said Eg Merh laconically, and turned to his sister. "Rava, would you like to go see?"

The young woman took the palm-wine bottle that they had just emptied drew away, leaping from branch to branch like a squirrel.

To Wang made a sign to his companions bidding them to wait, and retraced his steps; having covered a certain distance he lay down on a branch and listened; after a minute he got up, with a satisfied expression. In the distance, a long way behind, the sounds of the ax-blows struck by the route-clearers were echoing. He went back to his companions.

"Ker Mach," he said, "go back and guide the masters here, since there's a spring; they can camp here this evening."

Ker Mach, having made sure that his weapons were in good condition, was getting ready to leave when a terrible scream rang out from the direction in which Rava had gone. In the blink of an eye they were all on their feet, and bounded like tigers in the direction of the spring.

Suddenly, in the green velvet curtain of the forest, a profound gash broke the ground, interrupting the mass of foliage and creepers. On the other side of the ragged ravine, a rocky wall rose up thirty meters, and at the base of that gigantic wall of rock, a babbling steam of pure fresh water was running through the heaped-up blocks. To reach the bottom of the ravine the descent was easy, the terrain being steep but practicable, and lianas extending from the forest reaching down to the bottom of the abyss, in search of the moisture necessary to their existence.

Insensitive to the marvels of the location and paying no heed to the scenery, the Malays wanted to find out immediately where Rava was, and why she had screamed.

Terrible roars caused them to raise their heads. At the summit of the granite wall, twenty orangutans of large stature were standing. At the sight of the hunters they uttered cries and beat their breasts with their fists, producing a sound like the rumble of thunder.

Soon, their attention was drawn to the bottom of the crevasse, on the far side of the stream; a colossal ape was moving along the base of the rock, searching for a way out in order to rejoin his companions—and over his shoulder, folded in two, as Rava's body, hanging limply, as if broken. She was undoubtedly unconscious.

Finally, the ape found what he was looking for. An enormous liana descended from the top of the wall to within his reach. He seized it and began to scale the rocks, toward his companions, who were encouraging him with their cries. The Malays could not fire on the orangutan abductor without the risk of killing Rava.

"Fire on the others!" their chief commanded.

The rifles commenced a sustained fire on the apes. Two fell, disappearing behind the escarpment. At that moment, the huge ape arrived at the summit and set foot on the edge. He turned round, drew himself up to his full height and lifted his victim into the air—and the hairy giant uttered a roar, like a cry of war and victory:

"Ouha! Ouha! Ouha!"

Behind him, the great apes reappeared, and there was an immense, quasi-human and guttural acclamation, as if to a glorious leader:

"Ouha! Ouha! Ouha!"

X. The Virgin Forest of Borneo

The virgin forest! Those words generally evoke an idea of vegetative splendor, a place where gigantic trees support leafy foliage and starry lines of corollas. A luxuriant vegetation displays a thick carpet of moss and flowers; the sun, always radiant, illuminates that monstrous paradise, causing the most dazzling colors of fruits and magical birds to sparkle.

There is always a considerable distance between the enchantment of dreams and reality.

On leaving Riddle-Temple, the explorers' column had moved into a terrain that was fairly hospitable to marching. In the neighborhood of the Temple, the felling undertaken for the construction of the palisade had thinned out the forest. After a mile or so, however, the spectacle changed completely and the Muni-Wali brothers' woodcutters were obliged to begin the struggle.

Mabel, who had been astonished at first that they were setting out on foot, understood the material impossibility of using horses in the virgin forest—which is to say, a place in which, perhaps for thousands of years, the intense vegetation of the tropical regions has reigned as absolute mistress. The trees, whatever their species, do not grow in soil, but in a humus of plants and dead wood heaped up by time in chaotic agglomeration.

From a tree felled by age or by lightning, which rots on the ground in the midst of a mass of parasitic vegetation, shoots are born, which grow rapidly, reaching as best they can toward the sun, its light and heat—for beneath the virgin forest, the sunlight never penetrates. Infinitely extended toward all parts of the horizon, entangled branches and creepers link the crowns of the trees together, forming a kind of uneven platform of quivering vegetation through the woods, which light does not penetrate.

A greenish-blue penumbra reigns beneath that mysterious foliage. At the feet of centenarian trees, on a litter of decomposing plants, which is sometimes as much as twenty meters thick, enormous mushrooms and poisonous plants grow. Splendid orchids cling to the rough and worm-eaten bark of the trees, hanging down, their form and color indescribably bizarre.

In that abysm of vegetable debris, everywhere the ground offers a steep ravine, the torrential waters of tropical storms create marshes or swamps. There, lurking amid the heaped-up plants, swarms an entire society of horrible and venomous reptiles. The ground, by contrast, forms dry tumescences serving as the abode and realm of terrible red ants whose size sometimes attains three centimeters.

In addition to the reptiles, there are millions of flies of every kind and every size; it is not always the largest that are the most intolerable or the most dangerous. One can see spiders with bodies the size of hen's eggs scuttling, centipedes twenty centimeters long, cockroaches and superb fireflies that shine like stars by night.

All of that intense, hectic superb and horrible life flies and circles incessantly, in ferocious harassment. Up above, very high, toward the sun and the light, other creatures circulate, including birds of every size, with sparkling plumage shining with every color of the prism. The branches and creepers are heavily laden with flowers and fruits. Up above, there are cries and songs; down below, silence, decomposition and death.

Fortunately, from time to time, in the midst of that mortal desert, a delightful oasis appears.

What has created it? A tornado, or lightning.

A tornado uproots and breaks everything, sometimes over a space of several square miles, leaving nothing in a place where extravagant vegetation once reigned but a flat desert cleared of all growth.

Lightning pulverizes and ignites, after months of dryness; a fire ignited by lightning finds ready fuel; then the forest catches fire; it is a grandiose and terrible spectacle. The giants of the forest, eaten away by the fire from base to summit, explode like shells, projecting veritable jets of sap and resin, which burn like alcohol. Then, everything flees and disperses: insects, large mammals, reptiles and birds all escape, or fall victim to the scourge.

Then, where the formidable agglomeration of vegetable and animal life of every sort once rose up, there are immense plains of ash and scoria. However, a few weeks later, grasses grow, seeds arrive, borne from who knows where on the wind, and sprout in the soil fertilized by the fire. Soon, all that enormous life recommences. For a few years, however, there are veritable Edens, contrasted by their freshness and the light that still penetrates them, with the terrible dreadful forest that surrounds them—but the swarming life, wild and uncultivated, reckless and superabundant, invades them again; and beneath the heavy tropical sun, the frightful Hell of verdure, flowers, poisons, putrefaction and extraordinary beasts with nightmarish muzzles, eyes and paws, begins again.

XI. In the Burned Plain

Through the virgin forest the long column of hunters advanced, marching, sliding or crawling in the midst of that desert of luxuriant fermentations. Mabel, the superb creature of luxury, marched in silence, nauseated, her aching head enveloped in triple gauze, demanding by means of gestures the assistance of her two mendicant of amour: Archibald, red-faced, sweating and breathless but still solid in spite of it; and Silven Gorden, cool, dry, sure-footed and eagle-eyed.

The pioneers were, at any rate, were striving to render the route practicable. The Malays ahead of them were chasing away all the vermin of the bogs, which they filled in with bundles of sticks and tree-trunks felled by the axes of the Muni-Wali brothers' woodcutters. In spite of that, the column was scarcely moving forward three or four miles a day.

By chance, on the sixth day, they discovered a large plain: a vast area presumably denuded by a fire, of which no trace remained; a clearing without visible bounds, which extended as far as the eye could see to the horizon. That was a relief for the travelers. Harry Smith declared that they would rest there for a day while the Malays scouted ahead.

Since the abduction of Rava the hunters had been crazed with fury, and it had required all of Major Bennett's authority to prevent them from quitting the expedition in order to chase after the apes without delay.

Suddenly, a stream appeared zigzagging through the tall grass, and the troop of anthropoid-hunters paused to make camp on its banks.

XII. Ouha's Humanity

Beyond that plain, which extended for a dozen kilometers, the forest recommenced, but differently. The ground, which rose up at the horizon, silhouetted against a cloudless sky, was uneven and tormented, leaving traces everywhere of the volcanic origin of the region. The trees were more scattered, thick bushes alternating with arid, sandy spaces. Numerous springs emerged from the bases of the hills, running away in petty torrents or small cascades, soon forming a stream that hollowed out a bed in a more friable soil, going to join the river Am-Aukang fifty miles away, which flows into the sea a few miles from Imbuk. A sequence of undulations, alternating valleys with the slopes of the mountain chain, formed a long sequence of gradients before reaching the dorsal spine of the highest peaks.

Each of these valleys formed a green grassland, shaded by clumps of woodland, the essences of which were mostly useful or precious. Breadfruit trees, coconut palms, tulip-trees and wild bananas alternated with flame-trees with purple and gold flowers and tamarind-trees. Here and there were lethifers,[10] jambosas with refreshing fruits, yams with prodigious alimentary roots, precious sago-tress and durians with a fetid odor but a delicious taste. There were bamboos with tasty pith, and the chatny, a nourishing vegetable that grows everywhere in the Malaysian islands.

It was there that, for centuries, the race of orangutans had propagated, sheltered from the Dutch conquest and the island's natives. It was there that Ouha, the last offspring of a

---

[10] I have Anglicized the text's *lethifères*, but cannot identify what tree the author might mean; the word means "deadly." The jambosa is also known as the "Malay plum" or the "rose-apple." The "chatny" mentioned later in the paragraph is the source of the English word chutney.

human hybridization, reigned. The orangs' quest for woman does not date from our era; at all times, the anthropoids have abducted women and made them their mates. It goes without saying that assimilation was easy with an indigenous people of simian appearance.

Three generations ago, Ouha's ancestor had succeeded in inducting into his tribe a superb Malabar woman run aground, no one knows how, in Borneo, and who voluntarily abandoned the plantation on which she was employed, in order not to do anything any longer, and follow a magnificent ape into the forest. It was not rare, in that era, when slavery was still prevalent, to see a slave leave her master's plantation of her own volition for a superbly virile orangutan who took her fancy. The mentality of a native does not, after all, far surpass that of an orangutan, and for women there was a lubricious advantage, apes having a real predominance over humans in the respect.[11]

From that union, a singular hybrid was born, a mixture of degenerate ape and Oceanian woman. That ape languished and died young, but not without having fecundated a female orangutan, who produced a normal ape. The latter mated with one of his peers, and from that union Ouha was born, who manifested considerable physical similarities with ancestress. His stature was taller and straighter, his encephalum more developed; it was easier for him to walk upright, and his intelligence was more cunning than that of his fellows.

We humans are very proud of our intelligence, but with a little observation, we could see that every other living being also has an intelligence—to which we have given the name of instinct, although, in reality, it is an authentic intelligence that directs and regulates their needs, beyond which it is unneces-

---

[11] This allegation is utterly false, but is an understandable embellishment of the mythology of the great apes. Several naturalists reproduced the tales told to them by indigenes of orangutans stealing women, and anxious imagination did the rest.

sary for them to go, since their nature, their appetites and their amours demand no more of it.

Humans have, by degrees, arrived at a superiority, if it is one: a mind that generally tends to do everything that is harmful to their hygiene, their amour and the procreation of their species. Animals, by contrast, never do anything in opposition to good sense. Humans know that alcohol, opium and tobacco are bad for their health, and that they induce degeneration in the race, and yet they are ingenious in their manufacture and use them immoderately. Apes are certainly the animals most similar to humans, and easily assimilate our vices, but they are unfamiliar with them, and in order for them to smoke or get drunk, it is necessary for them to be taught by humans.

There is, moreover, in the mind of an ape, in addition to a tendency to imitation—which is primarily a kind of play—a cunning superior to that of humans, for it is able, thanks to its mask, to conceal itself perfectly. When a man thinks about certain actions or mulls over certain ideas that he would rather hide, in spite of striving to let nothing show, a slight curl of the lip or a gleam in the eye will betray him. An ape, however, offers no evidence at all. Only anger is capable of animating that expressionless face; suddenly without any warning, one of the animal's four arms strikes or grips.

With regard to Ouha, that was one of the characteristics of his human descent; his mouth had a vague smile, which emphasized the crease of his eyelids. Dr. Abraham Goldry had observed accurately when he had found an anatomical resemblance between Ouha and prehistoric humans. That orangutan was, in truth, almost a man, and considerably superior even to some white, black or yellow individuals of the human species. His incontestable supremacy over the others apes derived from that.

XIII. A Napoleonic Soul in an Ape

The orangutan sovereign Ouha, an anthropoid closer than any of his relatives to humanity, exercised over his ape tribe the absolute authority of a Caesar, Julius or Augustus, over humans tamed by his genius. No one, even among the strongest of those robust and lithe individuals who commanded incursions and led enterprises through the forest, followed by their feebler allies and clients, dared to disobey the orders of the King or oppose any resistance to his desires, no matter how tyrannical and imperious they might sometimes be.

Ouha, an autocrat of genius, knew how to make use of the slightest powers, to attach recognized superiorities to himself by means of prerogatives, genuine missions and even distinctions, grating them genuine simian troops to command, and giving places near to himself to those whose imperious sagacity distinguished them from the crowd. A veritable discipline, a simple mechanism of which the pride of chiefs was the pivot, regulated the thousand and some individuals, males and female, of the city of the apes.

Furthermore, in periods of calm, the dignitaries could indulge their slothful indolence on the reserves of fruits and provisions heaped up in abundance for Ouha, the idle sovereign, fond of hunting in the immense forest, making war on neighboring tribes, and ambitious above all for trophies taken from humans, to whom—perhaps enviously—he strove to get close and whom he pursued with a hatred or admiration, conscious or not, that became characteristic.

From the first year of his life onwards, the puerile ape, a caricature of a giant monster, had subjugated the tribe of orangutans to his already-sovereign will by means of the choice he made of escapades, from which a benefit, an authority for those of his tribe, always emerged. At that time, Ouha's innumerable family had been under the domination of a tribe whose faces were framed by black beards. Crafty and highly ambitious, Ouha had insinuated himself into the good graces of the old chiefs, especially one named Kom'itsch, who was venerated by tradition as the descendant of a very ancient race.

An expedition in which he and young adults recruited by him had raided a Dutch farm, from which he brought back objects fabricated by humans, had given him an influence in the ancient tribe that had enslaved his own. He had flattered the powerful, which he needed to do to become one of them and obtain a command. Then, on returning from a fruitful war, certain of the love of his subordinates, he had been able to foment discontents that had been long dormant—in the fashion of humankind—against the real dynasty of old chiefs, tyrants, predators and stealers of females from subject families. After a simulacrum of repression, he had assumed the leadership of the mutiny, until the triumph of his own relatives, those with red neck-beards.

As he had seen humans do while he had spied on them during his voyages to the valleys and plains, Ouha had selected as his palace one of the natural caverns he had discovered in the mountain-side, masked by brushwood and verdure. There he had stored the stolen pottery and clothes of his human victims, necklaces taken from Malays, vases and glassware, even weapons, the fruits of raids mounted on humans, which he did not know how to use. In addition, provisions—tributes levied on his subjects—were carefully accumulated there.

He knew how to use these tithes and trophies to ensure his power, by means of the self-interest and cupidity of the orangs he governed, ingeniously and shrewdly managing his resources and the wiles of his instinct. By virtue of an innate science, a reliable instinct, he attached the entire might of his tribe, rather than any faction or party, to himself; thanks to him, they became the lords of the forest, rich and feared.

An ambition grew in his soul as his ascendancy progressed, by virtue of having seen humans and having observed that, although they were inferior in brute strength, they were masters of animals, even of the apes made in their image.

Ouha, as sovereign, wanted to steal the prestige of humankind, and, having been vanquished—since he was always considered by the humans as an animal—to appropriate from the victors the means of domination.

Above all, he was strongly ambitious for his own precedence. Proud in his willful egotism, he dreamed of being, in the eyes of his own kind, a being different from them—as he thought himself to be, and truly was.

He succeeded in overcoming the instinctive terrors of his race, and tamed within himself the simian far of storms. Sometimes, when the sky lit up with lightning flashes, zigzagging between the high branches of giant trees, and the thunder rolled its clamors, like the noise of great rotten trees falling to the ground and causing it to shake, the terrified orangs saw, standing up on top of a rock or at the very top of a tree in the middle of a clearing, the silhouette of Ouha, defying the heavens.

Certain of the effect that a charlatanism of courage can produce, Ouha even made sweeping gestures, uttering cries as if he really had the power to command the elements, perhaps to direct the lightning, to be the conductor of the orchestra of the tempest.

Never having been punished for that audacity, Ouha's valor increased against other unknown phenomena, the terror of animal minds. His boldness was limitless and, doubtless by virtue of that very temerity, always fortunate. Thus drunks often come through danger successfully.

Uncontested chief and king, the supreme arbiter of his tribe's destiny, when he screeched his name, Ouha manifested the terrible menace or hope of the apes with the black beards and red side-whiskers, for the vanquished had swelled the ranks of the victorious tribe and their blood, over the years had mingled, without henceforth producing any antagonism between the two unified races.

Rival tribes and families no longer dared, unless they were very numerous, to attempt to steal the fruits or steal the females of Ouha's subjects. Powerful, he incessantly increased the domination of the simian city he governed.

As among humans, legends forged by terror and admiration are created in the obscure intellect of beasts. When a shepherd's dog in a region has proved his strength, beating the mastiffs of other flocks, or when a cockerel in a poultry-yard has grouped a larger number of hens has reduced his rivals to respect for his property, others avoid him out of fear, and the weak court him, seeing his amity and protection. Thus the orangs propagated the name of the all-powerful Ouha, the strongest, biggest and most audacious of his race, through the forest for several leagues around, just as human do.

During some of the long wanderings he undertook, Ouha ventured as far as the huts of Malays and even the white men's dwellings. It was during one of those excursions that, hearing the sound of axes clearing his domain, he took the risk of approaching, albeit prudently, and encountered Dilou asleep in the shade of a large tree.

To begin with, he was amused to see such a pretty little creature, more beautiful than and yet so similar to female orangutans. Then, from his troubled flesh the irresistible desire arose for an exceptional embrace, for the possession of that young flesh, less hairy than his own; and, coveting Dilou for his pleasure, he picked her up without difficulty with a single bound, as if he were picking a fruit, and carried her off.

After having enjoyed the astonishment of the apes in the presence of his conquest, he was able to profit from the alliance, sensing that the amorous conquest would make him even stronger. Would not the orangutans, devoid of rationality, respect him by reason of that superb alliance, which brought him closer to the tyrant of the beasts, the omnipotent murderer, the vanquisher of nature: humankind?

Then, very quickly, Dilou, having become his wife, became attached to the monster, her lover, with every fiber of her being; she testified her affection for him, compounded out of sensuality, fear and native submission, before everyone. Meanwhile, childishly malevolent, and sensing that she was protected, the girl loved to torment the great apes—hitting them, even wounding them, and making them serve for her amusement. Cruel and pretty, she was almost more bestial than them, even though she was a human.

Thus, Ouha alone enjoyed her favors. Ouha dominated his fellows in that too—a love without parallel in their short memories.

And then came the abduction of Rava.

More delicate, and of a finer beauty, the Malay woman similarly kept at a distance all those from whom—thanks to the protection of the abhorrent monster, the master who had subjugated her by force—she had nothing to fear. Besides which, Ouha, jealous of his wives and no less so of the privileges he had arrogated to himself, kept his subjects, including his courtiers, at a sufficient distance not to allow them to penetrate the childishness of the prestige he exercised from afar with a wise prudence.

Fire, of which he had been afraid at first, but had accustomed himself to approach, was already, in the uncomprehending eyes of his subject orangs, a fearful symbol of Ouha's omnipotence. He had taken objects and women from humans; he had, in addition, robbed them of that fearful unknown, flame, the devourer of giant trees, the light that put wild beasts and nocturnal creatures to flight—all those who were not humans but gods!

And the incursions and raids that Ouha organized were, in truth, increasingly productive.

By means of gestures and monosyllables, the hairy sovereign was able to disperse the apes he led on methodical conquests; he reinforced those who faltered with new strength, maintained reserves, and as able to guide is animal army through the darkness of the forest, because he had been able to render them docile, bending to his will the boldest of those who had dared to aspire to rivalry.

One that he had made a chief, to whom he confided real missions, had dared to carry on his shoulder a branch being a strong resemblance to a rifle, which he had picked up during one of his expeditions, but which he utilized as a scepter, not knowing how to use it in any other way. Ouha, making use of the carbine like a club, killed the impertinent with a single blow, and thus proved the lie of the usurper of his authority. Other salutary examples had followed, at intervals in which habituation was able to generate doubt with regard to a king against whom nothing could prevail.

Eventually, when Ouha discovered the march through the forest of a caravan of white men, among whom was a woman, the audacious orangutan immediately conceived in the depths of his soul, by virtue of so many efforts and contacts with glorified humans, like a king coveting a new crown, the supreme ambition of carrying off the white virgin. He would then possess, for his satisfaction, the three types of feminine humanity known to him and his kind.

As a petty king or a prince wants to marry the heiress of a powerful empire; as a Bonaparte, a soldier of fortune magnified amid the agitation of ideas and crowds, after amours in which his senses and ambitions have already found happiness and support in a creole, strives to hoist himself further by a noble marriage; so the dictator, king and Napoléon of the apes, the victorious hero Ouha, premeditated the abduction of Mabel, in order to make her his queen, attaining his own apogee by virtue of her possession.

XIV. Me, Ouha! Me!

Six days had gone by since the abduction of Rava. Three months before, Ouha had returned to his kingdom with his usual escort: twenty elite orangs, who made up his personal guard. Ouha's primitive tribe had once comprised about forty couples, but the simian emperor's conquests had added the vanquished tribes to the population. Presently, Ouha's numbered eight hundred, as many males as females. It was the largest agglomeration of anthropoids that had ever been formed.

Thus far, the conqueror had only dreamed of the domination of his own race, but his brief sojourn in Harry Smith's home had given him new ideas; strange concepts were battling in this dense brain. More than any of his other subjects, he had the particular gift of memory—not as highly-developed as it is in humans, but in contrast to other apes, in which the quality is completely lacking. Ouha could remember events dating back several months. Life at Riddle-Temple had left an ineradicable imprint in his brain, and since he had left, he had relived its slightest episodes without becoming bored.

One image, above all, pursued him: that of Mabel Smith. There was such a difference between the beautiful American and the women he had possessed, like Dilou, Rava and a few others that had died among the apes. He remembered a bright and fresh complexion, eyes of a color strange to him, hair that was reminiscent of living light. Dazzled, the ape desired that flesh, destined for pale men oddly enveloped in fabrics, who seemed to him to be feeble creatures, and yet superior to him.

Moreover, those gods incessantly opened their mouths to articulate a thousand different sounds, and seemed, between themselves, to be interested in unknown things.

The language of apes is, in fact, extremely simple: thirty words, which are guttural grunts rather than articulate language. Nevertheless, with those few words and very active

66

mime, orangs succeeded in communicating everything that is capable of interesting their species. A few of them even had a name, which they proclaimed while beating their breasts, which was a way of saying: "Me, Ouha!" or "Me, Uau!" or "Me, Brray!"

Those were the name of the notables of the tribe.

XV. The Chimpanzee Ko-Zu

About a year before, an ape that was not of the orang race had arrived in Ouha—which as not only the name of their king but the one by which the anthropoids designated the region. He was an emaciated and anemic chimpanzee, exhausted by fatigue. He had appeared one morning requesting shelter. The majority of the orang chiefs had been in favor of killing the stranger or chasing him away, but Ouha had come to the defense of the intruder and ordered his admission into the tribe. The latter, who called himself Ko-Zu, soon became the emperor's confidant and favorite.

Ko-Zu was no ordinary ape; he had been part of one of the troupes of an American showman. Admirably dressed, he had been the sensational star attraction of his circus; introduced to the public as a very civilized ape, he was the perfect imitation of a haughty gentleman in a suit, white cravat and top hat; he ate, drank, smoked, shook hands profusely and signed cards distributed to visitors with his own name. The steamship carrying the circus and his fortune had been wrecked one day on the reefs that surround a part of the coast of Borneo. What would become of the passengers? The chimpanzee, jumping overboard and clinging to a piece of wreckage, ran aground on the shore.

At the sight of the forests, forgetting his acquired civilization, he had plunged into them as if into a refuge. It was certainly an atavism, for until then, Ko-Zu had only known forests painted on canvas. He had been captured when newly-born, then raised and nourished by a native woman who did not differentiated between him and her own baby son. In the virgin forest, Ko-Zu was obliged to serve a harsh apprenticeship, his ape education paralyzed in worldly habits. Fortunately for him, his capers and bounds led him to Ouha's kingdom.

For a year, Ko-Zu had resumed simian habits, and, without having the strength and agility of an orangutan, he was capable of holding a distinguished rank among them. A confidant of the monarch, he and Ouha had exchanged their impressions so effectively, combining Ouha's recent adventures with those that the ape artiste had recounted to him, that they strove together to elucidate the mysteries of European life.

The meditative Ouha thought about that frequently when he went back to his palace—for, unlike the other orangs, whose shelters were constructed in the trees, he lived with his wives in a cavern comprised of several compartments. The monarch generally resided in the largest, the one that communicated with the exterior. Lying on a bed of leaves, or squatting with his legs crossed in the Oriental style in front of a large stone that served as a table, on which his wives deposited his meals.

The females lived in the second grotto, the harem being composed of three young orangs, Dilou and Rava. The king frequently went into his gyneceum, for, in contrast to the other orangs, he never coupled in public. That departure from simian protocol gave him a prestige and respect that no one dared contravene. The act of copulation was forbidden in the presence or vicinity of the monarch, who punished offenders severely.

Having returned three days before, Ouha strove to make his confidant understand what had happened at Riddle-Temple. He did his best to depict Mabel's person, and demanded of the traveler whether he had seen similar beings. Ko-Zu had certainly seen them; he had even had intimate elations with a few rich and blasé women who had sought new sensations in the chimpanzee's caresses.

Astonished, Ouha demanded details. So that species of divinity was a female? It had a sex, just like orangutans? Like Dilou? Like Rava? Ko-Zu opined with his head that it was the same thing, except for being less hairy, and perfumed by something unknown, which smelled vile.

Strange gleams appeared in Ouha's eyes. If he had known, he would have carried off the blonde female from Riddle-Temple instead of Dilou—but he still had time.

His emissaries had told him that the Europeans were continuing their pursuit, and that the invasion of the territory of Ouha as imminent. Ouha was indecisive. Should he wait for the attack or should he strike first? He had made a mistake. The time he had lost in bringing Rava back home and vanquishing the pretty Malay's resistance—he had only been able to possess her the first time by using force—had permitted the hunters to emerge from the forest and find themselves now in a more favorable situation.

In his favor he had the number of combatants, since he could put more than three hundred strong adults into the field, but he knew that his adversaries were carrying weapons that sowed death at a distance. During Rava's abduction one of the apes had been killed and another wounded.

XVI. The Autocrat

Then, having gathered is principal chiefs, Ouha sketched out the situation for them. Harr, the hothead, who had distinguished himself in the revolt of the red-haired orangutans wanted to march immediately to attack the enemy and annihilate them. By contrast, the sage Brray issued the advice to wait and only to attack by night, in the forest if possible. That was also the opinion of Rhou-Ou. The adversary did not know the region of Ouha, and had only advanced following the trail of Rava's abductors. It would not be difficult to draw them into one of the region's forests and there, with the trees and the lianas against them, to engage in battle with all the advantages.

"That procedure is excessively prudent," mimed Harr. "We fight in broad daylight, face to face! Let's make the invaders see that we're hairy, and better than them."

Kri-Kri and Flu-Hu, both young orangs of proven bravery, applauded frantically. Brray shrugged his shoulders disdainfully. "That's imprudent youth!" he seemed to be saying "What's the point of shedding precious blood unnecessarily. We can win easily, without risk. Why create widows and orphans?" And his gesture designated the females and their offspring arranged in a circle outside the cavern.

Out there, the she-apes seemed to be inferring what was happening in the council, for they could be seen agitating and chatting animatedly.

"Bah!" Harr retorted. "What do a few dead and crippled matter, when one can acquire immortal glory?"

"Glory!" said a white-haired oldster then, who answered to the name of Frréé. "A word devoid of meaning! You dream of glory because you hope to emerge from the battle unscathed, but if your body is rotting in the sun, sooner rather than later, what good is glory to you? Believe me, children, no good can come of war, and, may the great Ouha forgive me, it would have been wiser to leave those dolls with their families than attract the thunder-bearing humans to our land."

Ouha, thus challenged, turned an irritated face to the oldster.

"Who is the master here? What's the use of my power, if I can't do what I want? These humans have been imprudent in pursuing us this far, for I had the intention of going to them. This land is ours. If we allow them to do so, the white apes will drive us back into the western forests in future, after having decimated us, and perhaps a few of us will be unlucky enough to be imprisoned in iron cages. Believe me, we ought not to go to sleep in a shameful peace when enemies invade our homeland. I have been a prisoner of humans myself for a few days, and I know what I'm talking about. I've consulted you for form's sake, my friends. My decision is made. I want to extend the limits of my empire all the way to the sea and expel the invaders."

The quadrumane's gesture seemed to embrace the world. He continued: "I am the elect, the messenger, the representative of the gods. You owe me, by virtue of that title, a passive an absolute obedience. I shall fulfill my sacred mission, and I shall make orangutans the sovereign people."

They all bowed respectfully; some of them even prostrated themselves and came to lick his feet. Among the most servile was the reckless Harr. Belly-down at Ouha's feet, he started ferreting through the hair in search of game, of which he made a meal when the hunt was fruitful. Ouha soon pushed him away, gently.

"To satisfy your advice, I shall divide the attack. Harr and Kri-Kri, at the head of a hundred volunteers, will attack as they wish, but while drawing the Whites toward the forest, where Brray and Rhou-Ou will be waiting for them, also with a hundred combatants. The rest of the army and I will form a reserve, ready to assist either party in peril. Prepare yourselves. We'll attack at sundown."

Ouha having spoken thus, in mime, the council withdrew and the chiefs busied themselves assembling their troops.

XVII. Interlude, with Sapajous, Mandrills and Baboons[12]

Between the mountainous group, the general quarters of the orangutans, and the camp of Europeans and Asians, there was a forest about ten miles in extent. Because it was on a more elevated plateau, that forest offered an appearance quite different from the one that the troop of orang-hunters had just come through, with so many difficulties.

The trees with the most precious essences were here represented by mahogany-trees, ebony trees, parasol pines and, in the dampest part, bamboos. The harder soil had resisted the invasion of parasitic plants; only dense thickets of mastic-trees and plants resembling of thorny reeds opposed the march. The foliage was swarming with birds and monkeys.

Among the latter, the genteel sapajous were particularly abundant, their mischievous faces and laughing eyes glimpsed in every tangle of branches. At time, they passed by in hundreds like a whirlwind, in a panic, frightened by a mandrill or a baboon, which, less alert, was threatening them from afar by grinding its teeth. Then, their fear having passed, their resumed their games and frolics.

Since the valley, all the varieties of quadrumanes had been excited. The coming of the humans had disturbed all the inhabitants of this wilderness. So, keeping their distance, all of them watched, not missing a gesture of the intruders and trying to comprehend the motive for that biped invasion.

---

[12] Literary fauna rarely correspond to natural fauna in French adventure novels, and species are often found far from their natural ranges. None of the named primates is native to Borneo, and these must therefore be regarded as fictitious variants; I have retained the name *sapajou* rather than translating it into "capuchin monkey," as the term is obviously being used loosely or eccentrically.

They did not have to wait long to be informed, for the Malays, sent forth as scouts, did not return to the camp without having claimed a few victims intended to add some fresh meat to the routine culinary fare. But the insouciant sapajous continued leaping and capering, playing with one another or with rays of sunlight filtering through the branches.

XVIII. Stories of Elephants...

After a good night's rest—the first since they had left Riddle-Temple—everyone had woken up feeling restored and in a good humor. From dawn onwards, animation reigned everywhere, everyone doing their best to repair the damage caused by the past days of marching, either to their boots, the straps of their luggage, or their torn garments. Mabel, already back from the river where she had gone to take a reparative bath, was standing on the threshold of her tent contemplating the picturesque scene.

She had adopted a very simple costume, which showed off her youthful beauty and the grace of her figure better than elegant apparel: a short brown skirt from which her high-stockinged legs emerged, terminated by slender feet shod in brown leather. Her torso was molded by the folds of a pale brown linen jacket, gathered at the waist by a leather belt to which a revolver and cartridge-case were attached. Curls escaped from her white helmet, punctuating the impudent features of her face—energetic in spite of the delicacy of their lines—with gold.

On the route, in spite of the crushing fatigue and the ravines that had to be crossed, without paying much heed to the innumerable miseries of the journey, the biting insects and the suspected dangers, Mabel had joked, laughed at trivial incidents, with the hectic delight of an insouciant child amused by anything at all. Her gaiety cheered up the men. Those of the escort admired her respectfully and sought her veil with their eyes during those bad moments in which weariness weighs down the strongest and saps their energy.

In spite of the apparent coldness that Mabel was accustomed to display to her pseudo-fiancé Wilson, and her mischievous teasing, aware of her power, the young woman appreciated Archibald's real and positive qualities as much as his veritable affection. The intimacy of the journey often brought the three young people together, and Mabel, ever the coquette, tried to pay equal attention to Archibald and Gorden. The capricious young woman, after a few amiable remarks, for which Wilson was glad, gave a marvelous welcome to Gorden, whose mind, more alert than Archibald's, found means of rendering the monotony of the much less fatiguing by means of a humorous and encouraging comment, or a compliment as agreeable as a flower.

Often, an anecdote, a story of hunting or adventure, concluded with a gallant observation, and the American woman, not remaining indifferent, would reply with a genteel smile, which irritated Archibald and encouraged his rival.

For a week, Mabel had been complaining. The fatiguing days of marching had become too monotonous for her taste. She wanted incidents—dangers, even. Thus, the emergence from the interminable virgin forest, always the same, was very welcome.

The new landscapes contrasted advantageously with those of the preceding days—but Mabel did not regret them. Past fatigues rendered a little rest in a less brutal nature doubly agreeable. And now the Malay hunters were returning to the camp. Having taken their booty to the cooks, they headed toward the Americans' tent.

It was the first time that one had been set up there, and that was not the least attraction to the little sapajous, which dared to approach from tree to tree and bush to bush, almost to within arm's reach of the travelers. One of them even dared to take a little mirror that Mabel held out to it, and the young woman was amused for some time by the surprise and grimaces of the graceful animal.

In the meantime, To Wang had separated from his companions. He came over to Major Bennett, the only one apart from Silven Gorden who understood the Malay language.

"Is there anything new?" asked the major.

"Yes master; we've encountered the free men."

"Have you seen the prisoners?"

"Yes, our sister Rava. She wanted to come to us, but the free men dragged her away with them."

"How many of them were there?"

"A dozen."

"If they aren't too numerous, things will work out of their own accord. Do you have a plan?"

To Wang shrugged his shoulders. "First we need to know how many there are, and where their village is."

"What? What's that you say? Their village?"

"Yes. The free men make their shelters in the trees, and in groups, as we do on the ground. When we've identified the place, I'll make my plan."

"And you think it's in this forest?"

"I know that we've seen Rava and twelve orangs. That's all. I've come back to tell you and to find out whether we're resuming the march tomorrow."

"Wait."

Having made his friends party to the Malay chief's report and having received general assent, the major went back to To Wang.

"You can continue your search. We'll leave tomorrow at dawn."

The indefatigable hunter bowed and signaled to his men. They returned to the forest, drawing in their wake a whole swarm of curious little monkeys.

On this occasion, the excursionists found themselves comfortably seated at dinner time before a copious and pleasantly varied meal.

"Finally," said Goldry, "we're going to get to grips. I feel quite excited. Just as long as nothing unfortunate happens to my friend Ouha."

"Your big ape," said Mabel, "merits a stern punishment, firstly for his past conduct, and also to make him more tractable in future."

"It wasn't him who was most at fault. We were wrong to mock him."

"What a pity! Must one avoiding laughing, simply because one is the owner of one of these animals?"

"Animals!" snorted the doctor. "That's what you think? Personally, I respect Ouha, my contemporary, like an ancestor."

"You might think that, but don't say it," said Silven Gorden. "For myself, I confess that I've never seen these great apes without experiencing a kind of malaise. There are truly too many similarities between them and humans for one not to be strongly impressed—especially, you know, when they're mortally wounded. I saw one of them that had been shot by one of my friends; I watched him die. He looked at us with such a reproachful expression that Paddy MacFerdan swore that he would never shoot at an orang again."

"What are you doing here then?" asked Archibald, ironically.

"I told you when we set off—to protect Miss Smith if any danger threatens."

Archibald was about to reply, but Mabel got in ahead of him. "Thank you," she said, dryly, "but I'm capable of looking after myself."

"I know that you not only have the beauty of Diana, the divine huntress, but also her intrepidity. There are, however, unexpected dangers for which the support of a second might be useful, and I wouldn't be ashamed, in case of peril, to appeal to your courage."

Mabel smiled. "You can count on me."

"Well," said the major, "we're in a region where it's necessary not to rely on any aid. There are situations where temerity becomes folly. Look, I'll tell you the story of one of my youthful adventures; I declare without shame that I was afraid. It was at the time of the Dutch campaign in Borneo. I was serving as a lieutenant under Colonel Werspick.

"For three days we had been crawling, as we've just done in the forest, with the differenced that we had to clear a path ourselves. So, when we halted, we fell like dead weights into a veritably brutish sleep. Then, one morning, I was woken up with a start by a frightful clamor. Around me there was a terrible chaos of broken branches, cries of agony, gunshots— and amid that noise I heard, for the first time, the trumpeting of furious elephants. Fortunately, an enormous tree-trunk provided me with a shelter between its massive roots, into which I hastened to disappear. And this is what had happened...

"As morning approached, a family of elephants had wandered into our camp: a male, a female and a calf, which was already a good size. Among the sentinels was a Scottish volunteer. I can still remember him—his name was George Barnard, and I liked him a lot because we were the only ones, apart from the colonel, who spoke English. So, poor George was on guard when the elephants arrived. Until then, he'd only seen them in zoos. As the animals were heading for the camp he was afraid for him comrades and he fired at the male, which was in the lead.

"The animal, wounded, became furious, as did his companion and the child. Then there was absolute carnage. The men, surprised in their sleep and woken up, like me, in that tumult, fled in all directions. The colonel, with an astonishing presence of mind, tried to rally the lads and get them to cover behind a mass of rocks that provided a measure of shelter for our camp. He succeeded in assembling the majority of them in a sort of cul-de-sac, whose entrance was too narrow for the elephant to get through. That only took a few minutes, but fifteen cadavers, horribly trampled, were already lying here and there, mingled with objects of all sorts that served the needs of the campaign.

"Eventually, not seeing any more enemies, the elephants calmed down and went back into the forest. Then I came out of my retreat and set off in quest of my comrades. The first cadaver I encountered was that of poor George, literally flattened like a pancake. I fell to my knees beside him and dissolved in tears. I stayed there like that for a long moment, as if unconscious.

"Warm breath on my face brought me round. A gigantic elephant was swinging its trunk in front of me. It was then that I was afraid—an atrocious fear that turned me to stone.

"The elephant looked at me, its eyes sparkling with anger. Was it the one that had been wounded, which had returned to its victim? Or was it a new arrival? I thought that it was more likely to be a new one, for it seemed to understand what had happened, but didn't have bloody feet. Eventually, it took another step. Its eyes and trunk inspected the Scotsman's cadaver; then it looked at me.

"Then, with a supreme effort, I raised my joined hands toward it, and my face, steaming with tears. It looked at me for a long time, then turned its back and slowly went back into the forest. Then I fell on George's cadaver, and fainted—my God yes, just like a little girl.

"Result: we continued our journey through the forest, but with half our weapons and ammunition, our food and tools destroyed, and our cooking-pots in pieces. Fortunately, the crate containing the quinine had escaped the disaster. It's thanks to that stimulant that we reached our goal, and were lucky enough to win a victory...

"Thus far, we haven't encountered any elephants, and I wouldn't wish that an you."

XIX. ...And Tigers

"Do you think," asked Dr. Abraham Goldry, "that if the sentinel hadn't attacked them, those elephants would have attacked you?"

"I don't know, but I don't believe so. Even I the wild state, elephants aren't cruel, and you can see that they aren't insensitive to pity. So I only kill one of those animals when it's absolutely necessary."

"Good! We already have one eccentric who wants to spare the apes. Now the major is recusing himself with regard to elephants. So we only have tigers to put on the list."

"Oh, no pity for them!" said Gorden.

"Aha!" said Mabel. "There's an exclamation that seems to indicate another story. Go on, Gorden, get on with it. Besides, it's the custom among hunters—and mine too, I hope— to bring back from that kind of campaign not merely a tiger-skin but a fine terror, like the major's."

"Don't make such wishes, Miss Smith! They bring bad luck."

"Bah! Are you superstitious?"

"My dear child, we're in Malaysia, the land of a thousand gods, genies, devils and whatnot. How can you expect anyone not to be a little afraid of the unknown?"

Mabel Smith cut him off with a burst of laughter. "The tiger, Gorden, the tiger!"

"Since you desire it, so be it. It was a few months after my arrival on the island. Not yet being very familiar with the hundred-hectare concession that had been sold to me after the death of the original owner, I had undertaken a methodical inspection, in order to get the best possible return out of it.

"My property was traversed by a narrow but very deep gorge, at the bottom of which was a small stream. One morning, I set off to follow the watercourse, with the aim of discovering whether it was crossable in certain places, or whether it was necessary to establish a few rope-bridges. I was mounted on a superb chestnut mare, mild and docile. She was going at a good trot, whinnying joyfully in the morning breeze.

"Suddenly, I felt a violent impact behind me, and my mare stopped so suddenly and unexpectedly that I was thrown over her head and fell into the gorge. Instinctively, I clung on to the brushwood, which deadened my tumble. Nevertheless, I arrived at the bottom quite quickly and took a header into the steam—which at the point where I fell, was some five or six feet deep. I hauled myself out, with a great deal of difficulty, and immediately began to climb up the other slope—for the roars I heard overhead were scant encouragement to go that way.

"I took nearly an hour to climb up the other side of the steep gorge, having to go back down several times to search for a more accessible spot. Finally, I set foot on the rim. On the other side, two superb tigers, accompanied by two cubs, were making a meal of the cadaver of my unfortunate mare. Fortunately, the tiger, when it pounced on me, had missed its mark, for its head had struck me in the back when it leapt on to the rump of my horse.

"I had no weapons, and I was obliged to watch the wild beasts' feast, without being able to intervene…and since that day, I've sworn a war to the death, with no mercy, against those felines. As soon as a tiger is signaled to me, I don't quit until I've killed it. I'm on to my sixteenth."

"I'll catch you up!" Mabel exclaimed. "I've only been on the island a few months and I've killed two of them."

"You're destined, Miss Smith, to claim numerous victims," said the ever-gallant Englishman, "and it's not those you kill who'll have the most to regret."

"You're on the lookout for madrigals as I am for tigers. Well, what if we were to go hunting in the plain? Perhaps we'll be lucky enough to encounter an interesting animal. Your two stories have given me an appetite for destruction."

"At your orders," said Archibald—who, having no cynegetic exploit to relate, was dreaming of accomplishing a few.

"Then," said Mabel, joyfully, "I propose an exploration of those little woods that precede the forest."

XX. The Vulture, the Snake and the Torrent of Ants

It was decided that the woodcutters and Gorden's adventurers would serve as beaters. It was a genuine pleasure-party; the region was full of game; gunshots fired on every side announced an imposing tableau for the return. For two hours the hunters devoted themselves to their work with joyful hearts. No dangerous animal had been spotted, so the initial vigilance had relaxed considerably, and everyone wandered at hazard, in isolation. Mabel, in particular—who was irritated by the attentiveness with which her two worshipers watched over her—exercised her ingenuity in order to give them the slip and take her chances without being under surveillance by her bodyguards.

The Nimrods had gradually drawn nearer to the forest. The adventurous young woman slid into a kind of rocky gorge, strewn with enormous trees and thorny thickets. From time to time she stopped to listen, anxious on the one hand to hear some animal, and on the other, to keep track of the sound of gunfire, in order not to get too far away from the hunt.

Suddenly, she stated. Like a falling stone, a large vulture swooped down from the sky upon a prey that was invisible to the young woman. A minute later, she saw it take off laboriously from a rocky escarpment, holding a snake at least two meters long in its beak. Having arrived at the summit, it spread its broad wings, ready to fly away, carrying the reptile, doubtless reserved for a family meal.

Mabel took aim and fired. The animal, hit in the head, dropped dead. The intrepid huntress set off to climb the rock in quest of her victim. She succeeded, and examined it. The vulture was a magnificent specimen of that carnivorous species. Extended, it was more than four meters from one wingtip to the other. It was dark brown on the upper part of its body, pale blond underneath, with a formidable beak and claws.

There, she thought. *That will make a superb trophy in the dining-room at Riddle-Temple.*

The difficulty was carrying it, for it weighed at least thirty kilos. She called for help, but was not heard. She fired a few shots, with no better result.

"Bah! I'll leave it here and send someone to fetch it."

Thus resolved, she was about to descend from the when a strange noise attracted her attention. She looked down, and her hair bristled. A kind of black torrent was now flowing at the base of the enormous block, which it enclosed in its waves. At the same time a characteristic odor rose up to her.

The black tide was a migration of ants, and Mabel was not unaware of the danger that threatened her, for in the passage of those terrible insect dissectors, everything disappeared, sliced, torn apart and devoured by millions of ferocious little creatures, the largest of their kind, being nearly two centimeters long.

Already, the rock was surrounded by a column more than six meters broad. Attracted by the odor of the vulture and its leaking blood, a few ants were starting an ascent; if they drew the bulk of the army with them, the rock would be submerged and Mabel was doomed.

She seized the cadaver of the bird and threw it down, as well as the snake, as fodder for the jaws of the innumerable devastators. In a very short time the two cadavers had been stripped, and nothing remained but their skeletons, fleshless and gleaming.

For more than two hours, the black flood flowed around the foot of the singular pedestal. Mabel, in anguish, followed the march of the infernal column anxiously.

Finally, she heard shouts and gunshots, and the young woman replied to them with a rifle-shot. A few minutes later, Archibald, Gorden, the doctor and Mabel's father, Harry Smith, arrived at the edge of the ravine, accompanied by twenty hunters. Archibald, the American, was about to launch himself into the moving river of ants, but Gorden held him back. It would be certain death, without saving the young woman.

With a rapid glance, the Englishman assessed the situation. At a sign from him, one of his men attacked a eucalyptus whose stem rose up as straight and smooth as a mast to a height of twenty meters; circling the enormous trunk with his flannel waistband, three meters long, he went rapidly up the tree, bracing himself with his bare feet. He reached the top and started down again, cutting the branches as he came. The eucalyptus was reduced to the state of a greasy pole; subsequently attacked at its base, it was cut down and up-ended like a bridge between the hunters and Mabel's refuge.

The latter, who had been watching her rescuers' work anxiously, did not waste a second. Scarcely had the tree touched the summit of the rock than she launched herself on to the improvised bridge and came to fall into her father's arms. In spite of her efforts to master herself, her sex got the upper hand, and she collapsed in a nervous flood of tears.

Four hunters unrolled their waistbands, on which she as laid, and, lifted up by eight vigorous fellows, was rapidly carried back to the camp. On the other hand, the hunt had produced copious results: deer, wild boar, monkeys and birds of all sizes, representing at least four hundred kilos of various meat. Everyone got busy skinning and plucking. Fires were lit on all sides, promising abundant and copious roasts for the evening meal.

Mabel had retired to hr tent, where she was resting. Her nervous excitement gradually calmed down. Dr. Goldry administered a cordial that was both calming and restorative, accompanied by remonstrations—which, after the terror she had experienced, the young woman accepted without too much irritation.

As the day drew to a close, the Malays came back to the camp. They had not observed anything worrying, and judged that they could resume the pursuit through the new forest; To Wang affirmed that they ought not be more than two or three days march from the great apes' refuge.

XXI. The Invisible Companions

The next morning, the little army had resumed its appearance of two days before, and everyone prepared to penetrate into the new sea of verdure, which promised to be more easily accessible than the first.

Mabel, completely recovered, drawn toward peril by her recent excitement, manifested a great joy when the immense forest appeared close at hand: the virgin naves between columnar tree-boles, a natural cathedral that no one of her race had ever penetrated before.

After the plain with its scattered clumps of trees and thick bushes, the caravan passed beneath the arches of giant tulip-trees, and palm-trees whose crowns disappeared in a tangle of lianas, golden yellow, red, brown or greens ranging from pale emerald to dark. There were myriads of strange plants, multicolored orchids and spiny cacti in various forms: some as round as the heads of ogres, florid with red patches, like bloody lips or wounds; others with harsh, sharpened leaves like menacing darts brisling with spines. Here were giant mushrooms, pink, violet and white with leprous brown patches; there and everywhere flowers with bizarre corollas, their gaping mouths studded with sapphires, rubies, peridots and amethysts; there was metallic foliage, bronzed, oxidized, some seemingly varnished, furry or moist.

More slowly now, obliged to pause by incessantly-renewed difficulties—rocks, torrents, steep ravines—the caravan advanced with difficulty into the forest, which became denser and darker by the hour.

The sun's rays scarcely penetrated, here and there, the interlacement of verdure and creepers, the tresses of the great woods. In the penumbra, the twisted trunks of the trees seemed to be giant phantoms and aged, immobile monsters lying in wait for living prey.

An anxiety born of the perpetual gloom, the darkness and the unknown, gripped the voyagers, especially the whites, who missed the customary glare of daylight.

Sometimes, immense trunks felled by old age, the ruins of trees, blocked their route. Their interstices had been populated by avid plants, grown from seeds carried by the wind, and blooming flowers extracted their life from death. Unseen snakes sometimes hissed, whose slithering could be heard in the dry leaves. The calls and songs of birds became rare in the thickness of mysterious naves.

Most of the time, they marched in silence; at times, the orangutan hunters exchanged a few whispers, reminiscent, as if by instinct, of hushed words spoken in obscure churches. The route became more arduous as time went by; in the inextricable tangle of undergrowth and thorny scrub, it was necessary to resume the quotidian labor of hatchets and sabers, which cut through the ironwood and the coarse fibers of ebony and mahogany; then they heard the protest and flight of frightened animals, the bounds of wild beasts scared by the sight of so many humans, suddenly disturbed in their quietude.

They followed a nameless river all day. In the water heavy caimans lay dormant, like slimy paving-stones. They were all gripped by the grandiose majesty of the place. Mabel no longer left her place between her father and Wilson, while Gorden liked to supervise the hardest endeavors, to which everyone except the young woman lent a hand.

"Are you still finding the journey so monotonous, Miss Smith?" asked Gorden, smiling.

"No, the forest seems to me, according to the time of day and place, to be a huge amorous brunette, or a marvelous blonde."

"Yes," Gorden murmured, "A dreamer, sometimes she lies down limply in the hollows of valleys, or along the slopes, or else, virginally, she defends herself with all her thorns and all her thick branches, like a woman; she's a coquette; she attracts, reaching out her arms, but rejects you as soon as you try to penetrate her."

"She has the tresses of a goddess," Mabel murmured, "and sometimes, illuminated clearings like laughing mouths. She's chaste, veiled with verdure; but suddenly, immodestly, she displays her beauty; she's proud of knowing that she's so magnificent."

Major Bennett laughed at that enthusiasm. He confessed that he was getting old, and knew it. Combine with that the lack of habitual comfort, to the point of suffering, and—would you believe it?—it was, most of all, the endless whining of his wife that he missed.

Gathered together in the evening camp, after To Wang had made the necessary observations and determined the route, the Americans had their meal, chatting about previous voyages they had made and civilizations they had seen.

Mabel was seriously annoyed; Wilson had asked her, smiling, whether she had been afraid during her adventure with the ants; she sulked throughout the next day.

For two days, however, it seemed that everyone had sensed the invisible presence of unidentified creatures around the caravan. Exhalations of breath, unusual noises, the cracking of branches and confused rumors made the Whites and the men of the escort shiver.

Several times, To Wang, the recognized leader of the expedition, sent out scouts to explore the surrounding area; the bushes were searched and the forest beaten in all directions during a thousand and one halts and pauses, but nothing justified those fears: no enemy, no trace to put the humans on the track of any danger.

Mabel, anxious in spite of her constant effort not to let her unease show, taunted Wilson every time he came back from one of these patrols.

"Was it wild pigs, Archibald? Why didn't you kill one or two?"

"No, I didn't see anything. I heard footsteps, though; last night, I even thought I heard breathing to one side, overhead, quite distinct within the sounds of the wind and your bivouac.

It was like the breath of another camp, very close to ours. I woke Bennett and your Father. Gorden heard them too."

"Who?"

"But I thought I was dreaming," said Smith. "It was a nightmare, I told myself, and went back to sleep."

"Who was it?" Mabel asked, again. "What beings were they?"

"I don't know," said Gorden. "We didn't find anything. To Wang claims that there are snakes that follow humans, which are never seen." The young man laughed and concluded: "Perhaps it was the spirits of the forest that we've violated."

"The fairies are following us, without showing themselves," said Mabel.

The major snorted. "I don't know which of us is the craziest. I too heard footsteps in the trees."

Artfully questioned one by one, for fear that terror might grip the escort, each of the men n the troop affirmed that he had heard the same sounds of footfalls, simultaneously muffled and heavy.

The insouciant Malays smiled. "Spirits hunt by night, in the plains and forests, but brown men close their eyes in order not to offend the gods who pass by with any human gaze."

Al night long, sentinels kept watch around the fires. That same day, although hallucinations were scarcely explicable in such strong minds, noises more prolonged than the customary voices of the forest had resonated; then everything entered once again into the great silence populated by songs infinite in their nature, without any precise symptom aiding the voyagers in giving a name to the vague peril, the unknown evil, from which they thought, inexplicably, they were suffering.

The impression remained, however, in spite of everything, that they were being watched and followed.

XXII. The First Encounter

After three days of marching through the new forest, the hunters seemed no further forward, and Mabel, especially, was manifesting an impatience that was translated into mocking or irritated remarks toward her two flirts. Dr. Abraham Goldry too found the time long, and increasingly regretted having irritated his pupil Ouha and allowed him to escape.

Toward the end of the third day, as they were setting up camp in a kind of clearing devoid of large trees, which the coolies and woodcutters had stripped of bushes and small trees with great blows of sabers and hatchets, Harry Smith was the first to see the Malays—who had, as usual, gone out as scouts—emerge from the forest.

They were running in terror, howling: "Alert! Alert! The free men!"

Behind them, there was a frightful racket. Stones and enormous whistled through the air, hitting two of the running men, who fell, struck dead. After a momentary shock, everyone was armed and on the defensive, quickly forming a rampart of bales.

They did not have to wait long. From the edge of the clearing, fortunately well-cleared, surged the army corps of Harr and Kri-Kri.

Guided by the two bellicose leaders of the volunteer troop, the orangutans advanced rapidly, each one supporting himself with one hand of the ground and brandishing an enormous club in the other. Twenty meters from the retrenchment, the two chiefs drew themselves up to their full height, struck their chests, which resonated like gongs, and uttered formidable screeches—war-cries to which the orangs all replied with similar screeches—and they all surged toward the hunters, who, almost at point-blank range, launched a violent fire against the men of the woods.

The coolies, retired to the rear, reloaded the weapons and passed them to the combatants, but they soon became useless and hand-to-hand combat was engaged in places all along the front line. The coolies, understanding that the white mens' defeat would be their ruination, threw themselves into the battle and fought with the rage of desperation.

The merciless battle lasted a good quarter of an hour, after which, the two chiefs Harr and Kri-Kri having been killed, the anthropoids retreated. They had lost about thirty of their own. Then, at a sign from Wilson, echoed by Gorden, the Europeans and the Malays set up and aimed the two machine-guns, which, a minute later, riddled the orangs, unfortunately regrouped, with bullets. Bewildered, unable to comprehend that avalanche of projectiles, they spun around and crumpled in dozens. Finally, the survivors took flight, pursued by the hunters' bullets, leaving sixty of their number strewn on the battleground, as many dead as wounded.

Victory went to the white men, but they had paid dearly for it. Twenty men had perished, and thirty more had been wounded. In order to guard against a new attack, Gorden and Archibald had a rampart of earth erected by the coolies, simultaneously hollowing out a trench and a refuge for the riflemen.

There was also the matter of dressing wounds—mostly head-wounds or broken arms. The doctor, aided by Mabel and the Malay women, was actively engaged in that all night long, while the men were organizing the defenses, burying the dead and finishing off the wounded orangs—for it was impossible to take a single one alive. One of Gorden' men risked himself imprudently; he was grabbed by an orang's inferior hand, which seized his abdomen and eviscerated him in the blink of an eye. That was one more death to add to all the rest.

Large fires were lit at the four corners of the entrenchment, to illuminate the edge of the forest, and a careful watch was kept thereon. The night passed, however, without any further incident. In the morning, the convened council decided to send back the wounded, who would be a hindrance and could not render any service, under the guidance of the two married Malays, Sing Mah and Ehhi Facu, with their wives and an escort of thirty coolies. They were to return to Riddle-Temple by the route cleared on the outward journey, and wait there for the return of the expedition.

After the departure of the wounded, the hunters sent a few advance scouts into the forest, but with the greatest precaution. They returned to the camp without having made any disquieting observation.

XXIII. Dialogues

"It could be that the bulk of the band are further away. If we go into the woods to pursue them, they'd have the advantage over us."

"And there must be more of them, for we didn't see Ouha among these, and that gigantic orang must be a chief. If there are other tribes against us, the situation becomes critical."

"But with our coolies, who showed themselves to be very courageous, there are still more than three hundred and fifty of us. That's more than enough to defeat an army of apes."

"Besides, what guarantee do we have that, if we beat a retreat, we won't be pursued?"

"We have to recapture Ouha" said Mabel.

"We're continuing the hunt, then?" said Gorden.

"Let's get on with it!" Miss Smith concluded. "Forward march!"

They ate in haste. The Malays resumed their posts at the head of the column, and they plunged once again into the forest. Progress was slow and painful. Involuntarily, at the slightest sound, the hunters raised their heads, and alerts were all the more frequent because a host of small monkeys of all kinds accompanied the explorers—but that was, at the same time a reassuring sign, for all monkeys fled from the anthropoids.

XXIV. The Abduction of Mabel

Darkness fell without their being able to find a location like that of the previous evening. They were obliged to camp in the heart of the forest. The leaders decided that they would sleep in shifts; that way, everyone could get even or eight hours sleep. The first watch took guard-duty under Gorden's orders. The second would be woken up by the major, the third by Archibald. It was impossible to light big fires, the forest being too dense, the ground dry and covered in brushwood, without the risk of a conflagration. They only lit what they needed for cooking, in a carefully-cleared space. After the meal, everyone lay down as best they could. Only Mabel's tent had been erected, not without difficulty.

For three hours, the most profound calm reigned in the forest. The attentive men on watch had no need to fight of sleep; they knew only too well what danger might fall upon them.

Sitting at the foot of an enormous mahogany, Gorden pricked up his ears, for a few moments, strange movements appeared to have been taking place the treetops. Dead dry branches were falling to the ground in an abnormal fashion, for not a breath of wind was troubling the atmosphere. Some distance away from him, a gap in the foliage permitted rays of moonlight to pierce the darkness.

Suddenly, he shivered; in that semi-darkness he saw shadows moving; they were advancing silently through the high branches. He aimed carefully and fired. It was like a signal. Instantly, the forest was animated. From all directions enormous branches and stones began to rain down on the camp. Immediately, everyone was on their feet.

Gorden's voice rose up, imperatively: "No one leave his position or fire at hazard! Spare your shots! You, Wilson, switch on the searchlight!"

A minute later, a luminous beam swept over the trees surrounding the campsite. It was just in time. Everywhere, the blows of the orangutans' clubs resounded, followed every time by a cry of agony. The orangs, dazzled and fascinated by the unexpected light, stood still, as if petrified as soon as they were illuminated. The hunters took advantage of that to take aim, but without Gorden and his friends being able to take account of the cause, the rifle shots became increasingly rare.

Suddenly, there was a slight noise above his head. He looked up, and understood—too late. An orang, suspended by its arms above him, stretched out one of its feet with lightning rapidity. The Englishman felt himself lifted up like a feather, spun around and thrown into the distance. Fortunately for him, he fell into the dense thorn-bush, into which he sank like a coin into a piece of rotten wood. The shock was so violent that he fainted.

Archibald continued to swing his projector, to which all those remaining in the expedition rallied. For a moment, calm seemed to have been restored. Only strident appeals for help could be heard. Then, suddenly, there was a formidable screech:

"Ouha! Ouha! Ouha!"

The name was repeated by numerous voices: "Ouha! Ouha! Ouha!"

Archibald directed the searchlight beam in the direction of the acclamations.

Horror! The electric light illuminated, in full, an enormous ebony, all of whose branches were laden with orangutans, and, on the stoutest one, Ouha was facing up to his hunters. In his arms he held a white form: an unconscious woman, Mabel Smith, whose long blonde hair spread out like a flamboyant aureole over the torso of the colossal anthropoid.

"My daughter!" Smith howled. "My daughter! Don't shoot! Don't shoot!"

"Fix bayonets!" cried the major. "Charge!"

Everyone surged forward. Archibald, having reached the ebony, stood there, foaming with impotent rage. The trunk was devoid of branches to a height of six or seven meters from the ground. It was impossible to reach Ouha and his companions.

Suddenly, the searchlight was overturned in the shadows behind them, demolished by an invisible hand. It went out. Everything was plunged into darkness again.

A few hours later, the day dawned. The bold hunters were then able to assess the extent of the disaster. While the father, Harry Smith, the poor billionaire, deep in despair, sobbed in Archibald's arms—who was brutalized himself by rage and pain—To Wang gathered the survivors of the expedition and took a roll-call. The Malays were the least depleted; seven of them remained. There were only twenty-two coolies, eleven woodcutters and thirteen of Gorden's adventurers. As for the servants from Riddle-Temple, they had all perished. Of the expedition that had comprised, on departure, four hundred and forty-four individuals, only fifty-three remained.

The orangutans could not have lost many combatants; at any rate, they had taken their dead and wounded away.

To Wang had tried several times to remind his masters of the duties that were incumbent upon them. His efforts were wasted; the surviving white chiefs were incapable of resolution.

The Malay chief could not comprehend that stupid despair. Had they gone mad? In the meantime, he ordered that the dead be collected, and had a great deal of brushwood cut.

Silven Gorden, withdrawn from his thorn-bush still unconscious, and taken for dead, was placed on a pyre by the Malays along with Bennett. As for Dr. Abraham Goldry, he had disappeared.

All the cadavers were piled up on To Wang's pyres. He set fire to them, and then the entire troop beat a retreat, leaving behind them a barrier of flames.

XXV. Escaped from the Fire

The next day, the men retreating from the orangutans arrived in the open space where the first battle had taken place. They camped there again. The commotion of the retreat had finally brought Harry Smith and Archibald round. They wanted to go back. Between them and the orangutans, however, a barrier of fire now extended.

After a few hours rest, the caravan, decimated, depleted and almost annihilated, was about to set off again when a call for help, coming from the forest, made them turn around.

A man, or rather a human rag, bloody and smoke-blackened, emerged from the thicket and came toward them, staggering. It was Gorden, left heaped with the dead on one of the pyres. The fames had recalled him to life; with a superhuman effort, he had disengaged himself from the cadavers, and, through the fire and smoke, had succeeded in emerging from the furnace.

Fortunately, as it turned out, the wind pushed the fire in the direction of the anthropoids. He had picked up the trail of the expedition and, half-dead with fatigue and thirst, had finally caught up with it.

XXVI. Talk of Revenge

Ten days later, the remainder of the hunters got back to Riddle-Temple, where they found those wounded in the first battle.

That evening found Archibald Wilson, Silven Gorden and Harry Smith united in the ground-floor drawing-room, where Betty, still in tears, served the tea.

Gorden was the first to break the silence. "What do you intend to do, Mr. Smith?"

Harry Smith shrugged his shoulders sadly. "I don't know. My head's numb."

Gorden thumped the stable with his fist. "Stand up!" he cried. "Stand up!"

The two men jumped, alarmed.

He went on, violently: "Stand up! Are we going to recoil before absurd fatality? In life, everything is against us—nature and our passions. Is that any excuse for lowering your head and giving up? Act! It's necessary to act! To produce our accomplishments and intellect required thousands of generations, but now that we're gentleman, ought we, like our ancestors, to bow down before the phantoms of destiny, and when we're thwarted in our actions, good or bad, retreat? No! A hundred times no! We must fight, fight to the death!

"We've seen Miss Smith inert in the monster's arms, but there's no proof that she's dead. It's probable that, at this moment, she's subject to the same torment as Dilou and Rava. Ought we to abandon Miss Smith, leave her enslaved by an ape, remain inactive and renounce any rescue attempt? We've been beaten. Is that any reason to remain so?

"We've behaved like imbeciles. To fight the apes, we need to become apes ourselves, live their life, follow them, track them, weaken them by means of hunger—and that's feasible, even easy. I nearly perished by fire; it burned me, but enlightened me. Let's follow them to their lair, and every time

99

the wind is propitious, set fire to their domain. Let's destroy the forest, which is their shelter and their abundant granary, with torches. With the apes destroyed, nature will repair the damage. If we can't save Miss Smith, at least we'll avenge her by annihilating the accursed apes."

"Gorden," said Archibald, "you know that I love Mabel. If, thanks to you...to your initiative, at least...she's saved, I'll give her to you..."

"Thanks," said the Englishman, coldly. "Miss Smith alone can decide between the two of us."

Mr. Smith intervened. "I was almost ready to behave like a coward. When do we leave?"

"Oh! First we have to gather the necessary forces. In a week. In the meantime, let's pay off our men; they'll be useless to us in the strategy we're going to adopt.

A brown head suddenly appeared at the drawing-room window. "To Wang has heard everything," the Malay said. "He demands vengeance. The apes have taken Rava. We too want to see both of them again, Miss Smith and Rava. Do you want us?"

Gorden reflected.

"No," he said, eventually. "But you and your men can make your own way. We'll give you weapons, and what you need by way of provisions. If we meet up at the final objective, we'll help one another, but I think it will be better if we're as few as possible."

"So be it," said the chief. "Give us weapons and food; we're leaving in two hours."

"If you bring back my daughter," Harry Smith shouted, "you'll have a million rupees."

The hunter's eyes gleamed. "Hope!" he said. "Hope!"

Two hours later, in fact, the seven Malay survivors left Riddle-Temple, well equipped with arms and food-supplies— which is to say, a small bag of rice each.[13]

---

[13] This plan, by virtue of which two separate rescue expeditions set forth, scheduled to arrive in the orangutans' lair,

XXVII. Beauty and the Beast

Birds are, at present, chirping in the clear half-light of the mauve and violet forest. Songs and unknown calls are mingled. The branches are golden and silvery, the leaves emerald, topaz or amethyst. The hopping movements of invisible creatures crackle; all the voices of wakeful nature are singing.

During the eternity of the night, Mabel Smith has trembled, gripped by horror, terrified. For a long time, it seems to her, she has been dead; at any rate, she is bruised; her entire body is aching as if from blows received and violent embraces. She has been dreaming...no, she is remembering a real nightmare: an ape, a powerful monster, had abducted her, carried her off in his frightful hairy arms.

She is alone, completely alone in the midst of woods that are singing with all the voices of the creatures that live here. Her father? Wilson? Gorden? Where are they? Is she far away? Can she find them again? It seems to her that a circle of iron is burning her, and making her a diadem of torture; she can scarcely collect her thoughts, her memories. Bewildered, she studies her torn garments, makes sure that she still has her revolver and cartridges in the case at her waist.

Anxiously, Mabel searches her surroundings with a fearful gaze, the terror of seeing the monster, her abductor, nearby causes a shiver to run through her entire being. She has not been asleep, but she was too weak, overwhelmed by emotion, an indescribable lassitude. She felt herself placed on the ground. It seems to her...she believes that she recalls...warm hands, breath brushing her; but that was—the young woman

---

seems replete with dramatic potential; for whatever reason, however, the author forgets all about it and reduced the two expeditions to one. He could have removed this chapter entirely, thus obliterating the inconsistency without leaving a significant lacuna in the narrative, but did not do so.

would like to hope—the aftermath of the horrible nightmare, since she finds herself alone, lying on thick moss.

She can still hear footfalls, though, the heavy tread of a crowd around her. And words still resonating in her ears, or syllables, at least, whose meanings she does not know. She does not dare to move, to make the slightest gesture, for fear of seeing a monstrous population of orangutans surge forth, like the one that carried her through the woods over frightful precipices.

Atrocious visions populate the America virgin's brain. What good are her father's billions here?

Finally, with infinite precaution, for fear of the sound of a broken branch or rustling leaves, which might betray her, she looks up.

The clearing is illuminated by morning light. It is perfumed by flowers—enormous lilies similar to European lilies, whose broken stems emit milky fluid; purple flowers, between stout indented leaves, where the dew remains, in little diamantine drops; and violet, yellow and brown orchids, some reminiscent of the faces of animals, seemingly lying in wait for prey.

Mabel stands up, takes a step, and, hidden by the bole of a enormous mahogany, advances her head. But she hears sounds as if imparted by human lips; she turns round. Coming from all directions, between the trees, tumbling with atrocious grimaces, simultaneously ironic, menacing and risible, apes surround her, crouching down and staring at her with their enormous sticky eyes, luminous coals beneath the crumpled eyelids of lubricious old man.

Mabel utters a loud scream and recoils.

Other quasi-human beasts are there too, behind the beautiful blonde American: the apes extend their arms toward her, their claws hands, and grunts, like the admiration of primitive humans, greet her.

They are making gestures of desire toward her; she thinks she can even distinguish the human gesture of kisses blown to her slender loveliness. And many of the monsters are

102

sniggering, passing enormous sanguinary tongues over their brown lips, like ferocious gourmands.

Screeches and cries of anger burst forth above Mabel's head; she raises her eyes toward those frightful voices. And suddenly, she feels herself picked up, while the great apes, crowding around a newcomer, howl like acclamations two guttural syllables:

"Ouha! Ouha! Ouha!"

Then they all disperse.

Mabel, lifted up, loses consciousness again.

Reopening her eyes, she looks around, amazed both to find herself alone and by the gloom, only pierced by two luminous beams, as if descending through the air-vents of a cellar or through the portholes of a ship into the depths of the hold. In her buzzing ears is the memory of an animal crowd, cries and laughter, explosive and sinister.

Has she been recovered by her own people? Rescued from the apes, is she finally safe? She dares not call out, nor explore her retreat. Perhaps, weary of the nocturnal combat, her father and his friends are asleep nearby?

Mabel was afraid of being disappointed, of not finding them. For a long time, she hesitated, in great fear of causing the illusion of hope to fly away. Weary of doubt, however, in order to break the yoke of anguish that was gripping her heart, in an infantile voice, frightened by the silence and the darkness, she called out:

"Father!... Archibald!... Silven!..."

Only the stony echoes of the cave replied—and it was her own voice that the rocks sent back.

In the meantime, her eyes had become accustomed to the half-light. She was lying on a mass of dry brushwood in a grotto, whose walls she could now make out. In crude strata, blocks of quartz, in which a ray of sunlight lit up shards of mica and the somber glow of garnet were stacked, joining up with an undulating vault, as if the malleable minerals had melted and swelled out in places. From channels in the rock, colonnettes rose up from the ground to the vault, from which droplets fixed in stone fell in festoons: stalactites clad in patinas of moss. In the interstices, flowers and lianas had grown, dull and delicate, by virtue of never having drunk bright light.

Suddenly, Mabel shivered, on hearing the rustling of invisible creatures. She suspected the frightful presence of reptiles in the cave. Terrified she listened to the buzz of insects resonating in the silence, and the voices of the earth around her, in the solitude and abandonment.

The energy of her nature took over, though; by an effort of will, the young woman forced herself to make a tour of her precarious shelter—perhaps her tomb.

Mabel tried to climb the rocky walls in order to reach the luminous holes, but the rock-face was slippery and as vertical as a wall; the grotto's eyes were too high for her to be able to reach them.

She discovered fruits of the forest beside her bed, arranged in ingenious piles: guavas, red and violet berries, manioc pulp and bananas on large leaves.

Who would have such solicitude for her? Had she fallen into the hands of a native tribe? She had difficulty believing that beasts, the orangutans, would go to such trouble, would have the instinctive consideration of humans in her regard. She felt hunger pangs, which she appeased with a few fruits. A calabash of fresh water was placed next to the agrarian aliments.

No matter how hard she tried, she could not discover the entrance to the grotto. She listened for a long time, in all directions, perceiving murmurs like a shrill crowd, dull sounds that appeared to be muffled.

Mabel sat down, expectantly. Was she a prisoner? For sure, but whose? She knew that the savages of Borneo rarely killed female captives once the flame ignited by the heat of battle was extinct—but an idea more terrible than death imposed itself on her mind: that of living among those primitive humans, of belonging to them, of being a slave submissive to their caprices.

She would have prayed, but she scarcely believed in any but natural powers. Her conscience clear and her heart firm, she controlled herself solely by means of the force of her character.

Sadly, she recalled Riddle-Temple and familiar scenes; then she waited, with o other desire, for the moment, but to know her fate and to resist it with all her strength.

An intense light suddenly burst forth opposite the place where Mabel was sitting on a block of stone. Like a whiplash with gold, silver, opal and ruby tresses, sunlight struck the walls of the cave.

A hairy mass, a creature like a badly-molded human, robust, with a broad chest, enormous jaws and a narrow skull— an orangutan, in sum—appeared, and, waddling on two hands, came toward her, squatted down and made signs to her.

The beast seemed dressed in a linen robe by virtue of his thick fur, hanging down in long wisps. The enormous head was swaying, the eyes rolling: two black diamonds mounted in gold, for which the wrinkled red pupils made a hideous matrix. Two black hands were suddenly extended toward Mabel, with long hooked fingers with curved nails.

At first, the young woman had remained still, as if petrified, beneath the gaze with which the beast was covering her, but at that gesture, a scream of anguish and horror and an appeal for help escaped her mouth, and she leapt backwards.

The standing orangutan considered her, and it appeared to Mabel that he looked at her sadly, in an almost human fashion, and she became less fearful. She recognized Ouha.

Several recent wounds marbled the ape's fawn-colored fleece, one on the shoulder, another—frightful, and swollen by a patch of coagulated blood—on the chest. Ouha was indeed the abductor of the previous night; the one whose steely arms had borne her away through the darkness. In the indescribable sentiment of terror that chilled the beautiful American, Wilson's joke, when he wanted to dissuade her from taking part in the expedition, came back to her:

"They don't devour women, or eat their flesh at all—but would you want an ape for a husband?"

Mabel allowed the orang to approach her, firmly resolved—she kept one hand on the holster of the revolver that she had, providentially, retained—to die or to kill Ouha, if any excessively ardent audacity threatened her. But she took account, remembering the previous day and the dawn, of the multiple danger; other monsters were surely not far away: an entire city, a simian tribe, whose prey she was. Who could tell? Patience and cunning might save her.

Ouha continued to stare at the blonde Mabel with eyes that were infinitely gentle, in spite of the gleam of covetousness. He was articulating syllables, veritable words, which were certainly explaining a desire, perhaps a plea.

With his long hands, brown on one side, with black palms, Ouha made gestures similar to those of humans, in a mime of admiration. The hands sketched the oval of an imaginary face, the eyes, the lips; he seemed to be trying to explain his thoughts—things, at least that he represented by signs.

For a moment, she was tempted to laugh, because the embarrassed beast in front of her scratched his narrow cranium, comically and ridiculously. Ouha stroked his thighs, murmuring in a raucous voice, which he attempted to soften, words of prayer, anger, supplication and command.

Finally, Ouha disappeared, making his exit through the gaping opening in the cavern wall, and allowed two female apes to go to Mabel, who looked at her, felt her, astonished by the feel of her clothes, her soft hands and her pale face.

Her initial read having dissipated, Mabel understood that the anthropoid monsters had no designs on her life, at least for the moment. She studied the scarcely-articulate language of her two jailers, astonished by the gentleness of their movements toward her.

The opening was sealed again from outside, by a block of granite.

The beams of light descending from the vault were attenuated; the young woman presumed, after the day's ordeals, that worse anguish awaited her in the dusk and the approaching darkness. Her two guards were agitated, addressing hoarse words to her, accompanied by signs—and the two beasts, with gestures of respect and dread, continually repeated the two syllables:

"Ouha! Ouha! Ouha!"

They sniggered in Mabel's face and, pointing to their parted legs, repeated a word—what did it signify?—pointed to their breasts, their sex, miming kisses or bites.

And disgust overwhelmed the virgin.

The monster came in again. He dismissed the jailers with a gesture, striking them brutally with one of his posterior hands.

Mabel, trembling, felt herself caressed; the monster's breath brushed her face.

As Ouha leaned over her, she had the inspired idea of launching her fist at the wound in his chest.

Ouha uttered a cry of pain, and raises his enormous hand—but he let his arm fall again into empty space, and his bobbing head took on a melancholy and heartbroken expression. His eyes became misty. He stared at the American woman, caressing her for a long time with his black diamond pupils encircled by gold. Mabel understood that it was not death, but true love that was coming toward her.

Then, she felt her strength.

She had, thus far, played with the love of men; she was about to have to exercise her power upon a brute. In spite of the horror of her situation, a smile of audacious pride brushed her lips. What was she risking, after all? Only death—for she was firmly resolved not to submit to the Beast's caresses. She was armed with a revolver. If she were about to succumb, if she were defeated, she would kill herself.

Still squatting in front of her, Ouha seemed to be seeking to read the expression in her eyes, and Mabel was struck by the intensity of the intelligence shining in the colossal orangutan's eyes. In that frightful mask, the eyes were alive, astonishing luminous and eloquent. The American woman understood, on seeing that gaze, that she had nothing to fear from the violence of the wild beast. However, it was necessary to occupy the anthropoid's mind in order that desire should not get the upper hand over the apprehension that he seemed to have of doing the wrong thing.

She took two bananas from the bed of leaves where they had been placed, and offered one to Ouha, keeping the other for herself. The orang seemed delighted by the offer. He watched the young woman peel the fruit and raise it delicately to her lips. He copied Mabel's gestures carefully, and, instead of swallowing he banana whole, he savored it, as he had seen his prisoner do. He was so comical that Mabel had difficulty not bursting into laughter, but she remembered Ouha's anger at Riddle-Temple, and restrained herself.

After that fruit, others followed, and then others. The meal, uniquely vegetarian, was scarcely satiating after the fatigue of recent days, but she saw nearby the pith of the bread-fruit tree. She took a morsel of it and raised it to her mouth. She pulled a face. Ouha, who continued to imitate her, grimaced too, but infinitely more successfully. Mabel, who had never eaten that precious vegetable, but who had heard mention of it, knew that it was necessary to dry out a fragment that pith and roast it.

In order to indicate to Ouha that she wanted a fire, she collected three large stones, which she arranged as a hearth beneath one of openings in the cave, took a handful of brushwood, put it between the stones and mimed striking a match. Ouha knew what she was doing, because he had seen Smith and his guests light cigars.

The orangutan scratched his buttock, then his head; then, abruptly, he got up and disappeared.

XXVIII. A Little Mandolin Music and Tea

A few minutes later, he came back, but he was not alone; he brought the chimpanzee Ko-Zu with him. At the sight of the American woman, the latter made the gesture of raining a non-existent hat, and bowed with the grace of a true gentleman. Mabel, flabbergasted, returned the salute. Ouha looked at his companion in astonishment, and, as if Ko-Zu's expansive gesture had displeased him, gripped him brutally by the arm and dragged him to the hearth. Then he took a twig from the ground and made the gesture of striking a match, after which he signed an instruction to the chimpanzee to light the fire.

Ko-Zu, embarrassed, turned toward Ouha and started a very animated conversation with him. Ouha appeared to approve. The chimpanzee immediately went out, and Ouha sat down again beside the hearty. A few more minutes went by. Ko-Zu came back in, and held out to the stupefied Mabel a little sculpted silver box on which Indian deities were depicted: a box full of wax matches.

Mabel started. She recognized the box; she had seen it in the hand of Dr. Abraham Goldry. How had it come to be in the hands of her abductors?

Meanwhile, Ouha, seeing that she was not lighting anything, made a gesture of impatience. The young woman, reminded of her situation, struck a match; a few moments later, a bright flame rose up between the stones of the hearth. That seemed to amuse the two apes enormously. They drew nearer to the fire, and were soon rubbing their hands voluptuously.

Over the flame, Mabel extended slices of the precious starchy substance, which, when dried and roasted, loses its acridity and becomes succulent.

Mabel made the distribution. She was at home, receiving visitors. Ko-Zu, remembering good manners, from the European viewpoint, sat down in the Turkish fashion, extended a large banana leaf over his knees and politely received the morsels that the mistress of the house handed to him. Ouha looked at the elegant gentleman askance, but did his best to imitate him. The meal was quite cheerful; the manners of the two guests amused Mabel, who forgot her situation a little. Where did that singular animal come from?

Suddenly, Ko-Zu slapped his forehead in a casual gesture. Bowing to Mabel, seemed to ask her permission to leave, and then disappeared.

Mabel turned to Ouha and, by means of a lively mime, attempted to interrogate him. Ouha appeared to understand that she was asking about Ko-Zu, and he pronounced a series of more-or-less articulate sounds, doubtless words, accompanied by an explanatory mime that she found incomprehensible.

In any case, Ko-Zu came back, carrying a wickerwork tray bearing a number of objects, which he deposited triumphantly in front of Mabel. On seeing them, she felt tears rising to her eyes. They were, alas, the relics of the catastrophe. There was no more doubt about it; the apes really had been victorious, and all the Europeans had doubtless fallen under the blows of the anthropoids. She really was Ouha's prisoner, then. What ought she to do? Continue the ridiculous struggle for life or put an end to it straight away?

Her right hand settled on her revolver. At the same moment, however, a strange sound attracted her attention, and, her eyes involuntarily going toward Ko-Zu, she burst out laughing. Would that irritate Ouha? But the impulse was stronger than she was. She might have been killed on the spot, but she was unable to refrain from that nervous and inextinguishable laughter. There was good reason.

Ko-Zu brought out a mandolin that he had been hiding behind his back, and started strumming the strings delicately, opening his mouth as if he were singing and rolling his eyes, showing the whites. It had been one of his principal turns when he was an artiste in the Perkins Circus. Every time, Ko-Zu had unleashed tempests of laughter and bravos.

Finally, the piece came to an end. The ape stood up, bowed gravely to the right, the left and the front, and walked away backwards, still bowing. Mabel, exhausted by laughter, was weeping.

To her great astonishment, Ouha was not annoyed. On the contrary, he was looking at the young woman with a very satisfied expression. Seeing his prisoner finally calmed down, he stood up, and bowed. He was about to leave when he bumped into Ko-Zu, who was coming back in. The virtuoso had made a false exit, and was coming back for his curtain call. Seeing that his audience was not thinking about that, he came to sit down again and politely indicated the tray to Mabel.

On the tray there was a kettle, a packet of tea and a bottle of whisky. There was no sugar. Under the attentive eyes of the two apes, Mabel brewed the national beverage. To sweeten it, she had the idea of squeezing a little mango juice into the kettle, and, that fruit being very sweet, it did an adequate job. She poured the result into a calabash, drank first, and then passed it to Ouha—who, in a brotherly gesture, left a little for Ko-Zu. The latter had been eyeing the bottle for some time, but Mabel, fearing that alcohol might lead her guests to some drunken stupidity, confiscated it—to Ko-Zu's great disappointment. Ouha supported the American woman's decision, however, and dragged the chimpanzee outside to calm him down.

XXIX. The King of the Apes

For three days Mabel remained imprisoned in the cave. Every evening, when the light from the vents in the vault began to fade, the jailers mimed what she divined to be her destiny. Then the Master, the giant orang, arrived and chased away the two females. For long minutes, the Beast stood in contemplation before Mabel.

Once, when he hazarded a gesture toward her, and a vague inclination of desirous empery, the young woman struck him so hard with a stick she had picked up from the ground, directly on the site of one of his wounds, that a croak of anger and pain exhaled from the ape's gigantic mouth, where sharp ivory teeth bristled in the bestial red jaws.

She thought she was doomed, and mentally resolved to sacrifice her life—but the Beast soon mastered his anger and, crouched at the woman's feet, uttered plaintive and puerile complaints, moaning soft syllables that attempted to express persuasive pleas. With infinite gentleness, Ouha seemed to be giving in; he was begging to obtain what he could have taken by force.

Had he divined the resistance that Mabel would oppose to him, and that he could not succeeded in vanquishing her? If she were dead, Ouha would have to renounce his desire. With the instinct of a near-human brute, the superior orangutan found the road. He never came with empty hands but, like and infatuated swain, brought his captive the most beautiful fruits of the forest, which he presented to her in evident homage.

From the yelps of the female jailers, Mabel gathered that the two endlessly-repeated syllables "Ouha," with which the orangs saluted the master when he appeared, were his name, and that all of these animals had one of their own, like humans. In her mind, the terrible creature, the orang abductor, the lover whose frightful assiduity she dreaded, also became designated, as for his peers and subjects, as Ouha.

Mabel Smith decided to undress. No modesty prevented her from being seen by the apes. She thought she would keep her clothes for the hoped-for day when she would reappear before human beings. She took off her short brown dress and her belt and the Indian underskirt that she had adopted for the voyage.

The monster came in as she was undressing. Mabel did not interrupt herself, but continued to remove the pieces of her civilized costume one by one.

She was afraid of being completely nude, however, under the near-human gaze of the Beast. From the corset, almost a girdle, amid the ruffled whiteness of the crumpled slip, her bosom emerged in firm and rhythmic globes, swelling, immaculate cupolas of alabaster, into which two crimson rose-petals had fallen. Her culottes, like bouffant britches, floated above her knees over the blue-tinted flash of garters retaining long back stockings, emerging from boots laced to the calves, comprising gaiters.

Interest by the young woman's gestures and state of undress, Ouha was careful not to disturb her; avidly, he watched Mabel with eyes desirous of these unknown beauties, tranquilly unveiled, which he hoped eventually to penetrate.

With an instinct superior to that of his fellows, Ouha had noticed how Mabel, having nothing to do, had collected flowers from the walls of her prison. One day, he arrived with a heap of corollas in his hairy arms: lilies of the forest and clusters of variously-nuanced umbels, daturas and orchids, in an enormous sheaf. He had scattered them at the young woman's feet.

Mabel, beautiful and pale, beautiful and blonde, radiant with youth, in the superb springtime of her sexuality, radiant in her slender, supple grace, seemed, in confrontation with the monstrous orangutan, amid the scattering of violet, brown, pink, white, red and orange flowers, like some marvelous and impudent fairy from the distant civilization and refinement of human beings.

Gently, Ouha grasped Mabel's hand and drew her toward the opening of the cavern, which had not been sealed. Soon, the infanta was standing, holding flowers, beneath an arcades of branches, in the midst of an animal people, clamoring enthusiastically:

"Ouha! Ouha!"

And pointing at her, the beasts cried:

"Bouff! Bouff! Bouff!"

She understood the admiration of the crowd of quadrumanes, and that the orangs found her beautiful.

Around the giant—Ouha surpassed all the apes of his tribes by the extent of his head and shoulders—climbing or tumbling from branch to branch, capering in crazy leaps, the apes pressed forward, with manifest signs of respect, arms extended above their heads toward him and toward her, humbly bowing their enormous heads, like a caricature of the way in which human courtiers behaved.

With an instinctive majesty, Ouha held in his hand an object that the young woman had some difficulty in recognizing at first, so worn and disfigured had it become by virtue of unknown avatars. It was a rifle stolen from a trapper, the butt notched in many places: a trophy taken from vanquished humans. He stood there, holding it by the barrel with the butt in the air, like a club; it was undoubtedly his scepter, the emblem of the power he exercised over his fellows.

When the audacious orangs approached, prowling around him, he scattered them with a gesture of that human weapon. Evidently, the apes, conscious of Ouha's superiority over them, obeyed him by virtue of a respect mingled with fear. He also had a kind of slit leather belt, stolen in the course of his raids on humans.

Ouha, King of the Apes, held Mabel Smith by the hand, and all the orangs bowed down to them with various cries of astonishment and admiration—and there were also covetous gleams in the pupils of the wild beasts, flames of ferocious flattery, searching the young white woman's semi-naked body, all the more alluring and irritating for her nudity being incomplete.

Hanging from Mabel's belt was the revolver from which she was never separated. The thirty cartridges that she still possessed would certainly not have sufficed to facilitate a crazy escape; even if she had killed more than twenty of her enemies, others would have caught and disarmed her; she would not have escaped their claws, their enormous and powerful jaws. Even if she had contrived to flee by means of cunning, how could she have found a route to civilized lands? And how could she have succeeded, even if she knew the way, in making the journey, in suffering hunger, in resisting thirst, in defending herself from the thousand ambushes and countless perils with which the route was strewn? But the weapon remained precious in order to evade an immediate peril, or even, in the case of excessive suffering, to free herself from a captivity that she could no longer bear.

Orangs suspended from branches above the beauty, with one hand clenched or with their entire bodies thrust forward, testified to their wonder with onomatopoeias of evident admiration. Females, somewhat to the rear and the sides of the assembly of apes, displayed peevish and furious faces between the trunks and branches. By their mimes they expressed their amazement at a creature almost of their kind, but whose face and breast were white and pink, denuded of hair. They passed their hands over their brown faces, tugging the wisps of their fleeces, uttering cries. And incessantly, with repetitions of the name of Ouha, extensions of their spines and grotesque inclinations of their hilariously bestial heads, raising their arms in gestures of admiration, they murmured:

"Bouff! Bouff! Bouff!"

Mabel judged from the gestures accompanying that syllable that the orangs were definitely saying that she was beautiful

Gamboling around, the frightful creatures, whose laughter displayed their ivory teeth and powerful monstrous jaws, began to dance sarabands of joy. The terrible Ouha, his club resting on his shoulder, occasionally place one of his hands on Mabel's bare shoulder, scarcely protected by the thin shoulder-strap of her slip, as a sign of possession.

He alone remained grave, his bald head streaked with severe and worrisome wrinkles, and let syllables fall from his lips that were doubtless orders, for Mabel Smith noticed, every time, the departure of an ape, the appearance of a newcomer or the almost-inarticulate reply of one of those surrounding them.

Mabel Smith had recognized the little Dilou, but the latter did not appear to recognize here—or did not want to, perhaps out of respect for Lord Ouha. The young woman had reverted to the savage life; her hair tangled and stuffed with dry leaves, she directed a hateful stare at Mabel, sensing a rival.

Dilou ground her teeth and displayed her closed fists, one by one, and her hands clawed with bitten and curved nails, chipped by bestial endeavors. She shouted angrily at the placid Ouha, who, with a mocking expression in his eyes and his lips parted by an indefinable smile, seemed disdainful, refusing to punish her with a scornful indulgence.

Wearying of Dilou's ill humor, however, he displayed Mabel to her and pronounced a few imperious syllables, pointing at the white woman and then the black woman.

He had given an order.

Dilou, like a submissive whipped dog, with the constrained expression and glowering gaze of a slave yielding to a stronger master, Dilou came toward the American woman and took one of her white hands; she placed it momentarily on her forehead, then crouched down at her feet, slightly behind Ouha and Mabel.

Another woman was standing there sulkily, with no possibility of doubt, looking at the Orang with dull eyes. This one had the coppery skin of the native islanders, and the fine attributes of daughters of status. Like a Greek earthenware statuette, with slender legs and firm and delicate figure, her body silhouetted in a succession of graceful curves, her breasts young and meager, modeled in bronze-colored flesh, she was almost a child, barely nubile. Cold and dignified, with the impassive forehead of a proud slave, she looked Mabel Smith up and down, taking in every detail, and the American maid thought she saw a hint of pity in the young native's gaze.

An amazement, in which there as terror and also hope, at least of survival, gripped Mabel. What were these beings, she thought, who attached humans and kept women as slaves? Must she submit to such horror or die?

"Dilou! Rava!"

Thus the Orang, the King, designated with demonstrative gestures the young black woman and the silent Malay. With the master's permission they went away, already savagely, to plunge into the forest. Dilou repeated her name, striking her breast to indicate and affirm her personality.

Curiously, the apes surrounded their king's beautiful captive. Their admiration and the covetous ardor of their pupils irritated Mabel, ashamed now of the human element of those simian gazes. By caressing themselves, the orangs translated their admiration for the forms they beheld; leaning back against tree-trunks or standing upright, the beasts allowed their disturbance to show, nodding their heads, their eyes half-closed, some sighing, risking gestures and becoming enraptured.

One of those nearest to Ouha gradually came closer to her, seemingly watching for a moment when the abductor was not paying attention of Mabel. Emboldened, more audacious than the others, the orang extended one of its long dark arms, and suddenly placed his hand on the young woman's flower, as if by way of a caress. Touched, she leapt backwards, drawing the revolver around which her fingers remained clasped with lightning rapidity, and shot the animal.

At the sound of the detonation, the frightened apes dispersed, recoiling, to say the least—save for Ouha, whose eyes went from Mabel's living fragility to the inert mass of the orangutan. Sentences composed of veritable words, curt and monosyllabic, a terrified chatter, filled the corner of the forest where the orangs lived. Ouha, meanwhile, turned over the stiff cadaver with vitreous eyes. Frightened, the horde howled, with threatening gestures. Covering Mabel with his body, Ouha drove away the boldest with a terrible sweep of his scepter-club, picked Mabel up by the waist and carried her off.

The apes prodded the cadaver, putting their fingers into the hole in the skull, with whistles of terror and plaints—testimony of fury, fear and mourning.

XXX. The Magical Jewel

Once back in the cave, Ouha made Mabel understand that she had nothing to fear, but, designating the revolver, he demanded to see the weapon. The young woman hesitated. To refuse, however, might be dangerous. To kill Ouha, as she had indiscreetly slain the orangutan, would be very risky. Besides which, it is very rare that an anthropoid can be killed by a single shot, and the instantaneous death of the lubricious individual could be considered a miracle.

Kill Ouha? She would do better to blow her own brains out, for the entire horde of male and female orangs would be against her. Mabel turned her back and rapidly removed the five remaining cartridges, which she shoved into her cleavage; then, turning round, she handed the pistol to the quadrumane.

Ouha turned the weapon over and over, aiming it has he had seen others do, put his finger on the trigger, seemingly amused by the repeated click of the hammer. Afterwards, disappointed by the lack of any result, he handed the weapon back to the young woman.

Having slipped a bullet into the chamber with the skill of a conjuror, she immediately fired at a calabash, which exploded into smithereens. Ouha jumped. Nonplussed, contemplating Mabel, he seemed to be asking her for an explanation, and by means of a very expressive mime, the American virgin explained to him very carefully that the weapon could only be utilized by her.

After a few minutes of profound meditation, Ouha reached out his hand again, demanding the revolver. There was no means of refusing. Ouha took the weapon and made as if to leave.

Then, for the first time, Mabel dared to seize him by the arm, and, with the other hand, grabbed the revolver. The ape held on to it, though, and, pulling free, made it understood that he feared that the young woman might hurt herself with the dangerous implement. Mabel dared not insist; not having the requisite strength, she resolved to employ cunning.

Inviting Ouha to sit down beside her, she offered him bananas, of which the orangutan was fond, and to whom dining together seemed a great favor. Mabel was counting on the probability that Ouha would make use of both hands to eat, and, in consequence, set the gun down beside him; it would then only be a matter of making him forget it.

What a disappointment! As if it were the most natural thing in the world, the orang gripped the revolver with one of his feet. Then he peeled his banana tranquilly. Mabel was obliged to play her part, and, in order to deceive the ape with regard to the importance she attached to the murderous jewel, she prolonged the meal and made Ouha understand that she would be glad to have, once again, the society of the chimpanzee, the worldly clown. The anthropoid understood and went out to seek his confidant and friend.

He soon returned, accompanied by Ko-Zu and his four wives—Dilou, Rava and the two spouses of his own species.

XXXI. A Marvelous Concert

Ouha sat down first, and invited his guests to take their places. Mabel, slightly nonplussed, resigned herself to the role of hostess, circulating fruits and grilled breadfruit. Dilou and Rava seemed delighted by the reception, and struck up a conversation with Mabel that was a triumph of polyglotry.

Only the two orangutans seemed put out, for Ouha and Ko-Zu made it their duty to give them a lesson in good manners and etiquette. One of them, Ma-Ma, having taken it into her head to search for her body-lice, received a scolding from the master, who remonstrated with her. Always keeping one eye on Ko-Zu, Ouha never missed any of his gestures, and copied them immediately.

In response to a general demand, the chimpanzee was obliged to fetch his mandolin and mime one of his great numbers. Then Dilou, accompanied by the artiste Ko-Zu, sang a nursery rhyme that had remained in her memory. Rava, not wanting to be outdone by Dilou, began a long Malaysian chant, which she accompanied with wooden castanets. In their turn, the two she-apes gave voice to lugubrious groans accompanied by a jazz band of thumps on the breast. It was quite a concert.

The American woman, who enjoyed all kinds of eccentricity, did not want to seem incapable in the eyes of the apes. She took the mandolin from Ko-Zu, which she knew how to play well enough, and played a prelude of brilliant pizzicato. Then she launched into a song from an American operetta, which she sang with such gusto and expertise that it was a veritable triumph. Her guests were under her spell; Dilou and Rava had eyes moist with emotion, and the four apes were rubbing their breasts frantically.

As Mabel's vibrant voice had been heard outside, the entire tribe had gathered around the opening of the cave. All the orangutans, attentive and breathless, gave voice to a dull rumble when the young woman's voice died away, and that exterior thunder attracted Ouha's attention. He turned round furiously.

After that, there could be no tranquility in his realm without all the curious and loquacious coming to listen at the door. Mabel intervened and made him understand that she wanted to be everyone's friend, and that those brave individuals had a right to play their part in the celebration.

The monarch seemed to yield to her reasoning. Picking up the scraps of the feast by the handful, he threw them majestically to his subjects, who fought over them.

Mabel Smith wanted to see what ascendancy she might obtain over the apes by means of art.

She plucked the mandolin from Ko-Zu's hands again and, advancing to the threshold, she started to sing a brisk and cheerful American melody at the top of her voice, whose chorus was:

> In every good girl,
> Even the most genteel
> There's something wicked.

The crowd of apes drew back as she walked toward them, singing. They seemed subject to a strange impression, in which fear and admiration were mingled. Evidently, this creature, apparently so frail, whose mouth sent them sounds simultaneously so powerful and harmonious, seemed to them to be a divinity by whom they were dazzled.

XXXII. Her Majesty the Queen

Meanwhile, Ouha and the others, in order of precedence, emerged from the cave, and the four apes, in imitation of Ko-Zu, mimed the chorus. Having recovered from their stupor, the orangutans were confronted by the white woman, their king and the other three apes of his court, rolling their bewildered eyes and frantically plucking phantom instruments. In their turn, they opened gaping mouths to imitate the magician, who, slightly vexed by that unexpected effect, stopped singing.

Immediately, the mute choir ceased its grimacing. Ouha, drawing nearer to her, placed his enormous hands on Mabel's head. He seemed to be saying to his subjects: "This woman, this marvelous songbird, is mine, Ouha's, and mine alone! Woe to anyone who touches her! She is mine, Ouha's! She is your queen!"

The gesture had been accompanied by a few guttural syllables. The whole was understood by the apes, who filed in front of the group, howling:

"Ouha! Ouha! Ouha!"

They all made their breasts resound with formidable blows of their fists.

When that ceremony was concluded, Ouha, with his arms extended, went through the forest in order to make Mabel understand that the kingdom was his, and that henceforth, Mabel might enjoy it freely.

Even carried out by apes, that kind of recognition of power did not lack grandeur. Mabel was a sacred queen, and without taking account of it, she was flattered thereby.

From that day on, she was able to go out, to come and go as she pleased. In addition, she made Ouha understand that it was not prudent to leave her unarmed, and the condescending monarch returned her revolver: the magical jewel.

XXXIII. His Harem

As the king, the undisputed leader, by virtue of his brutal muscular strength and near-human intelligence, Ouha, like any polygamous sovereign of a primitive civilization, possessed his harem.

As ambitious petty kings of an age to take a wife strive for an alliance with a powerful family, some dynasty in the shadow of which they might increase their influence and the size of their domain, Ouha, the great orangutan, disdainful of vague females, had coveted women and he had gladly, on occasions propitious for abduction, captured Dilou and Rava in order to possess them—and finally, Mabel. His power was displayed by such conquests, which raised him above his race.

Dilou had rapidly adapted, among the anthropoids, to an existence little different from that of her ancestors: eating, drinking, singing song, running, being beaten, submitting to the caresses of the strongest. The difference between the gestures and the primitive language of her ancestors in a remote area of the Gabon and those of her abductors was not, after all, very obvious.

Her grandfather, a redoubtable leader, had spent his days in front of the royal hut, in blissful idleness, eating fruits and bloody flesh, or crouched down, nodding his head to the sound of flutes. At solemn feasts he walked coiffed in an old red kepi that a European had given him, holding, like Ouha, a blunderbuss in the guise of a scepter. For the idols, blood was shed on the sand in front of his hut; captives or subjects were sacrificed, according to the whim of the sluggish monarch, cruel at times. By night, obscene sarabands were danced, rounds and mimes of coarse amour, and warrior scenes that often terminated in blows and blood.

As for Rava, since an enormous hairy hand, a gag of oboe and sinew over her bruised lips, had choked off her desperate cry for help, she had found herself, astonished to be

124

alive, surrounded by gray, brown and black muzzles, grimacing around her. And as she had circled the cave in which the supreme orangutan had imprisoned her from dawn till dusk, like a captive wild beast, Ouha, without coming in, had obsessed her with the nightmare of his flame-like eyes and his ashen face, framed by the abrupt sides of the vent in the rock.

Female jailers had guarded her, until the moment when the monster chased them away with blows of his hairy hands; and on the third evening, Ouha had thrown the young Malay woman violently to the ground, and she had submitted passively to his embrace. Since then, like a resigned slave, for whom all resistance is futile, Rava allowed herself to be taken at the conqueror's whim, without pleasure, in spite of the monster's gentleness, fearful of hurting his preferred captive and seeing her languish and die.

Rava no longer pushed Ouha away, merely retaining a dull hatred of her possessor, of the implacable lubricity of that formidable male, that hairy tyrant against whom her weakness could not prevail.

Twice, deceived by momentary solitude, when she believed the entire tribe to be distantly dispersed, Rava had attempted to escape. Recaptured and beaten, however, imprisoned and fed exclusively on a few fruits and water, without offering a glimpse of a tear, superb in the dignity of defeat, she had submitted once again to the vile caress. Now that all hope of flight was gone, and, judging her tamed, the apes left her free to wander, she exercised her ingenuity to make her miserable existence tolerable. She wove loincloths with lianas, primitive garment to protect her nudity, not so much from gazes as the thorns and sharp twigs of the forest. Then she used the same ingenuity in making snares to catch birds or snakes, or designed to catch little rodents and other forest game by the neck or the paw, in order to nourish herself on them.

She also hollowed out calabashes in order to collect palm-wine and preserve aromatics; since her childhood among her own people Rava had known the art of extracting from

125

plants the pigments with which the natives painted their bodies—the blues and reds with which they heightened their eyelids or decorated their arms, faces and torsos with cabalistic signs and tribal badges. She thought that, by doing that, she would not lose status in her own eyes and would prove her femininity.

Long deprived of customary nourishment, Rava had searched in vain for a means of making a fire to cook her prey, but she eventually found flints, and discovered flammable essences in the woods. The first time that branches set in a hole in a rock had caught fire at Rava's hands, the horrified male and female orangutans had fled with cries of unprecedented terror, gesticulating furiously. Only Ouha, after the initial alarm, had dared to come back and prowl in a feline fashion around the fire where, against a red and gold background, exulting in her victory, a prideful silhouette was freely displayed, a statue of living bronze: Rava.

Then again, the slender and lovely statuette, so fine, had been obliged to fight to conciliate the jealous Dilou. By virtue of the Malay's feminine concerns, her distance, and her visible disgust for her hairy lover, the black woman had calmed down, certain that no rivalry would come from the Malay woman and that she did not wish, in any way, to separate her from Ouha.

Driven by the keenest desire, for a being of a race superior not only to his own but also to that of Dilou, his first concubine, Ouha displayed in Rava's regard a persuasive gentleness, all the more so because he wanted to possess her more ardently. In his animal sensuality, he retained the anxiety of a colossus playing with a fragile doll, fearful of breaking her. When he had finished, he laughed, expressing his joy with articulating whistles.

"J'soi! Sitsch!"

On the other hand, he genuinely sensed, by virtue of his instinct, refined by his contacts with humankind, his prestige over his subjects growing. Only Ouha dared to approach the fires that Rava lit, to warm himself there in the morning and the dusk. Carefully, he drove away the apes who were fearful of the flames but who, on seeing Ouha's attitude and risking an audacity, wanted to draw nearer to them. He even affected an ease, a visible pleasure, by means of is mimes and gestures, in the act of warming himself—one of his royal prerogatives. He expressed the bliss of heat be means of the syllables: "Ffitch! Choo!"

With a repugnance she could not overcome, therefore, and a fear that time did not soothe, Rava submitted to Ouha, in accordance with the law of primitive and natural beings. She won Dilou's attachment by meager womanly services, moderated her jealousy by continually giving way to her and throwing her into the arms of the monster, their common lover, in the hope of escaping, thanks to her, the horrible embrace. Dilou's love for Ouha often saved Rava from monstrous caresses.

Then, the little Malay, some two years older than the Dilou, assumed for her black sister a measure of maternal care. When Dilou, who liked to run recklessly through thickets like an exuberant young beast, came back with her skin punctured by thorns, her and or feet bruised and bloody, Rava knew the leaves, pulps, flowers and salutary herbs that could heal her. One day, when Dilou had been bitten by a coral snake, the Malay woman had staunched the wound with her lips and cured the venom's unhealthy fever. Thereafter, Dilou loved Rava with a blind devotion, in spite of the intractable fits of rage into which she sometimes flew when the Malay, woman, for reasons of preservation, took from her hands some object she had fabricated or forbade her some harmful action.

Gradually, they had come to understand one another. At first, gestures had been their only translator, then sounds—those that are onomatopoeic are almost the same in all languages—and signs, according to circumstances, had formed their limited dialect. Their instinct furnished them with mutually caressing and coaxing words before they had precisely defined the relevant meanings. Dilou spoke her native tongue, ape and Malay; Rava spoke the few words usually necessary in her native language, and had imposed them on Dilou by her superiority.

When Mabel had arrived, a cry of almost-animal rage, little different from the clamors of the apes while fighting, had escaped the thick red lips of Dilou; her eyes bulged out of their orbits and her clawed hands reached out toward the new captive. The apes' admiration for that rival, manifested by the obscene gestures of their hands wandering over a projection of their hairy bodies, had brought the jealous anger of the little captive to a peak.

Coldly and phlegmatically, Ouha beat Dilou; Mabel, aided by Rava, protected her. Before the white queen, to whom he did not want to risk a refusal, within her sight, the magnificent orang caressed Dilou and Rava, and then, summoning a she-ape with a cry of "z-k-ch!" satisfied his lust again with cries and sighs of sensual joy. Stunned and frightened, Mabel stood in a corner, waiting, before allowing her eyes, weary of old fears, to close, to see the monster collapse on his bed of leaves and to hear his enormous jaws clicking.

Then, when she was too fearful of the male, silently, she went to take Rava by the hand, and then Dilou, making them lie down next to her, a little more tranquil because that living rampart of the two women separated her from Ouha.

Often, Mabel awoke with a start, having thought she had felt the Beast's breath brush her face, or the ignoble purchase to his hair hands on her intimate parts. Many a time, on awakening, she found the giant crouched behind her head or at her feet, almost human, holding his chagrined face in his hands, with a real and profound sadness in his eyes, those of a disdained lover.

By virtue of all these tender demonstrations of Ouha's toward Mabel, a dull resentment brooded, in spite of everything, in Dilou's simple heart. She dared not make her hated manifest for fear of being punished, but in a sly feline fashion, like the she-ape she had almost become, the black girl attempt to hurt Mabel without being seen. She took objects of which Miss Smith scarcely ever let go as soon as they were put down, while the American woman's back was turned. Many a time, during the young white woman's siestas, Dilou threw thorny branches at her. Rava was always there to protect Mabel; the Malay woman had blossomed since the arrival of her new companion, and sometimes even abandoned her native phlegm to laugh and play with her childishly, like a happy little girl.

One day, without paying any heed to Dilou crouched near the threshold of the grotto, Mabel was standing at the top of a path that went along a precipice where vague rocks undulated all the way down to a foaming torrent. Dilou, throwing herself between her legs, would have caused her to fall with an abrupt shock if Rava had not shouted, grabbed hold of her and held her back.

During the long days, the women took long siestas almost every afternoon in the strong diurnal heat. But twenty days had passed since the abduction of the American woman without Dilou having given up her malicious attacks on Mabel, in spite of the severe punishments inflicted by Ouha several times over. That day, the heat was torrid; its leaden fluid enveloped the silent forest, where nothing could be heard out the slithering of reptiles, and the hum of summer insects between the leaves; even the soul of the forest, the beasts, suspended their breath.

Mabel, glad of Ouha's absence, was asleep on her bed of leaves and moss, renewed every day by the king—for Ouha, noticing the care that the white woman took of her lodgings, made things easier for her.

At the noise of small stones shifting, Rava opened her eyes. Dilou was climbing up the rocky walls of the cavern by means of its projections. Grimacing, Dilou crouched down on a stone outcrop, almost directly above the sleeping Mabel's head. With fiery eyes, Dilou stared at the white virgin. Perhaps, in the obscure soul of Rava, a dull mistrust of Mabel still remained, as toward Dilou, both of them being so different from herself, so she made no move to prevent anything Dilou might do.

Rava watched Dilou and, curiously, spied on her every gesture, Having spotted a block of granite, the black woman rolled the heavy stone along a ledge. Finally, Rava stood up and, when she saw Dilou brandishing the stone, with great effort, above Mabel's head, bounded forward to snatch the block from the menacing hands and send it rolling far away from the sleeping beauty. The noise woke Mabel up; she understood, and her eyes thanked Rava.

XXXIV. Love Progresses

By dint of observing their gestures and the syllables of their primitive language, Mabel had come to understand the thoughts that the anthropoids translated into marvelous and precisely eloquent mimes of cupidity, desire, sadness, joy or anger, at the instant they felt those impressions, common to all beings.

Once the initial stupors and terrors of the early days had passed, she had also understood accurately what power she had, what ascendancy her delicate beauty could exercise over brutal strength.

By the murder of the audacious orangutan who had dared to advance his gesture toward the flower of her body, and whom she had shot, a salutary dread was established. Even Ouha, sovereign and suitor, despot and lover, dared not risk anything irremediable in her regard, convinced that she disposed of a force unknown to him, like thunder, in which there was fire, noise, and something that struck, which one could not see—a weapon whose secret he did not know.

Because of this mystery, the young woman remained, in the eyes of Ouha and his subjects, a redoubtable and benevolent enchantress, according to whether or not she was satisfied. Ouha was glad to have seen the admired white woman fight beside him, gaitered in her light brown boots, in lacy culottes, with a leather belt over the rigid armor of the corset or the crumpled slip falling in two symmetrical globes, leaving uncovered the alabaster upper body, scarcely flesh-tinted. During an invasion of neighboring orangutans, Mabel had wielded a hatchet, which she had discovered in a pile of booty amassed by the hairy king.

By virtue of that noble deed, Mabel had become a heroine to the apes, a living palladium, much like Jeanne d'Arc, the Maid, to the soldiers of King Charles VII before the walls of Orléans: a fetish surrounded henceforth by superstitious veneration. The entire tribe was convinced of the efficacy of her mere presence against anything. Twice, at their head, by Ouha's side, she had battled an enemy tribe victoriously.

Dilou, the black girl who had almost reverted to animality, had fought in both battles by Ouha's side, striking heavy blows with a knotted branch, or, according to her bestial instincts, enveloped by long contact with the apes, bounding with her claws extended, with ferocious cries, to bite an adversary's limbs, grappling in hand-to-hand combats in which her sinewy muscularity and the feline suddenness of her leaps often gave her an advantage over opponents that were much stronger and heavier, who were disconcerted by the attack and fled.

Rava, disdainful of such skirmishes, unworthy, in her view, of her human pride remained with the she-apes charged with guarding the royal cavern. During the whole affair, the Malay remained aloof from the combat, hieratically immobile at the foot of a tree, her face painted red and yellow, her eyelids dotted with red, elongated to join up with the arch of her eyelids

Suddenly, as if remembrance lying dormant in the ashes of her memory had been reunited in the little Malay, she had burst into song, in the bloody dusk, in the face of the setting sun. Her shrill voice, child-like and yet potent, intoned a chant to a staccato rhythm, punctuated by cries: doubtless a war-song of her race, springing from nostalgia for the human battles of which the apes' combat reminded her.

Ouha was wounded during that skirmish with the enemy tribe. Touched by is attitude, by the gentleness that the Orang King manifested in her regard, Mabel Smith had bandaged his wounds. The Beast had conceived a profound gratitude for the white woman, testified by a redoubling of attentions that was almost servile. When Mabel attached the benevolent leaves to his hairy torso with vegetable fibers she had collected, and when she applied damp cloths to the gaping lips of the wound, Ouha, without moaning, restrained the cries of pain that were on the brink of escaping him, gazed at her with wide-eyed submission, seemingly forgetting his tyrannical power at such moments, his superhuman strength abdicated to the hands of his beloved, that benevolent and desired divinity.

The American woman had now suppressed her indescribable disgust at Ouha's approach when a vertical gesture gave evidence of his sensual disturbance. The king, in spite of his long ardor, was afraid of the petty lightning that his prisoner could unleash.

One night, when she was asleep, she awoke oppressed by a heavy weight, as in a nightmare—but a form blacker than the shadows was, in reality, weighing upon her: Ouha, terrible and panting, whose muzzle was brushing her face; the entire brown mass of that gigantic body suspended above her svelte nudity; that erotic brute hideously braced on the four pillars of his hairy limbs.

Already, the long and muscular hands were gripping her, tremulous and seeking. How could she extract herself from such a vice-like embrace as the one in which the Beast was holding her? Paralyzed, she had no means of reaching the hiding-place in which her revolver was lying, carefully hidden. Rigid, her limbs atrociously twisted, she was like an inert cadaver, a solid blocks, taut and petrified.

Then, at the moment when the disappointed monster raised himself up slightly, the young woman struck the giant animal's long hard virility violently with her clenched fist.

Ouha bounded out of the bed of leaves, over the sleeping Dilou and Rava, and a loud cry of simultaneous pain and rage made the walls of rock tremble, resonating with repeated echoes. The two women, woken up, consoled him, Dilou, especially, in a childish negro-ape jargon, in which there were promises and questions, phrases of solicitude detectable in a tone ameliorated by coaxing words;

"Ber!...Hiens!...Ouha, pig!....Warr!...Zef!...Zefbel!...Me, pig!...Pig!...suck Ouha..."

All of that was almost lisped, with an infinite softness intended to console, questing at the same time, promising caresses and joys.

Another day, Ouha, thinking that Mabel as far away from the common dwelling, searched the cracks in the walls, trying to discover where the captive might have hidden the little magical and destructive jewel. The American woman caught him, mocking and enigmatic at the very moment when he seized the loaded revolver from among her folded clothes.

Ouha turned it over and over in his hands, unable to find the correct way to grasp the weapon in order to make use of it, brandishing it as if it were his rusty carbine, a mere club in his ignorant hands. Miss Smith took hold of the butt without him resigning himself to let go of the steel barrel—but she pulled the trigger with a finger that she immediately withdrew.

Terrified by the noise, Ouha hid, cowering in a corner, but then came to put his finger in the hole that the bullet had made in the ground. He made no further attempt to steal the lightning from the white captive—who was, in any case, his talisman, the symbol of his omnipotence. In spite of his disappointment as a lover with regard to the white queen, he was further convinced by that thunderbolt that he was, because of his three wives—the fire that they knew how to make, and the lightning that the ungraspable released—as much as by virtue of his own strength, the King of the Forest.

Then, during the long dog-days and the sleepless nights, Ouha stayed crouched not far from Mabel, following her slightest gestures with his eyes, or staring from the depths of his jet pupils set in circles of gold at the languid slenderness of the Adored, the woman he so desired to possess, but whose fragility defied him.

Thus, coquettishly, Mabel Smith, divining that Ouha was similar to human males in terms of his senses and admiration in the presence of a woman, used her beauty to ensure his conquest. Beauty would be saved from the monstrous desire of the Beast, whom, sometimes, inadmissibly, and with disgust, she desired.

Yes, Mabel was certain, in her precise perspicacity, of her power over the Orangutan that was as superior to other apes as Napoléon was to his contemporaries, Ouha, who hid beneath his primitive envelope the embryo of a soul of noble execution: Ouha, the formidable lover of women, a hairier, coarser and more rough-hewn man, a savage of genius, above his own kind by virtue of the conscious domination by which he elevated himself, by virtue of his pride, his strength and his extraordinary intelligence, to which, in sum, the primitive instinct of his raced has led him.

Was it contact with human beings had given rise to concepts and imaginations in that astonishing ape whose brain surpassed that of many humans? Or do certain animals carry within hem the seeds of ideas, the fetus of a soul? But Ouha, in the very tyranny of his will, seemed human, even more jealous of his prestige than his abductions. He was just, even toward his subjects, as soon as he had no quarrel with them. Politically, he divided in order to rule, creating rivalries by means of unequal favors, equilibrating the powers beneath him.

As the ascendancy of her weakness over the tamed Napoléonic brute became clearer, Mabel became the arbiter of his angers, the only being capable of igniting them or extinguishing them. Now, sure of Ouha's respect, mingled with dread, Mabel Smith occasionally favored him with a brief flattery of the hand. Mimed conversations or exclamations, onomatopoeias, and shrill cries completing gestures, became frequent between the orangutan and the American woman. One might have thought that, that by means of the attentions he paid her every day, every hour, the Beast wanted to beg pardon for retaining his beautiful captive. Fruits, flowers, all the riches of the forest—even animals similar to those that Dilou and Rava hunted so ingeniously—incessantly renewed, maintained in a superfluity of natural wealth the guest who would have been omnipotent had she not been a prisoner of the anthropoid tribe.

Meanwhile, taciturn, as soon as his vain desires began to torment him, Ouha remained immobile and silent for hours, staring through some gap in the foliage or, perched on one of the rocky outcrops of the mountain, filling his eyes and brain, where vague thoughts and great dreams were perhaps agitating, with distant horizons and celestial reflections regarding that which, being beyond is domain, was unknown to him.

Who knows, Mabel thought, *whether he might be imagining possessing me, in a distant world, in the midst of an imaginary décor, mutated into a human? How many humans, anyway, are less wise, less correct, is one might put it thus, capable of a cruelty of which that phenomenal orangutan has no notion outside of moments of battle?*

Tales of atrocities, between individuals or nations, of injustices and reprisals, sprang to her mind, where, by way of contrast, a number of instances of Ouha's clemency rose up. Ouha was doubtless energetic, but devoid of any tyranny that did not serve his power, and so gentle toward her, even in the presence of his subjects, as soon as the interests of his reign were no longer at stake.

Seeing him thus, so brave, and not without generosity toward the vanquished, seeing that he was even trying, thanks to her, to comprehend real beauty and grandeur, the extension of his instinct, raised to the level of intelligence, incessantly increasing beyond the limits of his species, a genuine esteem was born in Mabel's soul for the king of the apes.

Miss Smith, strong in the power of her limited, tender and chaste caresses over Ouha, the suzerain of the forest, had easily become his tutor. By virtue of incessant contact with Mabel, guided by that which she prevented him from doing and the actions to which the young woman urged him, Ouha increased his comprehension, harmonizing himself, in truth, under the increasing influence of the virtuoso who, by a sign, a caress or a promissory gesture, by her coquettish grace, caused his senses to vibrate and knew how to restrain them, also showing him his own interest, directing the apes through him.

Rapidly, Mabel, by her proud and gentle grace by her very fragility and protected energy, came to the point where she sometimes feared nothing, at certain times, but her own sin.

Nature, the supreme mistress of all creatures, was in the process of vanquishing the American virgin, awakening in that willful, undisciplined temperament the irresistible force of sexual sensuality, making her the bacchante of ancestral instincts, rapid dominatrices, effacing the virtue of a superficial and artificial civilization, ready to bring closer, to confuse and to marry, in a double spasm, the prehistoric man and the attractive and marvelous, adorably exiting and lovely daughter of an American billionaire, to couple them, bridging in an ecstatic groan of pleasure fifty centuries of civilization.

XXXV. Nuptial Preludes

The American woman often got up at daybreak to wander through the forest, studying and locating from every point of view all the picturesque sights of the region. On a few occasions she even left before dawn, to climb one of the surrounding mountains, and to watch the sun rise therefrom.

There was one peak of which she was particularly fond, because, directly to the east, a higher peak masked the horizon. With the rapidity of tropical zones, dawn did not exist, in a manner of speaking; the light surged forth suddenly behind that mountain, and everything was illuminated before the sun, masked by that barrier, had made its appearance. Abruptly, it rose; the mountain seemed to melt and allow a river of incandescent lava to flow.

Then, as the sun continued its ascension, the summit was clearly outlined against the blazing sky, and from every rocky spur, luminous rays extended to the zenith. Everything brightened, and as outlined in successive planes; there were golds, ochers, violets, from the most intense tones to the most tender and delicate gradations.

And every day, even though the atmospheric conditions sometimes seemed identical to those of the day before, the sunrise was different. The young woman sensed these marvelous splendors without analyzing them. She contemplated and admired; she enjoyed nature, so to speak, blissfully, as one eats or digests.

Sometimes, Ouha went with her. At first, the ape did not understand, but in a spirit of imitation, he struck the same pose as Mabel; soon, however, it seemed that, by virtue of contact with an intelligence more complete and more refined, his own awoke. Ouha's yawns became less frequent, his eyes more attentive. Once, for him, the sunrise had always been similar; now he took account of differences in the colors, in their shades; their diffusions interested him. That peak, which he had seen as violet the day before, was pink today; that snowy summit which, on some days, was pure white, seemed at other times to be ruby red.

One day, Ouha, putting his hand on Mabel's shoulder, pointed out a new spectacle with his finger, an effect of the sun that they had not yet seen. The young woman followed the development of his mind with great interest.

Similarly, the constant sight of the monster attenuated his ugliness. Thus far—she had been a prisoner of the apes for two months—Ouha had not appeared to suspect that she had a sex like his other spouses. For him, this woman was a being apart, who could not have any equivalent among other creatures. Having largely what he needed to satisfy his senses with his other wives. Ouha no longer had anything for Mabel but admiration.

Furthermore, he was fearful of the revolver, the weapon that had killed one of his best friends mysteriously, with a red hole in the skull: the magical jewel that only killed in the young woman's hands. He had made his decision; Mabel passed for his wife with regard to the tribe; she was the queen, of whom he was proud; he, Ouha, was admired and envied; it was believed that he had what he did not have; he was happy, or very nearly. It requires a great deal of luck to be happy!

Gradually, that restraint, which had initially reassured the American woman, came to seem a sort of disdain, from which, internally and not entirely consciously, her vanity as a pretty woman suffered at the same time as her senses. In that environment of free nature, they began to awaken. The sight of couplings—and that spectacle was frequent—exacerbated her flesh; her young and healthy blood demanded caresses. While her body, in that untrammeled milieu, took on a more robust development, her mind inclined toward impossible embraces. That disposition brought her closer to Rava, the only being of her sex who had, thus far, conserved an appearance of humanity among the apes. Rava had been obliged to submit, like Dilou, to simian coupling, but while the black woman had promptly reverted to the level of the brute, the Malay woman had remained a woman.

In fact, Rava was a woman of superior status, who a series of unfortunate adventures had caused to fall among "the Damned." In spite of the abjection of that fall, she had conserved her self-respect—which, among her former companions, had made her a being apart. To Wang had accepted the fugitive Eg Merh into his tribe when, after a quarrel over a card game, the later had shot and killed his opponent. The young man, arrested and tried, condemned to hard labor for life, had escaped and found refuge among the Damned. Then he had written to his family to reassure them with regard to his fate, requesting his relatives to do everything possible to obtain a pardon—which was possible, the law and the Dutch government occasionally oaring amnesties that maintained the prestige of the Metropolis in the archipelago, making it a kind of divinity that the naives both feared and respected.

Rava, who adored her brother, came to join him, thus serving as an intermediary between him and the family. Rava, being free, made frequent voyages to Brunei or Imbuk, bringing subsidies that rendered Eg Merh's exile less dolorous.

To her anguish in being Ouha's prisoner and wife was added anxiety with regard to her brother's fate. Had Eg Merh perished in the final catastrophe? Should she mourn him or retain hope?

Rava, therefore, belonged to one of the elevated castes of Malaysia; her education was fairly complete; she could speak and write Dutch fluently. Unfortunately, she only knew a few elementary words of English, learned from illustrated magazines in which an image was explained in two or three languages.

Thus, after some time, Mabel observed that her companion in captivity was, if not of her world, at least well above the condition in which she had previously supposed her to be. The two women became closer and, with the aid of a few common terms in their two languages, and by designating objects, the prisoners ended up comprehending one another and were soon speaking a picturesque Anglo-Dutch that was capable of translating all their impressions. Rava told her story, and Mabel affirmed her hope that, if her brother had survived, he would come to rescue them.

For her part, Mabel had not given up all hope of escape, thanks to her excursions through the forest. She had been able to go as far as the old battlefield. Over an extent of several miles the forest no longer existed. Heaps of ashes and a few charred tree-trunks marked the place. She had advanced courageously, searching the masses of debris, sometimes encountering human bones, weapons, objects of encampment, all burned and twisted by the fire, but their number did not correspond to the whole of the little army. There was a chance that some has escaped. In that case, perhaps those, knowing that the great apes did not kill women, would come to rescue them.

But time passed. Gradually, Mabel adapted to the savage life—strangely enough, more rapidly than Rava. The latter sensed it confusedly and strove, by reminding her of the past, to maintain her friend's memory of her homeland and family. But the reminders seemed rather to irritate the American woman.

In truth, Mabel was subject, at that moment, to a horrible crisis, and when, at certain times, she saw Rava sullenly obeying a summons from Ouha, she followed her with an almost envious gaze. She did not have the same impression, however, when it was Dilou or one of the two female orangs. The latter did not count, but Rava was a woman like her.

Why not her, then? The ape's platonic admiration annoyed her. At times, she almost desired that he would throw himself upon her to violate her. Of course, she would kill him afterwards, and then herself. In that case why not kill herself right away? Twenty times over she took the revolver out of its holster, but dared not. What? She was alive, full of strength, health and beauty! What would become of her? A heap of ashes that would return to universal life. Oh, if only she were sure of another life! Like many modern intelligences, though, she hesitated between spiritualism and materialism. Oh, if only she had had a religious belief, like Rava! She lacked faith; her mind, at present, was capsized. The American woman, refined by all the luxuries, was inclining, slowly, but more every day, towards a naturalism devoid of affectation and modesty.

Is there only one law of nature?

Humans, alone, have invented virtue in order to distinguish themselves from all other beings and mount a semblance of opposition to eternal laws; that hypocrisy irritated Mabel now and led her to hate humankind. The truth is that the creative forces of love were working within her dully. Habitude diminished horror, and that precious springtime beauty was ready, like everything in the world, to breathe and perpetuate itself, to participate in the universal thrust of life.

XXXVI. The Wedding Night

One night—one of those electric nights in which the atmosphere seems to be impregnated with lasciviousness—Mabel, drowsy and enervated, was writhing on her bed of odorant plants, which was renewed every day, and whose odor of newly-cut grass further obsessed her feverish body, unable to bear the contact of any garment. She had taken off every scrap of clothing.

It seemed that she heard a slight rustling close by; she opened her eyelids slightly. Fiery eyes were gleaming nearby. She felt hot breath running along her entire body; hard hands, made gentle for the caress, gripped her shoulders.

She made as if to pull away—but her senses were suddenly more powerful than her will, and, with full arms she embrace a hairy giant, who, with infinite precaution, extended himself over her.

XXXVII. In the Ardent Shadow

....
....
....
....
....
....
....
....
....
....
....
....
....
....

XXXVIII. Morning Relapse

When Mabel awoke in the morning, she had a moment of real despair. Heavy breathing nearby attracted her gaze. Lying on his side, Ouha was asleep, one of his long arms folded under his head, the other hand clutching one of his feet. That simian attitude rendered him more ridiculous. She considered his enormous face, his bloody lips, his blue eyelids, the small ears scarcely projecting from the midst of a thick brown mane. Was it to that monster that she, the aristocrat had surrendered herself? Of what clay was she made, then? She, Mabel Smith, the daughter of a billionaire, before whom all of Yankees manhood had knelt, was now the mate of an ape! That was too much. It was necessary to put an end to this ridiculous disgrace. She put out her arm toward the place where the revolver was.

That movement awoke Ouha; he opened his eyes. Wildly, the American woman seized the weapon and aimed it at the Beast. Ouha appeared to comprehend; his eyelids fluttered and his eyes took on an expression of infinite tenderness. He sat up on his knees, his long arms extended to either side of his enormous body, still gazing at the woman.

Consenting to death, as she had consented to love, he waited.

It was a decisive moment. To Mabel, it seemed that her brain was enveloped by a whirlwind of flame. Her crazed eyes examined the Beast; from the hideous muzzle her gaze descended over her lover; then her face turned crimson; she uttered a muffled groan; her entire body shivered—and she fell backwards, defenseless in her soul.

When she came to, she stood up painfully. She experienced an intense weariness, but the fever that had tortured her for several days had disappeared. She sat down and let her forehead fall into her hands. Thus, she had succumbed, this time without having the excuse of sleep and the night.

For a long time, she remained plunged in the abyss of her thoughts. The orangutan left her to her meditation.

XXXIX. A Reflux of Human Dignity

Suddenly, she raised her head. Someone had come into the cave: Rava. She advanced slowly, looking at Mabel with pitying horror. Then, the latter perceived that she was naked. Turning her back to the Malay, she hastily put on some clothes. Then she turned round and looked the young woman up and down.

"What now?" she said.

"You too?"

"Oh well," sniggered the American woman. "I'm as good as you, I think. And then, to be honest, I wanted it. I love him. I have the right to make of myself what I please. Go away! Leave me alone!"

Rava had let herself fall to her knees.

"Oh, Mabel, Mabel!" Her eyes filled with tears and she rolled on the ground, sobbing.

The American felt her reason vacillating. Her pride finally got the upper hand. She repeated: "I wanted it. It was me! It was me who wanted it!"

"May Allah protect you!" cried Rava. "She's gone mad!"[14]

Mabel burst into wild laughter. "Yes, probably, I'm mad, or I'm having a terrible dream. I'm no longer a woman; I've abandoned humanity. I've taken a step backwards; I'm no longer a woman, I'm a female, the mate of an ape!"

She burst out laughing again, and then said: "We must get away. Even if I die in the forest, I have to go. Otherwise...I believe I'll end up loving Ouha!"

---

[14] Although Rava calls upon Allah here, she will subsequently cite Buddha in the same fashion, and is described eventually as a "Hindu." It is not unusual in French adventure fiction for Islam, Buddhism and Hinduism to be confused, and treated as if they were the same set of beliefs.

"Oh!" said Rava, with a gesture of horror. "You're right, we have to go. But how can we? We're watched constantly."

"What does it matter? Let's risk everything for everything. If I stay here one more day, I'll no longer be able to go. But where's Ouha?"

"I think there's a council."

"Then let's leave immediately."

"We won't get very far without being recaptured."

"I have an idea!" Mabel exclaimed. "We need to flee by means of the river. The orangs don't like to get wet; the current is rapid. We're going to construct a little raft, quickly. We can be ten miles away by nightfall. The apes will think we're going to bathe, as usual. They won't suspect. Let's go."

Rava shook her head dubiously. Nevertheless, she hastened to pile what provisions there were in the cave into a basket she had woven, and they both went out.

XL. The Ape Council

There was, indeed, a council and on the far side of the clearing, a tumult was audible advertising a numerous assembly. The motive for the extraordinary meeting was that the orangs stored their provisions of bananas, guavas, banyans, etc., in a cave in the mountain-side, but for some time, the ape in charge of the food-supplies had been noticing losses. Sentinels had been posted, and the thieves had been discovered.

It was the entire clan of smaller apes that was guilty: baboons, mandrills and ouarines[15] had joined forces for the robbery. The apes, too large to slide through the opening that ventilated the cave, had recruited the little sapajous to their cause. The latter, thanks to their slender agility and dexterity, had formed a chain and passed the booty to those outside.

For a long time, hostility had reigned between the other primates and the orangs. The latter, heavier and more sedentary, continually had to suffer the thefts and pestering of the small monkeys. The orangs were certainly the stronger, but the others were multitudinous. Even Ouha had quarreled with the gang, who, in a pure spirit of mischief, amused themselves by exciting the orangs' wrath. The number of inferior monkeys had increased greatly because, thanks to the fire lit by Silven Gorden and his friends, all the animals inhabiting the forest had been driven back to the far side of the river, where the flames had stopped, into the region that as Ouha's domain.

Finding abundant nourishment in that country, and separated from their old forest by the burned zone, the monkeys had taken up residence there, to the great detriment of the orangs, whose domain was incessantly ravaged by the host of small creatures. For some time already, food had been getting scarcer, and now, to cap it all, these pillages were depleting

---

[15] Like sapajous, ouarines are New World monkeys, also known as howler monkeys.

the Orangs' reserves. There could be no more hesitation; it was necessary to drive out and expel the horde of raiders and punish them harshly, so that they would not come back.

So, as Mabel and Rava, unaware of the threat of war, prepared to flee, there was considerable agitation in the assembly. (The narrator will not say "parliament," for all citizens had equal rights there and could take part in the discussion.)

Fréü, one of the most distinguished orators, had taken the floor and, accompanying himself with a very expressive pantomime, explained the dangers run by the nation, confronted with this invasion of barbarians. Everyone shared his opinion in deploring the invasion of the fatherland. The words "Harr-ha! Harr-ha!" were continually on the orator's lips—or, rather, in depths of his throat. Harr-ha!—the fatherland—Harr-ha!—for which it was necessary to fight victoriously or die.

Fréü was an oldster, as was evident, not from his vigor or his stature by his white hide. Venerable, he had taken part in all the governments prior to Ouha's dictatorship. The latter knew that Fréü was an old imbecile, but as, before anything else, he was utterly devoted to the fatherland. Ouha held him in some esteem, and often put on an appearance of asking him for advice. The Ancient was becoming decrepit, though; his slack jaw often caused him to mumble, which excited the mockery of the practically-minded young orangs, who were always ready to launch themselves into an adventure without waiting for the lessons of experience, provided that there was a profit to be obtained from it.

This time, however, the patriotic fiber was vibrating in all of them; there was a sacred union in every heart. There was only one point on which it was difficult to reach agreement: the means of getting rid of the enemy. The latter's numbers, by comparison with the orangutans', was formidable. In fat, the Harr-Ha nation, including females and children, comprised no more than eight hundred individuals, and the enemy must be at least twenty thousand strong. Moreover, the orangutans, not being carnivores, did not desire the death of an adversary, from which they could not derive any advantage.

After Fréü, another orator took the floor. This one, named Brray, was a tall and sturdy orang, in the plenitude of age and strength, expert in the art of war. One could say that he had been dried out in the fire of combats. He had once been Ouha's adversary, being the former leader of the black-bearded orangutans; vanquished, he had accepted defeat with resignation, and before the common danger, he swore that if he were given command of the army, he would vanquish or die.

Ouha stood up and interrupted him. It was not a matter of electing a leader; he was already in place: himself, Ouha. It was a matter of discussing a plan of attack. The orangutans had the physical strength, but could they vanquish an enemy so numerous, and much more agile than themselves? It was to be feared that the enemy would avoid hand-to-hand combat, in which they would certainly come off worse, in order to fight at a distance and pepper them with projectiles. He knew, thanks to one of his spies, that the enemy had amassed enormous quantities of pebbles in the crowns of tall trees. They would be peppered without being able to reach the enemy, which, being lighter, could maintain themselves at a greater height on weaker branches, incapable of supporting the noble weight of an orangutan.

After this explanation of the situation, Ouha sat down again, and the discussion resumed. There were brilliant speeches. Many of them drew applause, but nothing useful emerged from those turns of verbiage and mime. If a European could have witnessed the assembly, he would not have found the slightest difference from those of his own country.

The meeting, begun in mid-morning, had not reached a conclusion by nightfall. The females and children, had brought he patriotic citizens something to eat. The latter had thus been sustained during the oratorical gesticulations, and, in the ardor of the debate, each one relieved himself without leaving his place—which, combined with the natural slovenliness of apes, made the parliamentary enclosure a trifle malodorous.

Ouha closed the session and postponed the remainder of the debate until the next day.

XLI. Dr. Goldry Is Rediscovered

Instead of going to the cave, the dictator, understanding that duty must come before love, headed for the river and went upstream, thus heading toward the mountainous massif that overlooked the entire region.

After a good hour's march, he found himself on a vast plateau completely devoid of vegetation. In the middle, there was an enormous hole in the form of a well. Ouha seized a gigantic liana, solidly attached to a spur of rock, which hung down into it, and let himself slide into the opening. The hollow was about ten meters deep, and in the direction of the river, evidently hollowed out by water, here was a tunnel extending toward the stream. After hundred paces, he emerged into a grotto illuminated by crevasses situated at a great height. Fine sand carpeted the ground, which was pierced here and here by stalagmites, some of which joined up with the stalactites in the vault, forming majestic colonnades.

From the depths of the grotto, a voice emerged.

"Is that you, my dear Ouha?"

"Yes, yes," Ouha replied.

Then, a shadow advanced from the back of the cave: a hairy man, Dr. Abraham Goldry, in person. Unkempt russet hair fell over his shoulders; a beard of the same color, extensively streaked with gray hairs, descended to his chest, as hairy as those of the apes. From all that hair nothing emerged but a cranium, polished like ivory.

"You've come very late, my dear Ouha," said Abraham Goldry.

"Impossible to get here sooner," said Ouha, accompanying his mime with a few sounds that vaguely resembled words. And without further delay, the king of the apes explained to the doctor the political events of the day and the orangutans embarrassment.

153

Evidently, those two strange beings understood one another very well. The man had almost become an ape, and the orangutan had profited a great deal from contact with the man. Doubtless remembering the scientific amity and profound personal esteem that the doctor had immediately testified toward him at Riddle-Temple, the orangutan had spared the scholar's life and had kept him prisoner. It was the inverse of his own adventure; the ape, in his turn, kept the human in a cave and conducted his simian education. The doctor lent himself to it readily, with a good grace, and hoped in time, by means of devotion and scientific sacrifice, to become a perfect orangutan, while remaining Dr. Abraham Goldry, thus collecting a considerable booty of incomparable observations for his studies of the origin of humankind.

When Ouha had informed him of the situation, he asked for his advice. The doctor reflected for some time, after which, he explained his plan to the orang, who listened attentively, supporting the explanations of his captive and friends with nods of the head.

"Perfect," he mimed, finally. "But only you can help me put the plan into action. Do you want to be one of us?"

"You're going to let me out of here, then?"

"You can come with me. Is your costume ready?"

"Yes, old chap—wait. You'll see."

The doctor went around a corner of the grotto, which formed a covert less well-lit than the rest of the cave. He stayed there for a few minutes, and then a superb red-haired orangutan appeared before Ouha's eyes. The king examined the new individual minutely, in whom the widow of the late Kri-Kri would certainly have recognized her husband.

This necessitates a few explanations.

During the attack on the European camp, the headstrong Kri-Kri, who was commanding the attack with his friend Harr, had been mortally wounded. He had dragged himself away from the battlefield, painfully, and, encountering a crevasse in a group of rocks on his route, had slid into it in order to die in peace. That is a habit among that race of apes; when they feel the end approaching, they retire to the most distant spot possible in order to die there. A petty bourgeois poet, François Coppée, has made the same observation with regard to the sparrows of Paris.

In winter, one does not see their delicate skeletons.
Is that because birds hide away to die?[16]

It was in that location that Kri-Kri ceased to live. The conflagration of the forest passed over him without consuming him, and it was in that tomb of stone that Ouha found him, thanks to traces of blood, when he came back with his fellows to collect from the battlefield those of his subjects who had escaped the flames.

Having the intuition that it might interest his friend, Ouha had taken the cadaver to him—a precious gift that the doctor received with transports of joy. He had been able to study the anatomy of an adult orangutan that had always lived in the wild, and had learned many things therefrom.

Ouha, always curious to learn, had watched the surgical operation, at first reluctantly, but soon with interest. The doctor explained to him the action of the nerves and muscles, the function of the organs and their role in the general economy. Did Ouha understand? At any rate, the lesson seemed to excite him—as for example, three years after the Great World War, in 1922, the theories of the German Einstein had enthused many people in Parisian salons, who had thus appeared to

---

[16] Champsaur must have attempted to reproduce these lines from Coppée's poem *"Est que c'est les oiseaux se cachent pour mourir"* from memory. A literal translation of the actual lines would read: "We do not find their delicate skeleton/In the April grass through which we run./Is that because birds hide away to die?"—the last line also being the poem's title. It is not clear why Champsaur refers to Coppée, with slight contempt, as a "petit bourgeois poète."

comprehend the relativity of time and space and even the non-existence of those two infinities, which were but one.

However, practical in the midst of his speculations, the skin having been removed with the greatest care, Ouha made his friend understand that he desired him to put it on, and the American doctor did his best to comply. Thanks to his medical kit, fortunately preserved, he was able to tailor and sew it, adjusting Kri-Kri's skin to his figure. The head, cleverly prepared, was fitted to the scholar's skull—who thus became the oddest of orangutans.

Satisfied, Ouha made a gesture of approval, led Goldry to the liana-rope, and signed an instruction to climb up. Alas, the new ape was not yet perfect. Having climbed up a few meters, the doctor fell. Ouha gave him a friendly tap, which sat him down on the ground. The orang scratched his head. What kind of a figure would his maladroit pupil cut among his subjects? Bah! He had been grievously wounded; he would use a crutch to support himself; that would spare him from executing the leaps and somersaults of his fellows.

That difficulty resolved, he put the scientist on his back and emerged from the grotto in the blink of an eye. When they set foot on the plateau, the immense landscape was lit by the moon, which was full—but it was about to disappear behind the mountains. The king and the doctor took advantage of its last rays to return to the orangutans' camp.

XLII. The Fugitives Are Forced to Return

During that day, so fecund in events, Mabel and Rava had bravely set forth, but, as Rava had foreseen, they did not get far. In fact, the agitation of the population testified that something unusual was happening. Scarcely had they gone into the woods, heading for the river, than they ran into sentinels who made them understand that it would be dangerous to go any further.

They went on, the sentinels not thinking that they ought to oppose by force the caprice of His Majesty's wives—but scarcely had they reached the river bank than a hail of stones descended upon them. Rava, hit on the head, fell down. Mabel, seeing a brave little baboon leaping from branch to branch brandishing a cudgel, had fired her revolver and killed it.

There were furious cries, then, and the rain of stones increased; launched from a greater distance however, they did not reach the young women. Supporting Rava, who had been stunned by the blow she had received, Mabel beat a retreat and went back to the cave, where she lavished the necessary care on the casualty—who came out of it, in the end, with a enormous bump on the head.

XLIII. The Alliance of the King of the Apes and the American Doctor

Ouha resolved not to wait until the next day to apply to the attack by the means indicated by the doctor. He went with the doctor to the apes' mustering-ground, a clearing situated in the heart of the forest, in an area that, thanks to its isolation between two hills, as entirely under the sway of the orangutans. Emissaries were sent to wake up the combatants and instruct them to rally there.

XLIV. The Ape Council: Nocturnal Session

Beneath the immense vaults of branches in gigantic arcades, which are interlaced and entangled in the darkness, are groups of shadows. In places, the full moon finds gaps in the vaults, and the mighty branches and trunks of the titanic trees writhe in a rip of light.

Enormous corollas hang down from the tulip-trees, their pistils twisted and almost animal darting protruding between the petals of the monstrous flowers; sweet perfumes mingle with the odor of putrid dead leaves and the reek of marshy ground.

The forest, noisy with a rhythmic breath, in which so many lives are palpitating—of wild beasts, trees, perhaps humans, flowers and birds—seems by night to be a body full of the ardor of female lust, beneath the sky constelled by myriads of stars, awaiting the lover who will come, from daybreak to sunset, from dusk to dawn: incessantly quivering beneath the sun or in the soft light of exotic nights, in expectation, the virgin forest, palpitating with so much life: its own.

In the naves of trees, phantoms with a hundred arms, formless and almost divine, vegetable octopodes whose branches and multiple trunks are the tentacles, the orangutans—the entire tribe—are gathered: caricatures of humankind. The notable apes have taken their places in the middle of the immense clearing, where, on the undulating grass, the tresses of the soil, the moonlight creates a large luminous semicircular space. The strongest—those whose limbs are the most robust or the mot agile—have taken the first row. Some are sitting or squatting with their hands on their knees; others are standing up, crowding together and jostling to get nearer to the leaders, uttering cries of appeal.

There are nearly two hundred of them.

Some, in order to dominate the assembly, have climbed on to branches, and mischievous or annoyed at not having obtained the coveted places, are raining fruits and broken branches on the others, the first to be seated, the strongest, whom they taunt with yelps, doubtless gibes, and mockery. Some of the larger ones, however, swiftly climb into the foliage in order to make the impudent shut up.

And here, standing tall, with his rifle, scepter and club in his extended right hand, is Ouha, with his three wives, one of ebony, one of living bronze and the white-fleshed Mabel, crowned with russet curls, clad in her slip, bunched up at the edge of her corset, her calves curved beneath the carefully pulled-up black stockings, emerging from the tan-colored boots, and short transparent trousers. Dilou, naked and gleaming, is carrying an enormous banana leaf; Rava is sad, serious and pensive in her dress woven from liana-fibers.

"Sksch! Sksch! Ouha!" Thus clamor, by way of a salutation, the palms extended toward the sovereign of the great apes: Ouha, the most robust, the most powerful, the most intelligent among them.

Silence falls while Ouha sits down, slowly and majestically, one foot set at the same height as his belly, the other hanging down from the decapitated trunk of a double tree, the second of which forms the back of the strange chair: it is the king's throne, almost in the center of the clearing, directly beneath the moon, whose laughing disk seeming to be looking down on the bizarre assembly from the height of a firmament of somber lapis lazuli, spangled with gold.

The women, at a sign from Ouha—the polygamous orangutan who takes his wives from among the companions and equals of men—sit down in front of him. like a living trophy to the simian glory that caresses his fiery eyes: black diamonds encircled by gold, in the crude setting of verminous and crumpled eyelids.

Immense fruit-bats fly away, frightened.

Now Ouha mimes with furious gestures, designating a part of the forest that all of them, nodding their heads approvingly, seem to know.

160

With wide-eyed amazement, Mabel—sitting between Dilou, who is rolling a coconut back and forth like a kitten, and Rava, indifferent, hieratic and pensive, supporting her chin in her right hand, staring into the distance—contemplates the sea of half-bald heads, black jowls punctuated by ivory whiteness, fangs overlapping lips and russet spines, bizarrely striped in places by the shadows of branches and leaves in the silvery moonlight.

In various attitudes, the orangutans are listening—or, rather, following the mime of the regal harangue. There are those among them like white-haired old men, their beards sticking out to either side of their jaws; some of them, having not lost an inch off their torsos, are standing up, showing off their huge, gangling, muscular bodies, fixing their attentive and shining eyes on the orator; others are leaning on their elbows, affecting serious and weary poses, letting their heads fall almost between their parted knees, as if bowed beneath the burden of grave thoughts; some are turning their heads from side to side, seemingly inattentive and mocking, babbling untiringly, wrinkling their black, brown, russet or gray muzzles over their terrible chattering teeth; a few, seemingly lost in distant brutishness, suddenly emerge from their apathy from time to time, approving with nods of the head or applauding, with their hands extended toward Ouha.

Several are scratching their behinds comically, and the most serious suddenly obscene, are caressing one another or themselves, without abandoning their serious expressions. And the contagious manual example of some is propagated from group to group. In a spirit of migration, the lust spreads and blossoms. Sudden spasms, joyful grimaces and blissful sighs momentarily interrupt an immobility swiftly resumed.

Mabel Smith thought she was witnessing an unexpected sabbat, but was troubled even so by those gestures, especially frightened by the resemblance of the simian faces to human faces, the parity of signs that might have been thought those of human madness. She did not know whether or not she was suffering a bizarre hallucination, witnessing, with the sensation of being awake, a nightmare both grotesque and terrible in its buffoonery: a senate of men disguised as apes, who, by virtue of eccentricity, were engaging in a parody of serious discussion, punctuated by lubricious wagers, follies, gestures and furious patriotic exclamations, broken and zigzagged like lightning-spitting clouds, by threats, fits of anger and screeches expressing, in an exaggerated fashion, all the human emotions.

Ouha, the respected sovereign, indicated a direction, a part of the woods, with signed calls for vengeance, and a bellicose excitement that signified combat. One syllable, from among the unintelligible sounds, reverberated in Mabel's ears:

"R'ran! R'ranich! R'rran!"

Mabel remembered the terrible fury of the orangutans on discovering their provisions of fruits—*bof fof!*—pillaged on returning from an expedition into the forest; other apes had passed by who, discovering the hiding-places, had stolen the roots, lianas and comestibles hidden in rocky granaries, in cracks in the stony flanks of the mountain.

Ouha was still gesticulating, in a bellicose fashion. Mabel now understood, from the signs of menace emphasized by the twirling of the rifle, scepter and club, the purpose of the fantastic, monstrous, bizarre council in the center of the moon-lit clearing.

Ouha having stepped down, a new orator seemed to be pleading, with expansive gestures, for an opposite thesis. Howls, a volley of insults, interruptions and clamors went up. Young orangutans stood up, and threats were sketched, addressed by one group to another. Then, one of the tallest seated in the first rank of the apes, leapt into the center of the assembly, his tall black silhouette looming up in the pale starlight.

Akutch, almost as venerated as the king, calmed the storm by his intervention. He pointed at the mutineers with his hand and appealed to them. The women, accustomed to these brief designations, understood the controversy. Mabel, forgetful of her sentimental tragedy, still struck by the human resemblances, smiled ironically, less appalled than amused by the original spectacle. She smiled. Who could tell whether the beasts' war might not lead them into civilized regions, whether some encounter might not assist her deliverance?

She smiled, among other smiles, at seeing a large ape beside Ouha who was looking at her persistently and who strangely resembled her godfather, Dr. Abraham Goldry. The poor doctor! What had become of him? Was he still alive?

For a long time, amid the hubbub of the crowd of orangutans, with lazy poses, the scratching of ears and behinds, seemingly disarticulated fingers rummaging in the mouths and nostrils of the audience, the assembly deliberated.

Then they all bounded around Ouha, and over the sovereign's head, the notable apes and their she-apes leaping like vertiginous acrobats from branch to branch with cries of joy and dancing rounds; and they all whirled, brandishing their fists or gnarled branches, doubtless toward the refuge of the thieves.

Shivering, Rava had got to her feet, and, striking the two flints that she always carried together, lit a fire of heaped-up branches. The moon was now setting behind the treetops, and the darkness was getting deeper, becoming dense where the crowns of the tall poplars, sycamores, giant red cedars and tulip-trees faded away.

Meanwhile, the females, in response to the cries of the disbanded council, had come down from the branches to the ground, amid the monstrous males, in order to draw them toward the city. Couples were swarming in the center of the clearing, lying down, interlaced—but the flames suddenly caused them to flee. Separated, the couples galloped in single file, and wide-open females passed from the hands that were gripping them to others.

In the halo of the blazing fore, staining the trees with gold and crimson and hurling reflections of infernal debauchery into the gaps between the trunks, Ouha remained superbly still, calm and erect, his upper right hand resting on Mabel's shoulder. The American billionairess, the flower of centuries of civilization, was standing between Dilou and Rava, the lovely and slender Malay, statues of ebony and bronze.

XLV. The Victory of Intelligence

As soon as the sun rose, Ouha's army was ready to take action. The king, the doctor and Ko-Zu represented the general command. The difficulty was one of communication with those turbulent soldiers, from whom a strict discipline and observation of orders received was necessary. The plan proposed by Goldry required few instigators, but it was necessary that they be supported by the whole army.

Abraham had understood immediately that a pitched battle was impossible against an enemy whose mobility and lightness put it out of range of any attack. It was necessary to use cunning. Knowing the curiosity and imitative compulsion that characterized the quadrumanes, he based his plan on that means of action. Thus, after multiple explanations to the most capable chiefs, the action commenced. It was the general command who were running the greatest danger.

To make the configuration that the battlefield was about to make more easily understandable, let us briefly recall the distribution of the terrain. The Orangs' domain was represented, above all, by the mountainous massif, inaccessible on the northern side, the massif being cut off steeply by the coast of Borneo for an extent of at least thirty miles. After that cut-off, the terrain descended, by a sequence of decreasingly elevated hills, to the median level of the island. To the east and the west was a sequence of small hills mingled with rocks and forests of tall trees, rich in fruits of all kinds; that was the true homeland of the orangutans, Harr-ha, bounded to the south by the river and the burned forest.

It was, therefore, a matter of forcing the enemy to go back over the river and then the zone of destruction. Now, the whole gang of little monkeys, having devastated the orangutans' territory and reserves, finding food increasing hard to come by, were spreading out eastwards and westwards rather than returning to the immense virgin forest from which they had come.

Shortly after the rise of the God who reigns in the sky and over the earth, surrounded by radiance, a little troop comprised of Ouha, Ko-Zu, Dr. Goldry and thirty young orangs set forth.

On Abraham's instructions, each of them carried on his head a basket full of bananas, hidden by branches and leaves; these green baskets would, as in Shakespeare, imitate a moving forest, serving the plan of campaign and also protecting the orangutans.

They wove their way around the clumps of trees that bordered the river, crossed it by leaping from rock to rock, and, after having wrong-footed the enemy by their maneuver, finally entered the burned region. Having arrived there, the orangutans looked back.

All the trees on the other side along the bank, were laden with monkeys, mandrills and sapajous, a curious and intrigued simian host, following the course of the ambulant bushes with thousands of keen and ingenuous eyes. The swarm of small monkeys of every species was weighing down the branches.

"So far so good," said the doctor.

He and his companions advanced further and further into the desert of ashes—or, rather, what had been a desert, for nature was already reasserting its rights, and vegetation was sprouting everywhere.

Having passed beyond the range of their missiles, but not so far away that the little monkeys would miss a single one of their actions, the troop of orangutans, following the doctor's example, leaned down to the ground and pretended to be searching for and picking fruits. The bananas carried in the verdant baskets played their role. Abraham, while playing his role like his comrades, never took his eyes off the monkeys.

Soon, a large mandrill, bolder than the others, came down from his tree and crossed the river He had no difficulty finding a banana dropped for his intention. He sat down and ate it greedily. Ten minutes later, a hundred monkeys had come to join him and search for the bananas that, imitating Petit Poucet, the doctor and his friends were sowing behind them. Encouraged by the example, thousands of small monkeys started fighting among themselves, in a mob, as to who would cross the river most rapidly, like Panurge's sheep in Rabelais competing to be the first to leap into the sea.

In less than an hour, the plain was black with small four-footed creatures searching the long grass for the bait of bananas, over which they fought with outbursts of anger and somersaults. Seeing the success of their ruse, the orangutans disguised as clumps of banana-trees increased their pace, heading at top speed toward the forest, still followed by the enemy army, which, while feasting, had not the slightest intention of attacking them. By nightfall, the orangutans had reached their goal and the baskets were empty.

Taking advantage of the last glimmers of twilight, they took refuge in a thicket and waited. Darkness caught the multitude of little monkeys by surprise. They now had the desert of the burned forest behind them; they were obliged to seek refuge in the forest, and, with the cerebral fragility and intellectual mobility of their race, they hurled themselves into its branches for the night, without suspecting that they had changed domicile and that they would have no memory of it the following day.

The doctor and his acolytes waited some time for all the little people to go to sleep; then, sure of not being observed, they retraced the steps of the journey they had made during the day. In the morning, they crossed the river, greeted by the acclamations of the orangutan nation. Thus was terminated, without shedding a single drop of blood, the invasion of the pygmy quadrumanes.

XLVI. The Beast and Mind

Taken back by Ouha, the doctor returned to his cavern, and the monarch testified his satisfaction by rubbing his friend's back. Goldry hastened to take off his simian envelope, in which he was stifling. Then the conversation began.

"So," the scientist said, "you also have Mabel prisoner, and you hid it from me."

"Mabel is my wife, and I feared that you would try to steal her from me."

"What an idea! From the moment that I became a postulant orangutan, why should I have any objection to my goddaughter being your spouse? All that I want is for you to make her happy."

"Don't worry; she has everything she needs."

"Hmm! Do you remember her residence at Riddle-Temple? There must be many things lacking here, and do you not know yourself how much more comfortable her life was at home than here? If I'm striving to raise you to a higher level, and I myself am becoming an orangutan, it's up to you to become a human..."

Ouha nodded his head. For the first time, he felt that the contact he had made with human beings as, in a sense, putting him outside his race—but would that be an advantage for him and his fellows, if he drew them with him by is example? He examined the doctor, who was certainly no Antinous, being tall, thin and angular, and cast a complacent glance down at himself, judging, privately, that humans were rather ugly animals, and that, from the physical point of view, he was considerably superior to them.

However, Ouha had one great advantage over his fellows: memory. He could recall his sojourn at Riddle perfectly, and the comfort he had enjoyed at that time. There was, most of all, a certain English armchair, in the depths of which he had sprawled voluptuously, while his friend Abraham explained one of the great natural laws to him, or Mabel, sitting at an item of furniture had made singular noises by tapping pieces of ivory partly lined with black wood.

While Abraham continued his speech, the distracted mind of the ape recalled the past, while an embryonic project was born in his brain. His character as a conqueror regained the upper hand, but this time, with desires well above his simian individuality.

After having become the absolute chief of almost all of the orangutan population, no longer having any against him but a few rebels, having acquired the blind friendship of a man of science, and having conquered a white beauty, he dreamed of the domination of the milieu in which he had seen them live, where he sensed that he would now not be out of place.

He could see himself, Ouha, comfortable swaying in the rocking-chair, savoring a fine cigar, with delicious beverages within arm's reach, while his wife, Mabel, seated at the piano, lulled him with the harmonious chords with which she sometimes accompanied a song trilled in a strong, pure voice. In the drawing-rooms, his subjects the orangutans were coming and going, clad in light garments similar to those that he had once been made to wear—which had inconvenienced him greatly, but which it had been necessary to suffer in order to get closer to that humanity he envied.

At times, stupefied by the variety of the images that succeeded one another, he passed his hand over his seething skull. How far away he was today from what he had been before his sojourn at Riddle-Temple!

As if he divined the thoughts that were whirling in his pupil's mind, the doctor redoubled his zeal, hammering away, as it were, at the ape's brain.

"My dear Ouha, I can see and sense that you understand me, and that justly entitles me to the glory of having created you. What a noble success it is for a scientist like me to see prehistoric humankind surging through the ages, picturesquely, to have lived with him the brutal and material life of the primitive being, and to lead him, in a few months, to the level of present-day civilization. From that viewpoint, you still know very little, and can't form any idea of what our great human agglomerations are like. Figures tell you very little, but imagine, for the sake of comparison, the army of little monkeys that you fooled so cleverly; I estimate their number at about twenty thousand. Well, some of our big cities contain a hundred times as many humans. I say that because it's necessary not to give you any illusions, to give you a false idea of your victory over us, for you only have dealt with a very tiny fraction of my race. Don't think that I'm telling you this by way of boasting; in spite of your remarkable spirit of domination, Ouha, the tiny number of your subjects can never acquire supremacy over humans. You can't have any idea of what the globe on whose surface we live is like, and how unimportant this island is relative to the immensity of the Earth."

"I haven't even traveled all over the island," Ouha mimed, "but I'll be content with that."

"Oh, you're always so ambitious! So much the better. I approve; such an ambition is, for you, a necessary emulation. The conquest of the island; there, to be sure, is an idea. I'll even help you, for there are no Americans in Borneo—which is two-thirds Dutch and one-third English—except Harry Smith, Mabel and me."

Ouha put a hand on his head. "You're mine."

"Hmm!" Abraham muttered. "I'm yours? Let's understand one another. An American is a free man and cannot be the slave of an..." He was about to say "ape" but stopped himself. "...A primitive human, a man anterior even to the Stone Age, for I haven't seen any of your subjects making use of weapons carved from flint. Clubs made from broken branches, not even stripped, and formless stones hurled by hand—that's all you've discovered."

"You're mine!" repeated Ouha, angrily.

"Ah! If you take that tone, my lad, we'll fall out. I know that you're stronger than I am, but don't forget that I'm cleverer, and that if I stay with you, it's a matter of friendship, not servitude."

Ouha seemed to understand. He softened his attitude, and wrung the doctor's hand.

"Good! Understand that, when I wish, I'll easily find a means to give you the slip. You interest me, as an enigma posed to science. I sense in you an intellectual force in conflict with your animality. I want to help you to cast off that envelope and take a great step forward in the scale of beings. But for your part, don't forget that I'm an American subject, a doctor of science, a professor at the University of Philadelphia, a member of several academies, and a laureate of numerous anthropological societies."

Ouha shrugged his shoulders and showed his monstrous fists.

"Again!" cried Goldry. "Opposing brutal force to scientific discussion! You'd deserve it if I left you to overcome confusion on your own, with your ideas of conquest. Rapine is sufficient. What could you do with your population of animals? Do you think that you know enough to raise them above their bestial level? Remember that you're an extraordinary exception."

"Yes!" opined Ouha, swiftly. "That's why it's necessary that no one equals me, for then I'd no longer be the master."

Abraham leapt upon the ape and embraced him. "That my lad, is very wise. You're definitely the Napoléon of apes. But think, nevertheless: what if you have no posterity that resembles you, to succeed you and continue your work? Humans don't work only for themselves, and must make provision for the future; that's the best way of being immortal. By the way, Ouha, what do you think about death?"

"Don't know," Ouha replied.

"That's what I mean," said Goldry, pointing to Kri-Kri's skeleton.

Ouha scratched his head energetically. Evidently, he did not understand. The doctor strove to give him an inkling of the end of life, movement and thought, but he ran into a complete indifference. Evidently, the ape had already seen many cadavers, slain accidentally or even without blows, but the mystery

171

of the Beyond said nothing to him, remaining outside his reflection and his anxiety. It was necessary to think about one's individual fate before death, but afterwards…the orangutan did not cross the boundary of his existence. He was a wise animal, who lived without thinking about his end.

The scientist remained thoughtful. Was that—the sentiment of survival—the secret of the first civilizations, careful preserving their dead and depositing weapons and food supplies with them in their tombs, for the Beyond? Rubbish, all of that.

"We'll come back to it," said Abraham. "It's not yet time to start a course in philosophy. You still have so many things to learn. *Sat prata biberunt.*[17] I think, in any case, that we've earned a little rest. Sleep here."

"No," said Ouha, "I'll go home. I'll come back tomorrow to discuss my future projects with you." He got up, shook the doctor's hand and withdrew.

Left alone, the scientist had something to eat, and then threw himself down on his bed.

---

[17] The quotation is from Virgil's *Eclogues*, where the full line is *Claudite iam vivos, pueri sat prata biberunt* [Stop watering, slaves; the fields have drunk their fill]. Like Goldry, Virgil meant the advice metaphorically.

XLVII. Voices Underground

Night, it is said, brings counsel. At any rate, the human brain ruminates, obscurely, the ideas of the day, as a cow ruminates the grass she has grazed. That was undoubtedly the case with the doctor, for, on awakening, he still had the evening's conversation with Ouha in mind.

That fellow, he thought, *will go far, especially if I lend him my aid. Have I the right to do that? In sum, I'm making enemies of my brothers, and I'm not very sure of my pupil's gratitude. Damn! It's a rude case of conscience, and more than one casuist would be embarrassed by it. Let's see, my old friend, what are you going to do? Take the side of the apes wholeheartedly? That would be amusing—but do you feel that you have the courage to die in the skin of an orangutan? In sum, the study that I wanted to make of the anthropoids is now complete; they're assimilable—but it will take many years to lead them to the mentality of that phenomenon Ouha. The best thing is to see what comes, while creating a means of exit in case of trouble. In addition, I have to find a way of questioning Mabel about her situation here...*

But the scientist thought that the best thing to do for now was the most urgent—which is to say, to continue his search. With that objective he went to the back of the cave, going down a steep slope.

At one point, two enormous heaps of sand had been piled up, as if throw to the right and left of a hole. The doctor jumped into it, and then, with the aid of half a coconut-shell, began to dig vigorously in the soil.

Abraham Goldry was a first-rate geologist; so, as soon as he arrived in the lodgings imposed on him by Ouha, he had made a rapid study of the cave's construction, and easily understood its origin. This entire region was composed of limestone mingled with quartz and sandy clay. Under the action of the rain, the soil, easily disaggregated, had given birth to a number of excavations, and the water filling them had ended up clearing a passage. Now, the grotto inhabited by the doctor had its slope on the side opposite the river; thus, it was easy to deduce that the waters had found an outlet here to another valley, or, after a sequence of numerous curves, flowed into the same course but much further downriver. The path followed by the rainwater was indicated by the sand it had deposited, and which, marked its track in the rocky or calcareous soil. It was there, at the lowest point, where the sand had accumulated to the greatest extent, that the ancient exit, now obstructed, must be located.

The scientist had been working for about an hour when the sand in front of him collapsed. Another few coconut-shell spadefuls to clear away and the path was open. Carefully, he slid into the opening. After a few meters, he was able to stand up and walk upright. The flow must still be continuing, for the sand was very damp and even, in some of the hollows, completely saturated. He advanced as far as the light filtering from the cave permitted, but, fearing that he might fall into a hole if he went on, he decided to retrace his steps. In any case, a sepulchral silence reigned under these vaults, and the cool air caused the naked explorer to shiver. Suddenly, he stopped, and lay down on the ground, listening.

From the depths, a noise had just reached his ears. He listened, making an ear-trumpet of his hand, and perceived a distant voice.

"Let's go back. There's no way out."

That voice was not unknown to him—but it was implausible. At the risk of breaking is neck, he risked going further forward into the subterranean tunnel.

Another voice said: "What if we camp here? We're safe, and the route's difficult enough for us to get a little rest."

"You're right. Let's light the fire, then, and settle in."

Goldry was still groping his way through the darkness. Soon, a bright light appeared a hundred meters away. Hastening his effort, he reached a gash through which he looked down on the most unexpected spectacle.

XLVIII. Major Bennett's Widow

In order to explain what follows, let us return to Riddle-Temple and White House.

Before setting out on a new expedition, it was necessary to settle up with the survivors of the first. After having paid them generously, Harry Smith, on Gorden's advice, drafted a brief report, in order to regularize matters with respect to Dutch law, the situation of the widows and orphans created by the white men's defeat, and, at the same time, to inform the government of the danger that colonists might be in of overly frequent attacks by the great apes.

Archibald, for his part, was given the delicate mission of informing Mrs. Bennett of the major's death and inviting her to come and take up residence at Riddle-Temple with her children. Harry Smith offered, in addition, to by White House in order that the widow and her children would have nothing to worry about.

Mrs. Bennett listened to the billionaire's envoy in silence, and when he had finished she showed him the door. Laconically, she said: "Scram!"

Archibald, nonplussed, tried to insist, but the Irishwoman did not give him the time.

"Peace! Peace! I'm all right here and I'll stay here. Do you think that imbecile William was useful for anything, and that it was him who kept the colony going? A good-for-nothing, ready to run off on adventures with anyone. I told him that billionaire would cause him nothing but trouble…and he has the nerve to offer me shelter in his home! Does he take me for a beggar? A Sulten can always earn a living. Go away, and tell those people that I'd rather die of starvation than owe them for a crust of bread. God bless you—and go to Hell!"

Having said that, Meg had closed the door in Archibald's face—but, returning precipitately to her room, she fell to her knees in front of the major's portrait and burst into tears.

When Archibald reported on his mission, Gorden said: "Let's let time soothe her pan. Mrs. Bennett has a heart of gold under her rather rude exterior. I think she'll get through it. Anyway, we won't lose sight of her. Now that's sorted, let's get on. Forward march!"

XLIX. A Moving Road that Carries You

The new expedition comprised only eight people, to wit, the Europeans Harry Smith, Archibald Wilson, Silven Gorden and Hubert Mamnuth—Hubert, whose name is figuring in the story for the first time, was the leaders of the woodcutters brought by the Muni-Wali brothers—and the colored men To Wang, Rava's brother Eg Merh, Mag Trih, a Malay half-breed, and Jacob Muni-Wali, whose brother Joshua had perished during the first expedition.

It had been agreed to commence the second campaign via the part of the forest already cut into by the Muni-Wali brothers' exploitation. It was a long journey, but the brothers' prospectors had discovered the zigzag of a river in that direction, whose shiny surface had appeared to them at intervals though the foliage, and which ought to lead, by going upstream, into the vicinity of the realm of the orangutans.

Two days after having crossed the cleared zone, the little troop was once again in virgin forest. The terrain was more uneven there and marshier. The waters, able to flow freely there, rendered the journey, if not easy, at least les unhealthy and less infested with reptiles. On the other hand, they had continually to scale rocks and cross deep precipices. They had resolved that, whatever difficulties they might encounter, in order not to go astray, they would steer by compass.

Finally, on the eleventh day of the march, a broad watercourse appeared—doubtless the one identified by the prospectors. What should they do? Follow its numerous meanders upstream or head directed westwards? The latter route, although more direct, was almost impracticable; the forest sometimes bathed in the middle of the current, which it obstructed with plants and aquatic trees like mangroves—the basal roots of whose trunks extended from one bank to the other.

Having tried to follow the bank, they were forced to give it up. Fortunately, the current, precisely because of all the obstacles, was not very rapid. They set out in quest of a clump of bamboo and constructed a light raft, just large enough to carry the little caravan.

On the fifth day, the little troop embarked, and, sometimes rowing but more often pushing themselves along with long poles, gliding between the roots and slender columns of the mangroves, began to go up the river, whose bed was extremely uneven. Often, islets of stone blocks almost barred the way, the foaming waves breaking against them violently. It was necessary, on occasion, to go around an obstacle on foot, carrying the raft. Once, they nearly had to abandon it; a barrier of rocks close the route beneath a waterfall several meters high and the two banks were so steep that the orangutan hunters took three days to find a means of getting out of the bottleneck.

To the fatigues of the voyage were added the dangers posed by wild beasts. Rarely able to protect themselves by means of fire, they had to spend the right in mid-river as often as possible, in an uncovered location. It was, moreover, necessary to spend several hours each day renewing their food supplies—without difficult though, there being no lack of game or wild fruits.

Finally, two months after their departure, they reached a vast plain lost in the immensity of the virgin forest, unwooded except for a few meager thickets and stunted trees. It was covered by grasses more than a meter tall.

L. The Camp on the Bank

"If I'm not mistaken," Gorden said, "We're now in the zone of the forest that was burned during our ill-fated expedition."

"We must be close to the lair of my daughter's abductors, then" said Harry Smith.

"Undoubtedly—and now, above all, we must increase our precautions."

"So what do we do?" exclaimed Archibald. "You decide, Gorden—our hopes rest on your experience."

With a gesture, Gorden summoned the two Malays. They drew nearer, and the three men discussed what to do next."

Finally, the Englishman said: "We need to cross over to the other bank, and find a refuge there from which we can scout out the entire region. Don't forget that our presence here must remain unknown to our enemies. As soon as we've located some retreat for ourselves, the two Malays will go out to search. They alone are capable of avoiding the orangutans. We'll wait until the moment comes to act.

The others agreed wholeheartedly with this opinion, and they crossed over to the other bank in the dead of night. An excavation between the rocks was their initial shelter there. Prudently, from time to time, when their food-supplies ran low, the adventurers went back downriver to go hunting some distance away, in order that the detonations of their rifles should not attract the orangutans' attention.

LI. Ouha Amuses Himself and Mabel Sings

To Wang and the two Malays roamed incessantly, exploring the entire region. They saw orangutans on many occasions, but without encountering Ouha or his harem. The days went by, however, without any result. Gorden had a great deal of trouble containing his impatience and that of his companions.

Finally, one evening, they understood from Eg Merh's radiant expression that he had news. He had been able to follow a group of orangutans without being seen, and had discovered their capital, about three hundred huts. Having returned to get food, he would leave again immediately, for he had found a place in the rocks from which he could see everything without being seen.

He came back again the next day. This time, Eg Merh had seen Ouha among his wives.

"Mabel?" cried Harry Smith.

"Yes, with my sister Rava and Dilou They're fit and well. Miss Mabel was singing, while the orangutan Ouha danced around her."

"My daughter was singing? Get away!"

"I assure you, Master."

"She's gone mad!" Archibald groaned. "Oh, the poor girl!"

"If that's true, damn it, it's going to be difficult to reach an understanding with her."

"What are we going to do?" moaned the unfortunate fiancé. "To think that she's so close to us!"

"Oh," the Malay interrupted, "from here to where the orangutans are it's four hours' march."

"Let's gain more ground," said Gorden. "Let's set out in quest of lodgings closer to the orangs. I want to see for myself. Afterwards, we'll assess the situation."

It was agreed that everyone would seek that shelter by himself, and that whoever discovered one would come back and summon the others with a rifle-shot.

LII. The Bats' Lair

Archibald was the lucky one. He went upriver, following the bank, as far as possible. After numerous obstacles obstructing his progress, he was surprised to find a beach of fine sand. Wearily, he lay down on it, gripped by a reverie that was not at all cheerful. He thought about Mabel having become the wife of an orangutan, Ouha.

Gradually, that daydream degenerated into a kind of torpor, and he fell asleep.

He was woken up by a bizarre sensation; it seemed to him that a fan was being waved over him, refreshing him with a benevolent breeze.

He woke up fully; a dozen large bats were flying back and forth over his exhausted body in the still-uncertain dusk, their membranous wings bumping into one another. The animals inspired a profound disgust in the young man. He leapt to his feet and whirled his rifle around him to chase the filthy beasts away. They spiraled for a further minute, some distance away, and then disappeared into a crack in the rock at the top of the sandy slope.

Archibald was about to leave when the bats emerged again and resumed circling. Then he had the idea of climbing the slope in order to cast a glance into the chiropterans' lair. He freed the entrance of the loose sand obstructing it with a few kicks, and, to his great amazement, saw a broad and profound tunnel extending into the bowels of the mountain.

What if this tunnel were to bring us nearer to the apes? he said to himself. *It would be a veritable windfall.*

The daylight was fading fast. He emerged and went back to the camp, where his friends were very anxious, for the night was already quite advanced when he arrived. As he had only had to follow the river in retracing his steps, however, he had found his way back easily. Immediately, he told his friends about his find. They decided that they would all go there at daybreak.

LIII. In the Entrails of the Mountain

After a solid meal, the eight companions set out. When they went into the tunnel, the tropical sun provided enough light through a few crevices, and they were able to advance quite a long way. The ground was covered with fine sand almost everywhere. They covered about two kilometers in that fashion; then the light abruptly ceased.

Until then, the terrain had been gradually rising. All the evidence suggested that they were in ancient tunnels once hollowed out by water in the calcareous regions of the mountains before the river had traced out its present bed. The phenomenon is much less rare than one might think. In France, for example, the gorges of Tarn and Padirac, in the same region, have the same origin. When erosion begins at the surface, it forms immense ravines through which the waters flow impetuously, but it sometimes happens that the upper strata are harder and more resistant; then the waters work underneath and hollow out vast subterrains, which dry out in time, like the one into which the eight adventurers had entered—which sometimes serve as drains during major inundations.

The eight audacious men were each equipped with an electric lamp capable of providing light for fifteen hours. That added up to a hundred and twenty hours of light, for until then they had scarcely made use of them. Archibald switched on his, and they continued to move forward. The direction was good—they were heading westwards.

Suddenly, Archibald, preceding his companions, stopped in front of a sheer declivity—a gaping opening at their feet. It might have been four or five meters deep, but its breadth did not permit the other side to be seen.

"What shall we do?" asked the young man.

"The situation is rather troubling," Gorden said. "If the tunnel goes on for several kilometers without emerging anywhere, we'll have made the entire journey for nothing. My opinion is that only two of us should continue the exploration. In the meantime four can go back to hunt and bring back provisions, and two can wait here."

The motion was adopted. The three Malays and Jacob Muni-Wali, the best hunters, went back. Gorden and Hubert Mamnuth went down into the crevice. Harry Smith and Archibald waited up above. It was agreed that, so long as it was possible, the four men would shout to one another at intervals, in order to maintain constant communication.

Having descended into and crossed the breach, Gorden and Mamnuth saw that the tunnel continued on the other side. They had some difficulty climbing the slope, but they succeeded, and continued along the tunnel. It had the same appearance as it had prior to the pit, save that the slope was a little steeper.

They marched for about two hours, and suddenly found themselves in an immense cavern of a truly magical appearance.

LIV. The Marvelous Grotto

Enormous stalactites hung down from the vault, twenty meters above, connecting up with stalagmites in several places to form majestic colonnades. The soft parts having been carried away by the waters the stripped walls of hard rock and stones were gleaming and scintillating in the light of eight lamps, all lit simultaneously for a moment in order to admire that splendor, launching fire of every color.

Through the center of the natural temple of gold and diamonds snaked a stream, the last remnant of the impetuous torrents that had created the marvels. From above, through a kind of vent encumbered by plants growing in fissures in the rock, came a blue-tinted light, as if through a vegetal stained-glass window, which lent fantastic effects to that basilica, a veritable masterpiece of elementary forces.

"Halt!" ordered Gorden. "Let's not risk ourselves in that immense crypt. If I'm not mistaken, other centuries-old corridors radiate from this crossroads, and we might get lost in that enchanted geology on the way back."

He attached a long thread to a stalagmite and then went on, with his companion, into the cathedral. The precaution was not unnecessary; numerous tunnels originated in that strange and formidable grotto. Compass in hand, Gorden and Mamnuth took the tunnel that led most nearly westwards.

"Oh, sir—look at that!" said Mamnuth.

There had been a rockfall. Rubble was heaped up all the way to a verdant belvedere, which one might have thought starred with emeralds, through which daylight was coming. The opening had surely been provoked by the collapse.

"Ah! This would be perfect if we had an exit up there. I'm going to attempt the climb."

Mamnuth launched himself on to the fallen rocks. It was long and difficult; the woodcutter had to go backwards several times, finding himself confronted by insurmountable blacks, but by going around the obstacles he finally reached the verdant lantern and clambered outside with the aid on lianas and roots.

Down below, Gorden heard a cry of joy.

From the depths of a valley that sloped down to the river, sparkling in the sunlight, Mamnuth could clearly see the city of the orangutans, whose numerous huts garnished giant trees. Mamnuth could even see a few orangs coming and going in the foliage. He slid into the undergrowth to examine his own location. He was on the summit of a fairly high mountain whose peaks, sheer on all sides, rendered it inaccessible—or at least difficult of attainment—to the apes.

To the north, in the opposite direction to the orangs' city, he was separated from the surrounding massif by a precipice of great depth, at the bottom of which a torrent ran. On the far side of the torrent the mountains rose up in increasingly steep slopes. That explained the creation of the caves and the marvelous grotto from which he had emerged. Before a seismic convulsion had created that abyss, the waters, following the slopes of the mountainous massif had slowly hollowed out a subterranean bed, which had been cut by that precipice during an earthquake. The waters having a new exit and a more rapid slope, the caves had almost entirely dried out.

Here, Mamnuth thought, *is an architecture fashioned for us by divine hands. We have only to retrace our steps for all of us to come and install ourselves in the diamond grotto.*

The descent was more difficult than the climb. Nevertheless, Hubert, the woodcutters' chief, rejoined his companions without any incident.

Three hours later, Gorden and Mamnuth found Smith and Archibald again, and immediately made them party to their discovery.

LV. A Revenant

Toward nightfall, the hunters came back, laden with game.

"We have enough food for four or five days," said Gorden. "We have only to take up residence in the marvelous grotto, and, after having drawn up our plans, we can get to work. I believe that this time we're sue of success—for thanks to these tunnels, unknown to the apes, we can be far away before they've detected us. If you agree, once we've eaten we'll leave for our general quarters and spend the night there."

Apart from Smith and Archibald they were all very tired, but the idea of a night in proximity to and occasional contact with the bats was repugnant to them. The band divided up the provisions and, as the route was known, marched at a good pace.

Thus, five hours later, the eight men emerged into the large cave, which the baptized, by common consent, Mabel Grotto. On that effort of imagination, they lay down on the sand and went to sleep, with the satisfaction of having made full use of the day.

When they awoke, the sun was already high, for the reflections of its rays, slanting through the opening in the vault, illuminated the entire interior of the grotto. In the sunlight, the walls of the cavern glittered like a casket of precious stones—splendid gems—and all the colors of the prism were confused there in harmonious splendor. The stalactites hanging from the vault, were colored in all the shades of white, tinted with blue, green, pink and lilac, as if made of clusters of topaz. The sand, mingled with mica, sparkled in places like molten metal.

After that breakfast of sunlight, and another more substantial, they all wanted to see the city of the apes and made the climb up to the belvedere. They came down again radiant; the campaign was definitely promising victory.

"What can we do to alert my daughter?" asked Smith, turning to Gorden.

"We'll discuss that—but I think this cave has other surprises in store for us. Now that we know where the apes' city is, I think we ought to continue the exploration toward the north-west. It will bring us nearer to our goal, and perhaps we'll find a more practicable exit here. Firstly, wherever we go, we need to make reference-points in order not to get lost, and so that, when we get back here after rescuing Mabel, we can get away *presto*."

"Let's get our bearings, then," said Archibald, "and get under way immediately."

Eventually, the eight found a tunnel leading in the right direction, but it was cluttered with blocks of stone containing diamonds, which it was necessary to go around or climb over. After three hours of difficult progress, they came upon an insurmountable obstacle; the tunnel terminated in a broad, high cul-de-sac, the top of which was lost in the darkness.

"It's a useless route," said Gorden. "We need to look elsewhere. It's a pity, because I'm convinced that the tunnel continues higher up, but we'd need a ladder."

"Or a knotted rope," said a voice falling from the ceiling."

"Eh?" said Archibald. "Who said that?"

"Not me," said his seven companions.

"Of course—unless the rocks are capable of greeting you, gentlemen."

"I know that voice!" cried Harry Smith.

"It's Dr. Goldry's voice," Archibald concluded. "Where are you, old friend?"

"*Excelsior!* Higher up, always higher up."

"You can't come down?"

"Not today—but I'll find a way."

"What are you doing here, doctor? We thought you were dead."

"Now you know I'm not. Stupidly, I was taken prisoner by the orangutans."

"With Mabel?"

"Mabel? Hmm…also a prisoner."

"You escaped?"

"No, I'm at home here. But what about you? What are you doing here?"

"We've come to rescue you—you and my daughter."

"That's a kind thought—but there's no urgency, for me or for my goddaughter."

"What do you mean? For you, all well and good—I know what an eccentric you are—but my daughter?"

"I'm not joking. Mabel and I are on the eve of becoming naturalized orangutans. My friends, if you knew all the advantages of the beautiful simian life, you'd come to share what you call our captivity."

"Abraham, you're lucky that I can hear you without being able to see you. I'd send you a specimen of civilization with my rifle."

Gorden intervened, incisively. "Let's not waste time with useless words. Dr. Goldry, are you with us or against us?"

"That requires reflection, my dear Mr. Gorden; first, I need to consult my goddaughter. For myself, I still have a great deal to do and learn here. I'm going home, gentlemen. I'll give you a answer tomorrow, at the same time."

"Abraham, wait!" shouted Smith—but the doctor had already disappeared, and the billionaire received no response.

"We have everything to fear from that eccentric," Harry Smith concluded. "I know him; he'd sacrifice my daughter for his beloved apes. It would certainly be better to by-pass him."

"That will be difficult now. Let's go back and look elsewhere. That won't prevent us from coming back tomorrow."

They withdrew, and we soon back in Mabel Grotto, the cathedral of diamonds.

LVI. Gold! Gold! Gold!

"While lunch is being prepared," Archibald said to Gorden, "let's take another look around. I can't sit still."

"Me neither. Let's go!"

The rivals, the Englishman and the American, John Bull and Uncle Sam, left their companions to rest, exchanging comments on Goldry's intervention.

Having gone around several of the sumptuous colonnades that gave the cavern the appearance of a vast basilica, coarse but precious, and climbed rocks sticky with silicious trickles, Wilson called to Gorden: "Look at this, my dear chap!"

He saw an enormous well, at the bottom of which were rocky masses half buried in the sand. Its edges, and a part of the wall overlooking it were shining in the light of the electric lamps like marble. Both men's eyes followed the shiny surface. At the top, near the vault, was a gaping black hole. In a few places, there must once have been fissures in the polished wall, which over time, had been filled by the sediment carried by the waters; they formed brighter streaks in the brown rock, which, from certain luminous angles sparkled with a surprising glare. With the point of his knife, Gorden detached a piece of that substance.

Having examined it attentively, he said: "Gold! It's gold!"

Archibald went pale. "Not a word about this find to our companions. Some of them would abandon the expedition, thinking of nothing but the discovery of the gold. I've seen comrades driven mad by the prospectors of the Klondike, abandoning everything—wife, children, family—to race after the sublime metal."

"For centuries," said Gorden, "this was a waterfall carrying gold with the chalk. The richness of these veins tells us that there must be a considerable mass of gold powder at the bottom of this well."

"Yes, I believe so. When we're rescued Mabel and she's made her choice, it will be a compensation for the loser."

"I'm afraid that we might both be losers, and that Mabel will prefer an ape to either of us."

LVII. Where An Ape Has Been...

Gorden sat down on a boulder and indicated another to his companion.

"Let's have a little chat."

"I'm listening," said Archibald.

"My dear chap, living and running dangers together brings men closer together, and, over and above amorous rivalries, can give birth to a serious friendship. I've had the opportunity to study you, and I'm sure of the honesty of our character. I don't know whether I inspire the same confidence in you but, for my part, I declare that I have a quasi-fraternal affection for you."

Archibald held out his hand. "Friends," he said, "in the face of and against anything."

Having returned the cordial handshake, Gorden continued. "Now I have the right and the duty to speak. I'm ten years older that you, my dear chap. In consequence, I've struggled against life and its passions; it was the chagrin of a failed love-affair that first led me to seek my fortune here, perhaps trying to forget. When hazard brought me into contact with Miss Smith, I was struck by a certain resemblance with the beloved I'd lost. With time and reflection, I've perceived that the resemblance was more fictitious than real. The truth is that Mabel was the first woman I saw after leaving England, and my imagination did the rest. The abduction of Miss Smith by Ouha brought a saner reasoning back to my mind and I perceived that I wasn't in love with Miss Smith, but with the appearance of the woman I'd lost. Since then, I've followed the expedition like an amateur avid for new distractions; I'm no longer your competitor, and I renounce the conquest of that new Golden Fleece. Unless..."

"Unless what?"

"Unless you renounce an alliance with Miss Smith yourself..."

"I will always love Mabel, as long as I live."

"Good—very good; those words are worthy of you. But..."

"But what?"

"The ape..."

"Ouha?" Archibald stammered.

"The orangutan who was the first to possess the virgin billionairess, the American woman with the golden fleece."

"That's horrible. I've thought about it many times; it terrifies my thoughts. Whatever the case might be, I'll do my duty, and I won't abandon Mabel to that horrible intimacy."

"I'm with you in that objective—and from now on, Archibald, you no longer have a rival, but a friend determined to do anything for the success of our project."

"Thank you, Brother. Now, I can face the future without dread."

"Alas, we're both rational minds—exceptions, like the eccentric and marvelous Mabel—and the sufferings of so-called civilized men are too abundant; that's why I'm afraid of the appeal of the natural life to certain souls overly desirous of new sensations."

"Whatever happens, we'll both have gained a fraternal friendship. Now, let's continue our research."

"Shall we go down into the well? It seems quite easy."

"Easy? No, but feasible. The best thing to do now is to follow the ancient path hollowed out by the waters. It must necessarily have an exit; thus far, we've been following these paths upstream; let's go downstream now, especially if they head westwards."

LVIII. A Cataract of Gold

The two men undertook the descent, rendered difficult primarily by the lack of light. The beams of the electric lamps did not extend very far. Finally, sliding and jumping from block to block, they reached the bottom. They found themselves in the middle of an immense arena of sand, with enormous rocky masses scattered here and there. They wandered around in search of an exit but without result.

"Let's go back to our departure-point," said Gorden, "and try not to go astray in all this rocky rubble."

They followed their footprints in the sand backwards, along the wall—which, fortunately, was free on that side.

"Let's check my hypothesis," said Gorden. "It won't delay us for long."

Indeed, at the foot of the ancient cataract, the falling waters had thrown a mass of sand sideways around their point of their fall, and along the wall, its depth was less than a meter. Hurling the friable soil to the right and he left, the Englishman rapidly laid bare a thick layer of gold powder, mingled with tiny nuggets.

Amazed and wonderstruck, the two men looked at one another anxiously.

"There's a colossal fortune here," said Gorden. "We'll come back."

Having shoveled the sand back over the gold powder and nuggets, they went along the wall of the ancient cataract for about three hundred paces; then, the chaos of sand and rocks resumed.

"We can see here," Archibald said, "what would become of Niagara Falls if, by virtue of some seismic phenomenon, the St. Lawrence was deflected from its course and the cataracts and whirlpools dried out."

"In nature, my dear chap, everything happens, comes to an end and recommences."

LIX. Mabel! Mabel! Mabel!

In every good girl,
Even the most genteel...

"Shall we go on, Gorden?"

"Let's. I have an intuition that we're going to find more tunnels, for at the bottom of that huge waterfall, among the frightful eddies and undertows of those masses of water, all the soft parts of the mountain must have been eaten away and mined. Many tunnels like those we've already come through must have been filled in by subsidence, but we have proof that some remain—and..."

"Look, there..." Archibald gestured toward a vast dark cave partly masked by an enormous rock. "Before we go into it, let's get our bearings, for if the excavation doesn't lead in the right direction, there's no point in going into it." He consulted his compass. "Due, North, Gorden, my friend—it's no good to us."

As they were going past the entrance, without going in, Gorden paused.

"Archibald, can you smell something?"

"Yes. One might think it were the odor of wood-smoke."

"Perhaps it's our fire, whose smoke, by virtue of some bizarre air-current, is emerging from here."

"Shall we try to find out how?"

They agreed to do so. After a thousand paces, the tunnel turned sharply to the west; at the same time, the odor of smoke became increasingly evident.

Suddenly, Gorden gripped his companion's arm. "Listen!" he whispered.

They both stopped, and picked up their ears.

"A mandolin!" said Archibald. "Well! What does that signify? If I were on my own, I'd think I was going mad."

"Let's go on, taking every precaution. Try not to sneeze in the chimney-flue."

They went on as slowly as possible, without making any noise; the chords became louder and louder.

Suddenly, a clear and delightful voice rose up, intoning a Yankee song.

In every good girl,
Even the most genteel
There's always something wicked.

The two men had difficulty suppressing a cry.

"Mabel! That's Mabel's voice!"

Another twenty paces, and stop! The tunnel was obstructed by a huge boulder that had fallen from the vault and blocked the corridor completely. Only at the top near the vault was there still a narrow passage, through which the smoke of a fire and the sound of the prisoner's voice were coming.

"Lend me your shoulders," said Gorden.

Archibald understood. He was the taller of the two. He set his back against the rock, after having put down his weapons. Gorden clambered up on the Wilson's shoulders; from there, by stretching as far as possible, he was able to catch hold of a sharp rocky ledge. He pulled himself up by the strength of his wrists, adjusted his equilibrium, gripped the rim with his elbow and got his head and shoulders into the gap. Once he was on top he observed that there was room to stand up, and did. The block on which he was standing having once formed part of the vault, there was a large hole there, in which twenty men could easily have stood.

After a few moments, his eyes having grown accustomed to the darkness—for he had prudently refrained from switching on his torch—he made out a ray of light ahead of him, at floor level. Gorden lay down on the uneven ground, and crawled toward the light, in the direction from which the smoke and music were coming.

The narrowness of the fissure only allowed him to see a part of the inferior cavern, but what he could see was not without interest. Directly facing him, squatting in the Oriental fashion, was the gigantic Ouha, drinking a fuming liquid. Beside him, on a tray of large green leaves, was a heap of fruits. A little way behind him was Dilou, seated on the ground, and behind her, standing up, was the Malay woman, Rava.

Mabel, undoubtedly positioned against the wall, was invisible for the moment. She was singing a new song when a new individual appeared in view: a female orangutan who, kettle in hand, was refilling the drinking-vessels. The song concluded in the midst of general applause.

Gorden judged that the audience must be numerous. The clapping of hands was mingled with the resounding blows of the fists with which the orangs struck their breasts, which resounded like gongs. Suddenly, the mandolin traversed Gorden's line of sight with lightning rapidity, while his attention was caught by another individual whom he had not noticed until then. It was a chimpanzee who, seated to the left of Ouha, the monarch, had caught the flying mandolin in mid-air.

For this matinee performance, the chimpanzee had put on an old jacket of unknown provenance and, for lack of a silk top hat, was coiffed in a carefully-polished tin can. Thus accoutered, Ko-Zu strummed the strings of his instrument frantically, mimicking what were doubtless the expressions of Mabel's features.

In is observatory, Gorden heard Miss Smith burst out laughing—and her gaiety infected the entire audience. The delighted Ouha picked up a banana and bit it in half, throwing the rest to the chimpanzee, who caught it and started nibbling it, without ceasing his grimaces and contortions. When the morsel was finished, there was further applause. Ko-Zu stood up, took off his hat, brushing it with is elbow as if to smooth the nap, and bowed all round.

The enthusiasm knew no further bounds then, and that enthusiasm undoubtedly overexciting the orangs, for there were gestures behind Ouha that displeased him. Seizing his scepter, placed beside him, he distributed a few blows to the right and left among his courtiers. That was the signal to withdraw. The assembly retired, and only the usual inhabitants of the cave remained: Ouha and his wives.

LX. Jupiter and Semele

Ouha turned to Mabel then, and seemed to interrogate her with his gaze. He made a gesture; Dilou, Rava and the two she-apes withdrew in their turn. And for the first time, Forden saw Mabel come into view.

Miss Smith, the billionaire's daughter, was almost naked; the ragged debris of a delicate slip, secured at the waist by lianas, scarcely masked her lower abdomen.

With one bound Ouha was beside her, and seized her in his arms.

Seated on a large flat mossy stone that served them as a divan, the lovers clasped two hands, while the other two wandered, stroking their legs; the enchantment of spring gleamed in their eyes, while vegetal seeds danced in the sunlight, seeking their gyneacea, pollen escaped from the stamens of anthers, in quest of pistils in the folly of April.

An amorous desire communed in their conjoined gazes. The mighty orangutan had taken hold of Mabel Smith, holding her seated on the moss, and titled her back in the clutch of his right arm, with her quivering hair in his lap, contemplating more ardently than white, feminine, ideal, divine flesh.

Doubtless finding that the residue of the fine transparent slip, held at the waist by lianas, was a sacrilege, in hiding a fraction of the most secret, coveted beauty, the ape tore the vestige away, and his hand covered the regal flower—and the young American billionairess, curling up, abandoning herself to pleasure, half-closed her eyelids in order better to savor the sensations.

In spite of the horror born of the unaccustomed nature of such a spectacle, did Gorden find a certain grandeur therein? He remembered a painting by Gustave Moreau, in which Jupiter, all-powerful and gigantic, holds on his knees the frail and slim Semele, daughter of Cadmus, King of Thebes, and mother of Dionysus, like a small, delicate object, like a flower, a rose of flesh, a rose-woman. Thus, Mabel and Ouha resembled Jupiter and Semele—but the king of the apes laid her gently down on a carpet of moss, and covered her with all the caresses of his huge, heavy, agitating body.

Gorden was livid. Anguish and disgust, voluptuous even so, twisted al his nerves, but curiosity held him, as if he were petrified.

Finally, recovering himself, he went back to the opening of the cave. Down below, Archibald was waiting anxiously.

Fortunately, Gorden thought, *it wasn't this poor amorous fellow who saw all that. It would have driven the poor chap mad.*

He let himself slide down the rock face, and came to rest in a standing position beside Wilson.

"Well?" Archibald queried.

"We can get Mabel whenever we want. A few blows with a pick-axe, and we can get into her home. Let's go back, my friend. We have no more to do, now, than to see Dr. Goldry again, and then we'll take action, with or without him. In any case, we'll keep quiet about what we've just learned. Given the scientist's mania for studying the great quadrumanes, our ancestors, and his liking for the orangutans—the free men twenty centuries behind the twentieth century of our civilization—he's capable of taking the side of the apes."

LXI. Toward Humanity

Far from giving up on recovering her liberty and seeing Riddle-Temple, her father and friends again, all of Mabel Smith's thoughts were directed to that goal: discovering the best route and having herself escorted, by Ouha and his subjects, toward deliverance. Previously, too preoccupied with her safety in the midst of the hairy monsters, especially given the animosity of the jealous females disdained by the chief, the young woman had not had the leisure to search for an effective means of escape.

To flee alone, through the thousand dangers of the forest, would have been folly. What resources could a woman discover, especially one who knew nothing about the country? How could she even hope to survive? Fruits and plants offered food on all sides, but she had to anticipate arid regions, infertile savannahs, and the danger of tempting but poisonous berries. As for hunting, she no longer had her rifle, which had been lost, and perhaps broken, in the battle between the expedition and the orangutans; her revolver and the few cartridges providentially preserved would not be sufficient to defend herself, if the journey were prolonged, against the eventually-inevitable perils.

In any case, in spite of the apparent liberty that the apes had afforded her since the early days, after her introduction to the tribe, she knew that she was carefully watched. As soon as she risked a stroll outside the orangutans' township, glimpsed faces, the friction of hairy bodies, cries—doubtless alarm signals—and the sudden emergence of a large ape, watching her from a branch, warned her of the impossibility of fight. Even if she had several hours start, with her progress impeded by inextricable thickets, she should have been quickly overtaken. Perhaps she would then be killed—or else, by means of what worse chastisement, what tortures, might Ouha the Terrible punish her?

As her influence over the sovereign increased, however, Mabel conceived a plan, built on what she had learned in the course of the journey while talking to Wilson about the expedition's goal. She knew, by virtue of having been interested in their progress, the difficulties of their route and the constant direction of their march, that they had to steer beyond the mountains, toward the south-west. Archibald Wilson, Mr. Smith, Major Benet and Gorden had been very nearly in agreement regarding that hypothesis; it would take at least two months, having crossed the mountain chain, to get out of the virgin forest. A chain of hills that rose up increasingly further from the plain, as if no longer to be stifled by the naves of trees, would serve as a precise reference-point. Mabel had also retained the information her two flirts had given her with regarding to steering by the stars, without instruments, on clear nights.

She knew that in the heart of the virgin forest, when the interlacement of the branches and gigantic boughs did not permit the celestial lighthouses to be used as signs, the grass, bent over according to the direction of the wind, the inflection of certain trees toward a point on the horizon that attracted them, and, even better, differences in the soil and successive flora helped distinguish the zones and permitted one to maintain an approximate direction.

Given that, the American woman took advantage of the respites granted by her solitary walks, sometimes with Rava, her friend and companion in simian marriage, to search for such landmarks of deliverance. Even when escorted by Ouha, she occupied herself in confirming her knowledge, and, and the same time, familiarizing herself—by studying the apes' precautions and being initiated by Rava—with the most frequent dangers of the forest and their remedies. She learned which plant healed the bite of the minuscule coral snake, what nauseating odor betrayed the presence of a rattlesnake, python or fer-de-lance. She was able to pick out the tracks of wild beasts and distinguish their imprints. If necessary, she had her weapon; perhaps impotent to save her, the revolver would at least spare her outrage or torture, when the time came that she judged that she was irredeemably lost.

In addition, Mabel put her ascendancy to work. After having explored the forest in every direction with the orangs or alone, sure of getting her bearings and maintaining approximately the right direction, she resolved to lead Ouha, by clever preparation, toward a chimerical enterprise that would get her closer to her goal.

She knew which instinctive levers acted most effectively upon the royal orangutan. Ouha, primitive but already half-extracted from his bestial matrix, possessed to a supreme degree the human virtue or vice of pride: the ambition and avidity to penetrate the unknown perceptible to his infantile soul, simultaneously tyrannical and puerile.

The American woman set out to penetrate Ouha's intimate reasoning, all the more so because the evidence of that amazing revelation became clearer every day. (She was unaware of his relationship with Goldry.) Ouha's personality, developed on a daily basis by circumstances and events, was capable of conceiving ideas, ripening projects and calculating their probable consequences. Mabel even judged him capable of an incredible discernment and an amazing lucidity. To Mabel, the imperious soul of Ouha, magnified by the science of power and his genius, seemed predestined for greatness—and the American woman, sure of her ascendancy and her influence, wanted to take advantage of Ouha's ambitious dreams, which she detected, caressed and increased.

In the evenings when, he was sitting next to Mabel, whose presence beside him he demanded as soon as he had finished his diurnal peregrinations, the young woman pointed out distant horizons to him, and described admirable countries by means of gestures and sounds whose meaning she had learned, evoking contests and battles, and then the repose of warriors amid the delights of the ravaged lands.

On the slopes of the mountain, she accompanied the king of the orangutans and, pointing out the direction of the promised land, seemed to model the prestigious fruits, the luxuriant vegetations. Out there—toward the south-east, where her people had long ago attained their goal—the great apes would find in abundance the clear waters of cool springs, red berries and melting bananas with pink flesh, palm-nuts and succulent golden-brown dates.

Without searching or difficulty, they would enjoy the luxuriant fertility of a land where everything existed in such profusion that, in order to possess those riches, they would have no need to tear their hands and leave shreds of their flesh on ferocious thorns. Then again, they would no longer have to fear incursions by other simian tribes. Out there, the apes could take over the habitations of humans and, when the conquest was concluded, live in bliss on the very fruits of the labor of the vanquished.

Thus, the white queen made promises shine, at the same time as she covered Ouha with praise and flattery. She talked to him, at those times, as if to an equal, affectionately and persuasively.

"You are great and you are strong, Ouha; no one is capable of resisting your energetic will and your courage. Your raised hand makes the most terrible denizens of the forest tremble. You are powerful and redoubtable. Out there, you would reign over a vast domain, more fecund with joy, beneath the radiant sky, outside the gloom of the woods to which tyrannical humans have confined your race."

Those were the sentiments that Mabel Smith, presently Mrs. Ouha, the queen of the apes, awoke in the monster, all the more vivid in him because new visions surged forth in that mirage, as visions of unknown splendor suddenly revealed, new to young minds, expand in the imaginations of children.

Ouha followed Mabel meekly, watching her gestures, striving to pierce the veils of distance with his sharp gaze; the vague dreams became more precise as he listened to the White Queen. But that spell-casting Titania, in that tropical summer night's dream, in Borneo, infatuated with a magnificent quadrumane Bottom, hairy all over, was nevertheless plotting to escape.

LXII. The Uncertainty and Meditation of a Scientist

Woman is often fickle. Foolish is the man who trusts her.[18]

Mabel Smith evolved, like all women. Her desire to escape was mitigated by the fear of losing her simian lover, whom she felt to be irreplaceable by a man. Such was her mental and physiological situation at the moment when her saviors were so fortunately ready to come to her aid.

Meanwhile, Dr. Abraham Goldry had been somewhat taken aback by the unexpected encounter with is friends. Having returned home and hidden the opening to the new tunnel by means of a large stone, which he rolled in front of it, he started talking to himself, in accordance with his habit, as all solitary individuals do.

"Here's a decision that's very awkward to make. It's certain that I can't stay here indefinitely. I'm well on the way to becoming an ape, but a thinking ape—a celebrated American doctor, expert in science and philosophy—is an abnormal being. Moreover, there's a chance that, in the long run, my philosophy might be absorbed by animality.

"To be sure, if all the orangutans were as intelligent as Ouha, I could perhaps start a school for the more cerebral apes, but really, that one must be an anomaly. The others copy and imitate with no mental reflection. Perhaps Ouha's children, if Miss Mabel were to bear him any, would be…oh no, that wouldn't work, because they'd be half-breeds, not orangs…damn it!

"It's the mental level of the apes that needs to be raised, or there's nothing can be done. I'd definitely have to make

---

[18] These lines, found inscribed on a window-pane at Chambord, were assumed to have been scratched there by the French king François I (1494-1547).

contact with them, educate them, instruct them, as I'm doing for Ouha. What should I decide? What should I do?

"Why did the others have to turn up just as my experiment is at a critical stage? May the Devil take them, and Mabel with them! Now there's a good idea! Yes, that's it. I'll help them to abduct my goddaughter, but I'll stay. Once rid of his white woman, Ouha will be entirely mine...

"Eh? What now?"

LXIII. The Widow of Kri-Kri, Slain in Battle

He stood there nonplussed. An orangutan had come into his abode, and a female orangutan: the widow of the unfortunate Kri-Kri. In a trice she had seized the skin of her dead husband, and as turning it over and over, astonished to find it so limp and motionless.

After the triumphant return of the vanquishers of the human invasion, the barbarians, the widow had applauded her spouse's victory more than anyone else, but, not seeing him among the heroes returning from the war, and thinking that he was dead, she had found a substitute—later, if she had a opportunity, her charms would make Kri-Kri forget the error resulting from too long an absence.

Having searched for her spouse throughout the region without result, after a long conversation with one of Ouha's wives, she had learned that the monarch went almost every day to the mountain, taking provisions with him. Undoubtedly, Kri-Kri was guarding a cavern that Ouha was keeping to himself.

Several times, she and Maha, one of the king's companions, as curious as all she-apes, had followed Ouha in order to discover his secret, but the master had spotted them and had inflicted such a stern correction that they had given up. However, after her beating, Maha gave vague indications to Mrs. Kri-Kri and strongly encouraged her to continue her research—and Mrs. Kri-Kri had spied on Ouha, prudently. Thus, she saw him emerging mysteriously from the cavern. Dread and curiosity had been in conflict for a long time in the widow's mind; she knew that Ouha was capable of killing her if he caught her spying on him. In spite of everything, the desire to know had got the upper hand over the peril, and she risked going into the lair. Having wandered around for some time in the meanders of that fantastic retreat, she had discovered the doctor, who was philosophizing in the nude, and the skin of the husband she regretted nearby.

At the sight of the she-ape handling those excessively flaccid remains, Goldry instinctively launched himself forward to recover his skin. He soon came off worse, though, and did not know what saint to call upon for aid when the widow's attention was attracted to an object that she had not yet noticed. It was Kri-Kri's skeleton, carefully reassembled by the doctor, and which, in his opinion, furnished the cavern with its finest ornament.

Mrs. Kri-Kri approached it, and seemed to fall into a profound meditation. With extreme timidity, she put out a hand, felt the skull and the jaw and moved the two arms. The bones, assembled with some difficulty by the doctor and only maintained by cleverly-placed pegs, did not resist the widow Kri-Kri's probing for long, and the skeleton collapsed into a confused heap. The doctor, gripped by a momentary fit of anger, without reflecting that he was naked and unarmed, threw himself upon the she-ape and shoved her away brutally. The irritated female turned round, and knocked Goldry over with one hand. He thought he was doomed.

On making contact with that soft white flesh, however, the orangutan had shivered. It was, for her, an unfamiliar sensation, which troubled her to the utmost depths of her being. Instead of being ripped into little pieces, Abraham saw the widow lie down beside him and rub his skin voluptuously.

The scholarly scientist was certain no Don Juan, but the frenetic contact inspired the Beast's desire produced in him, involuntarily, an effect that, to his great astonishment, became manifest. The widow Kri-Kri perceived it immediately and, flattered by the success won by her charms, did not hesitate for a second to take advantage of the windfall.

Goldry had not had such a surprise for years; a virility of which he had long thought himself incapable testified in favor of the human race in that regard. Obligingly, the doctor undertook a vigorous assault, but it was insufficient for the overly sentimental widow, who did her best to obtain a further success. In spite of everything, when the initial voluptuous flux had passed, Goldry seeing the frightful face of the she-ape leaning over him—him, the celebrated American doctor, honored by the members of several European academies—did not feel the slightest inspiration come to him. He was obliged, by means of artificial caresses, to attempt to calm the lubricious female—who, at any rate, lent herself to it with the best will in the world.

It was a trick; it permitted him to escape the overenthusiastic embrace of Mrs. Kri-Kri, who, lying there unsuspectingly, yielding entirely to that unexpected titillation, examined her lover, appearing to take great interest in his anatomy. Meanwhile, the doctor, with his free hand, had been able to reach Kri-Kri's skin, and rapidly wrapped it around the she-ape's head.

The scientist fled.

During the time he had been living in the cave he had familiarized himself with all its meanders. He did not have too much trouble, therefore, in escaping the widow's lustful moans. After a hectic but fruitless pursuit, she found herself back and the entrance to the cave. With the fickleness of her race, she forgot her momentary good fortune and, taking hold of the liana-rope, launched herself outside.

Unfortunately for her, she found herself face to face with Ouha, who, coming to visit his friend and professor, was disagreeably surprised to see that an intruder had penetrated his home. Without any further explanation, he inflicted a correction upon her such as none of her former husbands had yet administered.

LXIV. Discord Between Allies

That exercise had put Ouha in a good mood, in contrast to Goldry, who was upset by the violation of his domicile and his person. The Orang, increasingly obsessed by the idea of conquering Riddle-Temple, would have liked Abraham to tell him how to do that in a rapid fashion, with the certainty of success.

Goldry hesitated over collaborating with his pupil's plans, and tried to make him understand the reasons. Although all his sympathies were for his ape brothers, he could not forget that he was a human, and, moreover, an American citizen, and that he could not betray his friends and compatriots. Finally, he complained bitterly of the lack of confidence that had caused Ouha to conceal Mabel's presence until now.

Ouha seemed unimpressed by these reasons, and, displaying his scepter-cum-club, designated it as the decisive argument.

Abraham understood that it was necessary to temporize, and signified that it was necessary to discuss the matter with Mabel.

Ouha reflected for a while, then made signs to the doctor telling him to put on the ape-skin again and follow him.

LXV. Ouha, Mabel and the Doctor

An hour later, Ouha took the doctor into his harem. Mabel was on a fresh bed of leaves, asleep. When Ouha came in, she woke up, and seemed astonished to see him in the company of another orang. The latter, moreover, advanced deliberately and offered her his hand.

"Hello, Mabel."

The American woman started.

"Yes, it's me, Goldry, your old godfather, whom this rascal has been keeping prisoner for four months, without having told him that you were in his power."

Mabel blushed violently, and gathered a shred of clothing around her.

"Bah!" said Abraham, philosophically. "We're not in a drawing-room, and if I took off this ape-skin, which is a trifle large for me, I'd be even more scantily dressed than you."

Mabel was choked by shame, still unable to say a word.

Ouha considered them both with a suspicious eye.

"Calm down, my dear child," said the doctor, in a voice that he tried to render more inexpressive. "That perspicacious orang is watching us, and I know that he's got his mind fixed on conquest, first of Riddle-Temple. What do you think of that project? What line of conduct should we take? Ought we to aid him against your father or...?"

"My father!" cried Mabel. "He survived that terrible catastrophe, then?"

"Yes, he's alive—Archibald too, and Gorden, and others."

"Ah! So much the better—my greatest remorse was..." She stopped, having been about to say: *being the wife of his murderer*.

Abraham understood, and made an approving gesture.

"Chimène loves the Cid who has killed Don Diegue.[19] Your father is alive, Mabel, and your love doesn't have that Spanish spice. But quickly, where were we? If you wish, we can be free tomorrow, even though that would disrupt my plans. Certain events that have occurred today have decided me. Whatever I thought, we aren't made to live with apes..."

A growl from Ouha cut him off.

"I believe that fellow understands American. In brief, do we go, yes or no?"

"Since my father's alive, I'll go."

"Then all's working out for the best. I'll hasten to warn my friends. We'll arrange to draw the orangs away while we come to get you. We have a safe refuge, Mabel, and..."

Ouha intervened again; with a profusion of gestures he made it understood that it was time to talk business, and for him to have a voice in the discussion. What did Mabel say? Was she ready? Now it was him, Ouha, who was waiting. She had suggested ideas of conquest to him; he wanted to begin with Riddle-Temple. For him, the title of father had no more meaning than that of godfather, which Goldry attributed to himself. He, Ouha, wanted his wife to live in a more comfortable environment than the cave in which they had lived until now. He, Ouha, thought that he deserved something better. What did the two of them propose? What did he have to do to be sure of success?"

Having pretended to reach an understanding with Mabel, Abraham sketched out a plan.

"Ouha knows the way, since he's already made the journey twice. It remains to convene the council, to decide the means of mounting a campaign that will be rather a long one, and gather provisions. As for weapons, the orangs know no others but their clubs, which simplifies the question. The diffi-

---

[19] The reference is to Pierre Corneille's tragedy *Le Cid* (1638); the characters are based on the life of Rodrigo Diaz, "El Cid," who married Jimena, the daughter of Don Diego, whom he had killed.

culty will be making the orangs understand the necessity of carrying packages of food, although, given their habit of imitation, they will all take up their burdens the moment they see the chiefs bearing them...

"So, tomorrow, council meeting. Immediately afterwards, assembly, parceling of food, and departure the day after tomorrow for the river, the burned woods, and the forest. Perhaps it's the most dangerous route, but it's the shortest."

Ouha nodded his head, making it understood that he would convene the council for form's sake, because he was the master, and leave tomorrow morning.

Goldry exchanged a glance with Mabel. Would he have the time, between now and then, to warn his friends? Ouha signed to him to follow him.

"Where?" asked Abraham.

"To the council," said the autocrat—and he dragged the doctor away, leaving Mabel alarmed by the rapidity of the master's actions.

LXVI. Our Lady of Lust and Victory

Left alone, Mabel called Rava and told her what was going on. The young woman raised her eyes to the heavens and, crossing her arms over her bosom, thanked Buddha for having watched over her and not having abandoned her to the power of the apes. As for Dilou, who happened to be absent, it was agreed that they would not warn her until the last moment, and only then if they were certain that she would not betray them.

When the two orangs, the King of the Apes and Goldry, the doctor disguised as an ape, reached the council's meeting-place, it was already gathered, for Ouha had taken that precaution in advance. He took his place on his tree-trunk and opened the session.

Briefly, he recalled the origin of Ouha's monarchy. He alone had been able to unite and gather what remained on the island of the once-powerful Harr-ha nation, which internal disputes had reduced to what was united under his scepter. If, instead of tearing one another apart, the Orangs had fought energetically against the invasion of Humans, they would still be the masters of the island, for he, Ouha affirmed that the Harr-ha race had once ruled the world.

What should they do now? Should they remain penned in the mountains until the humans, still increasing in number, came to expel them?

"Expel us!" he concluded, with a fine oratorical gesture. "Where will we go, since this is our last refuge? They will destroy us, to the last ape. Ought we to wait for that catastrophe or should we avoid it by attacking first? The white men are still not very numerous on the island, and they alone are redoubtable. The yellow men are only too glad to be our servants; we shall take their women and reduce the males to servitude. What do we have to lose? Nothing, since we do not even have the certainty of conserving our meager independence. What do we have to gain? Everything: terrain cultivated by yellow men, whose fruits we shall be able to harvest; white and yellow women; comfortable shelters; and, finally, the assurance of an easy life without fatigue. However, I respect the free will of all, and I only intend to take volunteers. The tremulous can stay here with the old men, women and children—but those who remain will have no right to the booty and will have none of the favors I grant to those who obey me."

There was a silence. An old man, the sage Nhen-Nhen, got up.

"Great king, your wishes are commands. However, permit an old ape..."

"Don't bother," Ouha interrupted. "My wishes take precedence over all arguments. We leave tomorrow morning. Let everyone gather his weapons and whatever food he can carry. We have to cross a region devastated by our last enemies. It's wise to take food, at least for a few days."

The sage Nhen-Nhen got up again to ask: "Is the White Witch marching with you?"

"My wife, the Great White Spirit, will march with me at your head. She will assure us of victory."

Enthusiastic cheers resounded from all directions.

"Go on, go on," muttered Abraham. "Tomorrow, Our Lady of Lust and Victory, Mabel, will be safe, and you'll wait for her for a long time."

On that, amid political rejoicing, like a Roman Caesar ordering bread and circuses, Ouha ordered a large distributions of bananas and durians, of which the orangutans were very fond.

LXVII. A Desperate Hour

Afterwards, Ouha, the despot, dragged the doctor back to his abode again. Goldry tried to insist of returning to his own cave, but Ouha would not hear of it, and imprisoned him in his harem.

"All is lost," said Abraham. "I can't warn my friends, and that brute wants to set out on campaign before dawn. He's definitely not stupid enough. I disown him; he's not my pupil."

"It's my fault," said Mabel. "If I hadn't suggested these ideas of conquest, he wouldn't have thought of them by himself."

"What can we do?" groaned Abraham. "What can we do? Let's see—he's gone, doubtless to organize the recruitment of his army. What if I tried to get out?"

He headed for the cave entrance and darted a glance outside. Four orangs armed with massive cudgels were mounting guard. The doctor tried to open negotiations but the only response was a blow that nearly broke his arm.

Abraham beat a retreat and said to Mabel: Does he suspect our intention to flee? For want of speech, these animals have presentiments that don't deceive them."

Mabel did not seem distressed by the impossibility of flight. Dilou, in order to emphasize her evident displeasure at Abraham's presence, went out to chat to the sentinels, who were flattered by that mark of attention.

The doctor, content to be alone with Mabel and Rava, said: "That Dilou doesn't inspire me with confidence. She's capable of betraying us."

"No," said Rava. "She'd be delighted to remain Ouha's sole favorite."

"What can we do? What can we do, Mabel?"

"Wait. Ouha won't let you sleep here."

LXVIII. The Deserted House

At sunset, Ouha came back, satisfied. He had convinced three hundred orangs to make the expedition he desired, and had left them full of enthusiasm, under the command of his lieutenant, Ko-Zu.

Complete silence reigned in the grottoes. A strange anxiety gripped his bosom; he ran into the harem.

There was no one there.

Having looked everywhere, he let himself fall on to the ground and roared, so violently that Dilou came running, amazed to see the king alone in the cave.

After a few moments, Dilou approached meekly and attempted to calm his dolor with tender caresses. They awoke in the master, who was sobbing like a child, the memory of other caresses; he seized the unfortunate girl and threw her against the wall, fracturing her skull.

Ouha trampled her cadaver furiously, and then, impelled by a sudden hope, ran outside.

LXIX. A Wordless Rescue

The eight adventurers of the rescue party had waited for Goldry in vain at the rendezvous he had arranged. After an hour, Gorden and Archibald, accompanied by the two Malays, Eg Merh and To Wang, went to Ouha's cave, carrying ropes and levers of sturdy wood.

Archibald lent the others his back, and the three men went into the grotto from which they could see what was happening in Mabel's residence. At the moment when they started listening, Ouha came in with the doctor. They therefore heard the conversation of Mabel and Abraham, and the explanation of Ouha's plans. When the king of the apes went out, dragging the doctor with him, they consulted as to the course of action to take.

Having examined the place, they judged that it would take at least two hours to make an opening big enough to let the prisoners through. They set to work immediately, attacking the rock at the place where it seemed most friable. Fortunately, the found a surface that was conveniently cracked; by introducing the blade of a knife into the cracks, they are able to detach fist-sized pieces, without producing the slightest sound.

When Goldry and Ouha came back again, only a thin layer remained to be removed. As soon as Ouha had gone, they broke away the rest and threw ropes down into the grotto. The prisoners had only to put their feet into a loop fashioned at each extremity, as if into a stirrup, and then hold on to the rope. The four men lifted them up like feathers, in less than five minutes.

From the interior of the royal cavern, the primitive window, high up and set back, could not be seen. Without a word, the rescuers pushed the three refugees ahead of them and got them down on the other side; having remained on top, Gorden detached the moorings and rejoined his companions with a bound. Then Mabel and Rava threw themselves into the arms of their friends and embraced them, weeping. The males were no less emotional. Even Goldry was glad to return to humanity.

The Malays, being less demonstrative, were the first to give the signal to retreat, drawing Rava away. The whites followed.

Two hours later, they were all reunited, and Mabel was in her father's arms, in the diamond cathedral.

LXX. The Rainy Season

Mr. Smith did not take long to perceive his daughter's physical modifications. She had changed a great deal since he had lost her; her figure was no longer as slim; her shoulders and bosom had developed; her skin, formerly so pale, was bronzed. Her gait and gestures now had a primitive abruptness. She hesitated and searched for words. Nevertheless, she was overjoyed to see her father again.

Smith, fearful of a few replies that might be embarrassing for the young woman, refrained from interrogating her, and limited himself to talking to her about Riddle-Temple, how happy he would be to be reunited with her there, and telling her the story of their search and the fortunate discovery of the caves of the ancient mountainous massif.

Mabel retreated into an almost absolute mutism. It was only after a few days, in the presence of the delicate attentions with which her companions surrounded her, that she began to come back to herself. Finally, she took part, at least by means of a few bursts of laughter, in the enthusiastic conversations of the doctor, who never wearied of expressing eulogies to his friend Ouha—of whom, however, he added, "he had seen enough."

Mabel, who had lived in the midst of the great apes, taking part in their hunting and their battles, had even more to say than the doctor, but she kept quiet, revisiting intimate memories beneath her helmet of golden undulations, while the scientist, with his habitual thoughtlessness, exalted the qualities of his prodigious pupil.

They remained in the caves for a week, making preparations for the return. The rainy season had arrived and the river, considerably swollen, promised an easier return. They set about constructing a raft larger and more solid than the first, adding to it a detachable mast, at the foot of which was a straw tent woven by Rava and her brother, intended for the two women.

While this work was going on, Gorden and Archibald returned to the large cave of diamonds they called Mabel Grotto and, having climbed to the top of the crevice, had witnessed the departure of the Harr-haian army.

Ouha, recovered from his stupor, sometimes marched at the head and sometimes on the flank, urging his troops on; he had imagined that the fugitives must be ahead of them and hoped to catch up with them, or to get to Riddle-Temple before them.

The two men saw him cross the river and go into the burned forest; evidently, the army was following the itinerary of the previous campaign.

Two days after the army had gone into the burned forest, however, the sky darkened. In spite of his intelligence, the sagacity of the Orangutan monarch was at fault; he had not been able to record the meteorological changes of the rainy season in his memory. Even though he had suffered them every year, every year they took him by surprise, and it was under heavy rains that the most urgent reparations were made.

Every year, Ouha gave shelter in his grottoes to those of his subjects whose huts had become colanders. Every year, the great apes huddled in the shelter of their roofs of foliage, shivering in the dampness of the forest. That lasted two months, and then ordinary life resumed—and, with their customary insouciance, the apes let the next season come without having bee able to prepare for it. Ouha had been the first to try to maintain the habitations of his subjects in good condition; he knew that the period of downpours would come back eventually, but he did not know how to calculate and anticipate that epoch.

"That's a lucky break for us," said Gorden to Archibald, while they were both in their belvedere. "The rain will catch them in the heart of the virgin forest, and three-quarters of the army will stay there."

"I can't help feeling sorry for them," said Archibald. "Those people aren't to be scorned."

Gorden looked at him, smiling. "Did you say *those people*?"

"It's true that I can't look at those anthropoids without anguish. In truth, they resemble us too closely."

"Yes, but they're still apes. If humankind owes its origin to them, it took thousands of years and appropriate climatological conditions to arrive at that result—which is to say, us. Anyway, your simian sympathies would be considerably diminished if, like me..." Gorden stopped dead. "Bah! the main thing is to be rid of the obscene beasts. If we come back here later, without dolls with us, we'll have more room for maneuver."

The two men went back to the camp, and informed their companions of the result of their observations.

After a week, the eleven, including Mabel Smith, her father, Archibald, Gorden, the doctor, the Malays, Rava, were ready to leave. By then, the rising waters of the river had almost arrived at the level of the tunnel, and Mabel was able to embark without even getting her feet wet.

LXXI. On the Water

The two women had dressed as best they could in clothes borrowed from their companions and had installed themselves in the tent. They busied themselves preparing a meal. A large flat stone served as a hearth, and dry, resinous wood as fuel.

If Major Bennett had been able to make the journey, it would have reminded him of his return from the Borneo campaign in his youth, when, with a company of bold and joyful fellows, he had descended the rapids to join the Dutch fleet. The river was flowing impetuously, eating away its banks uprooting and carrying away thousands of trees and clumps of brushwood.

Sometimes, that mass formed an immense train of living and leafy wood that surged forth, smashing everything in its passage, colliding, becoming jammed in a bed until the force of the current carried everything away—and the mass went on, like an enormous battering-ram, shattering and breaking up an entire corner of the forest further on, which, swallowed up in its turn, would swell the fanatic catapult.

In the presence of such a peril, it was necessary to let themselves be carried away by the moving islet or to clear a passage, with a great effort of levers and hatchets. Then, when the difficult passage had been surmounted, the raft set off again with the rapidity of an express train.

The route, so painfully traveled on the outward journey, was covered in ten days; on the eleventh, the raft emerged into the sea. The mast was set up, and the coconut-fiber sail hoisted.

Four days later, the steamboat Inverness, serving as a ferry between the Celebes and the Philippines, picked them up and disembarked them at Imbuk.

They were safe.

LXII. A Little Calm and Rest

Six days later, they were at White House, where Major Bennett's widow received them, contrary to her habit, with the greatest cordiality—which did not prevent her from scolding her domestics and her children for their idleness and rudeness in the presence of the strangers. She insisted that they should all stay at the farm while Gorden and the Malays went to Riddle-Temple to find out whether the orangutans were already there.

"It's scarcely probable," Gorden said, "for it's only twenty-two days since they left, and the forest must have had surprises in store for them."

Indeed, there was not the slightest sign of orangutans at Riddle-Temple, and Betty Symian had no other anxiety than that of not seeing Harry Smith and Mabel again. When she knew that her young mistress was at White House, she had the tilbury hitched up and departed, in order to embrace her more rapidly.

Gorden and the Malays immediately organized the defenses, in case the orangutan army arrived. Emissaries were sent in all directions to appeal for and summon help. That done, they waited.

LXXIII. Toward the Promised Land

During the difficult journey through the burned forest, so awkward for orangutans, they were obliged to march like humans on the ground, bent over, supporting themselves on their hands, while clasping their clubs, each of them bearing on his shoulders a heavy burden of bananas, sago and other fruits and roots. In order to encourage them, Ouha carried his own bale, like all the rest. His example did not prevent complaints, for the great apes whom the people of Borneo call "free men" are not used to carrying kitbags like our soldiers.

Finally, they reached the virgin forest again, and the anthropoids were able to relax, running through the branches and lianas. Ouha too was glad to be able to launch himself wholeheartedly through the forest foliage, but it was necessary for him not to forget his duties as leader continuing to guide his soldiers along the right path.

Indications were rare; he had some difficulty locating, among the newly-regrown plants, the traces of the route cleared by the axes of the Muni-Wali brothers' woodcutters. Eventually, he found it, and for fear of losing it again, constrained himself to march on the ground. A few of his most faithful subjects escorted him, complaining, but following him anyway, obedient to their master. The bulk of the army advanced overhead. Sometimes, to encourage the chiefs, Ouha permitted them to rejoin their soldiers, spending an hour or two in the branches.

Thus, for two days, all was going reasonably well, when the first drops of rain began to fall.

LXXIV. The Enemy with Countless Feet

The anxious orangutans surrounded their leaders and demanded good weather with furious cries. Ouha made the most loud-mouthed shut up with blows of his club, and ordered them with a gesture to resume the march. For the orangutans, that march to the land of Cockayne had only represented an attack, a conquest, booty and food, and idleness at their discretion. When they began to suffer fatigue, and it was necessary to ration and conserve their food-supplies, they had not anticipated any such thing. The majority had squandered their provisions in the first few days and then thrown away the sacks of reserves, which were heavy to carry.

When the rainy season began, only Ouha and thirty of his most faithful adherents had kept their sacks, and the discipline of well-trained and battle-hardened troops. Soon, even among the captains, in spite of the spirit of imitation typical of their race, idleness and hunger held sway. The rain arrived, steady rain without an hour's pause, gentle or violent but falling incessantly, frightfully continuous, drowning the route and masking the already-limited horizon of the virgin forest, which was nothing but a mass of vegetation, even more luxuriant and exuberant. Beneath the rain, beneficent for itself, the vegetation expanded and dilated, taking on formidable proportions. The lianas grew visibly, invading everything.

After several days of that infinite rain, the few traces left by the woodcutters' axes disappeared; the soil, composed of the spongy and fermenting humus of a hundred generations of trees and various plants, gave birth to thousands of biting insects, voracious and venomous. The water accumulated in depressions in the ground, forming pools that were sometimes several kilometers in extent, in which an entire society of viscous, crawling, slithering creatures swarmed: enormous toads and snakes of every sort, ranging from the coral snake, scarcely as long as a pencil, with a fatal bite, to the gigantic python, between six and eight meters long, capable of strangling an ox.

On higher ground, the great wild beasts had taken refuge: tigers and panthers, and wild pigs of the peccary variety, pullulating and wallowing in the mire. Attracted by all that forest vermin, the great Indian vultures had arrived, and were living on all that fauna while doing their best to devour one another. Large herds of buffalo fled, seeking the high plateaux where they hoped to find their nourishment, passing by like whirlwinds, upsetting everything in their passage.

The rain fell, and kept falling.

The simian army, in disarray, like a mob of phantom wild beasts, their fur soaked and their bodies sweating, marched—or, rather, dragged themselves along—clearing a difficult passage through the tangle of lianas, the waterlogged branches sticky with moss, ungraspable by their four hands. Some deserted, hoping to be able to return home, got lost or continued wandering until they perished of hunger and misery.

The rain fell, falling tirelessly.

Still at its head, Ouha was the army's soul. They all felt that, and clung to his tracks. Sometimes, weary of the struggle, one of the great apes let himself fall at the foot of a tree, and, without the strength to defend himself, became the prey of some monster—a snake, a tiger, or even carnivorous insects, whose number prevailed over the giant victim's last remains of strength.

When would that misery end? When?

Ouha, lost, was only steering by means of a sort of intuition. Would that march to the conquest of the world, following a star—which, for him, was a march of love—last much longer?

The days succeeded one another; nothing indicated that the disastrous deluge would come to an end. They went on because staying where they were would have meant death, and the pitiless rain fell incessantly, extending its mobile curtain around them, limiting visibility to a few paces.

Little by little, the mass became clearer. How many were they now? Ouha dared not count his apes. They sustained themselves on roots, plants that were scarcely nourishing they were so saturated with water. The poor diet, fatigue and damp undermined the army's health; they suffered from fever, dysentery, infected bites, ophthalmia—which rendered their already-gummy eyes purulent—and the incessant assault of thousands of flies, living in all their wounds and rendering them putrid.

Oh, how far away they were from their departure, when they could already see themselves entering the promised land as conquerors! But all the orangutans trailed along behind Ouha, in the stinging rain, the funereal rain, through the sodden virgin forest, just as Napoléon I's veterans had once dragged themselves through the Russian snows.

Devoid of thought, with to visible objective, Ouha marched on, drawing behind him a troop of muddy, blood-stained specters covered in wounds, the skin of their hands worn down to the flesh washed and thinned down, so to speak, by the incessant rain.

Would that agony last for days or weeks? Was it close to its end? Had they been going in a circle of incessantly-renewed torture? They could not tell, having no notion of time. They had marched this far, they would march until, like the others, they fell exhausted, renouncing the horrors of the struggle for survival, and land in the marsh.

In the beginning, when a comrade weakened and collapsed, they had tried to lift him up. Now, they went on, indifferently, all of them, in the end, almost desirous of falling and resting forever.

It rained, and rained.

Finally, one day—how many days had their misery lasted before that resplendent morning?—the rain stopped. Ouha, having slid painfully to the top of an enormous pandamus, perceived the blue sky, and called out, screeching his cry of command and glory: "Ouha! Ouha!"

What remained of his army, some forty individuals, the strongest and most resistant, made further efforts, dragging themselves along, and the laggards soon rejoined their leader.

LXXV. The Triumphant Return of the Sun

One morning, the sun rose, as it had before the deluge, radiantly, in a cloudless sky. Over the treetops of the forest, a purer air reigned. Each of them felt revived, forgetting his past distress in order to experience nothing but the present well-being. Ouha ordered them to rest. He wanted to regroup. The apes chose a suitable location, and, for the first time in two months, were able to sleep well. They slept all that day and the following night.

When they woke up, they felt slightly more cheerful. Their pelts had had dried out; their eyes, closed for twenty-four hours, had been cleared of all the parasites that were eating them away. They set out in quest of food, and one of them was lucky enough to discover an entire clump of coconut-palms on a ridge, laden with fruits. That provender, healthy and abundant, which furnished them simultaneously with something to eat and drink, settled their stomachs and intestines.

They took up residence to that hilltop, from which he water flowed away rapidly, creating a sort of well-aerated oasis accessible to the sunlight. With their changeable minds and short memories, the orangs, forgetful of their former plans, thought that they had arrived at their goal, and resumed living their habitual life. Only one satisfaction was lacking: females—but the fatigues they had endured had numbed their sexual appetite somewhat, and the great apes rapidly came back to life, reconstituting their strength.

Ouha, however, had not forgotten, and racked his brains to find a means of continuing the enterprise. Nothing now remained of is project of conquest; he no longer had the necessary number of soldiers—but he wanted Mabel, his wife, and if it were necessary for him to go after her alone, then he would go alone, even if it were to fall inanimate and dead at her feet.

Ouha did not feel any anger against the infidel, and found it natural that she would return, by herself, to the luxury that he had dreamed of providing for her.

While his companions, coming and going, yielded to their whims or their needs, Ouha, crouched on a principal branch, remained pensive. Once, he was obliged to change his position, the sun having got in his eyes.

That ray of sunlight was, for the anthropoid, Newton's apple. He remembered that, in the homeland Harr-ha, when he had been on the threshold of his cave, the sun had risen to his right, behind he mountainous massif, and that, in consequence, the river, the burned forest and the virgin forest were in front of him. He therefore concluded that, being in the same position relative to the sun, he had the objective to be attained—Riddle-Temple—ahead of him.

With his war-cry of "Ouha! Ouha!" he summoned is companions, and gave them the order to stay in the same place, making them understand that he was going to explore.

Then he headed southwards, alone.

LXXVI. The Heart of a Faint-Hearted Lover

Leaning on the highest balustrade of the gallery of Rid-dle-Temple, Archibald Wilson was daydreaming. After an evening spent in the great hall of the ancient monument, in which Harry Smith had installed a large organ, with his companions in adventure-for, since their return, the eight companions whatever their social status, had been treated as equals by the grateful Mabel and Harry Smith.

The Malays, with perfect tact, knew how to assume their place without any affectation of humility. Frequent contact with Europeans had rapidly acted on that race, naturally intelligent, whom only religious superstitions had debased, in giving them a mentality enslaved by all kinds of credulities. The positive mentality of their companions had influenced them, and they had gained by it. Thus far, the three Malays, retained by Rava—who did not want to be separated from Mabel—had stayed at Riddle, but their departure was imminent. They were to go to Brunei, and then rejoin Silven Gorden in an attempt to return to the large cave in order to harvest its gold.

Archibald was thinking about that expedition and wondering it if might not be better to join the quest for gold rather than continue the pursuit of a more-than-problematic love with Mabel.

In fact, since her return to the paternal domain, the young woman's attitude with regard to her suitors had been so bizarre that Gorden, as he had already told Archibald, had not hesitated to surrender his place entirely. Although Harry Smith had tried to retain him, he had decided to go home. Left alone, a flirt devoid of competition, Wilson had striven to please her, with a good deal of care and grace. Mabel listened to him with an astonished expression, scarcely responding at all to his inflamed declarations.

Meanwhile, Archibald had singular returns to the past; he could not help thinking about the nature of Mabel's life among the orangutans, wondering what comparison might, in the future, be drawn between him and the anthropoid. The brave lad felt that it was his duty to marry Mabel Smith, attempting to erase from the young woman's life the terrible adventure and promiscuity to which she must have been subjected—for he assumed, naturally, that Mabel had only succumbed to violence. He dared not make the slightest allusion to that past, in order not to communicate his discomfort and embarrassment to the young woman.

Harry Smith, who was also suffering from the ambiguous situation of his daughter, would have liked the whole thing to be terminated by a marriage, and for Archibald to take his young wife to America for a while. It was evident to the worthy papa that staying in Borneo would not help her to forget the filthy catastrophe. Personally, he would remain at Riddle-Temple; the doctor seemed to have no desire to return to his homeland and was doggedly determined to finish the work he had begun on the great apes and their relationship to humankind, in the same arena.

Thus, everyone at the ancient Indian temple was carefully avoiding, in Mabel's regard, and reference to her captivity among the Orangs—but that very silence was a reason to think about it constantly. Evidently, her father and fiancé were glad about her rescue, but she felt that they might, perhaps, have preferred to regret her death than have found her living in a situation that she seemed to have accepted without horror.

Archibald felt the repercussions of all these mental fluctuations; he, most of all, was suffering from being unable to find a way out that would satisfy his heart.

LXXVII. The Offering

A slight sound made him turn around. A white form was coming toward him.

"Mabel!"

"Yes, it's me," said the American woman. "Don't get up, dear. We need to have a frank talk. As I've understood what you'll never dare to ask me, I've come to put an end to a discomfort that's weighing on both of us. You're hesitating to ask for my hand. I understand that well enough that, in your place, I'd do the same. Well, Silven Gorden has understood better than you everything that's precarious between us, and he's retired from the game. Why are you waiting for before doing the same?"

"Mabel," the young man stammered, "I love you...even so."

The young woman burst out laughing. "You love me. Marry me, then. But you're not unaware that you wouldn't be marrying the Mabel of old? Do you think you have the mental strength to forget? And the physical strength to be able to replace Ouha?"

"Mabel!" Archibald exclaimed.

"Well, what? I don't have enough hypocrisy to feign sentiments outside my nature. Was it a misfortune for me, that sojourn among the apes? I don't believe so; I don't feel that it was. Now, there are a number of social conventions that weigh upon me like chains. I know that the free life of the forests might soon have made a brute of me...but afterwards? What interest can your civilized life have for me? In myself, I only feel two desires: a life contemplative of free nature, and the satisfaction of my sense of womanhood—appeals that your civilization has repressed, but whose tide carries me away. That's insanity, you'll say, a mania—but it takes hold of you."

"Then you want to go back...out there?"

"Perhaps. I'm fighting it. But everything here irritates me and exasperates me—your habits, your pleasures, your games, the division of time, your semblance of morality, your so-called delicacies. In short, everything that once amused me annoys me now."

"Why?"

"Why? Because an obsession stronger than my reason, stronger that anything, is weighing upon me, physically and morally; because I know that, behind your great romantic love, there's nothing, fundamentally, but a desire to possess Mabel, and that you don't have the courage to say so frankly. Can you imagine, now, that I need the approval of a pastor to give myself? What do you want of me? A mate—or what is called among you a wife? A housekeeping wife, mother of a family? Children! A husband! A family with me!"

She burst into wild laughter, took off and threw aside her garments with a gesture of her hand and stood there, totally naked, in front of the astounded Wilson.

"With me, the mate of an ape! Well, what are you waiting for? You want me, my dear! Take me! I'm offering myself...so take me!"

And as Archibald recoiled, aghast, she leapt upon him and threw her arms around him.

LXXVIII. Affairs of Gold and the Heart

Early the next morning, a visitor arrived at Riddle-Temple: Silven Gorden, accompanied by a party of ten coura-geous pioneers. They had come in search of the three Malays, anticipating their departure. According to their information, the river was presently more accessible, and Gorden had had the opportunity to but a steam-launch with a very shallow draught from one of his compatriots, which optimized the conditions. It could carry twenty people and a load of four tons. That stroke of fortune had led him to bring forward the departure. He had sent the vessel to wait for them at anchor in the Strait of Makassar.

After breakfast—which was cheerful, everyone having, that day, reason to be more-or-less satisfied with life—Gorden told Wilson, that he wanted to speak to him in private, and the latter took him to his room.

"You can imagine that I don't want to disturb your quie-tude, my dear Archibald, but I have something important to tell you."

"What is it, Gorden?"

"The orangs have been seen in the forest, in the direction of the Muni-Wali plantation. Be on your guard! Personally, having only been able to play a ridiculous role in this adven-ture, I'll take advantage of it to go in search of the gold—but that discovery was made together, and I ought, therefore, to settle matters with you and decide what your share of the ex-ploitation of the deposit will be." When the young American made a dismissive gesture he went on: "Don't give up your interest in the affair. If you marry Mabel Smith, whose fortune is considerable, it's preferable for you to be able to go into the marriage with a comparable sum. I've taken the necessary steps with regard to the Dutch government. The State will be content with 25%. I therefore reckon that, given the risks and the expenses I have to bear, I have the right to 50%. That leaves 25% for your share."

"But I don't have any more right to it than my other companions."

"You're free the share it out as you wish. Only you and Harry Smith are eligible, since the others were part of the expedition—but Mr. Smith's fortune is already an embarrassment to him. As for Dr. Goldry, he has no right to anything, not being a member of our party at that time."

"As you wish, then."

"Thanks," said Gorden. "That acceptance reestablishes a certain equality between us. By withdrawing my competition in the matter of Miss Smith, I placed myself, morally, in a state of inferiority relative to you. This restitution, in gold, restores the equilibrium. Perhaps I'm not fulfilling all of a duty I assumed, and I'm paying compensation in gold."

"You have a singular fashion of evaluating our moral qualities—but I'm still astonished by the facility with which you renounced Mabel."

"I've already told you my reasons. There's one that overshadows all the others."

"You've said too much—or not enough. Miss Smith's future husband has the right to know everything."

"You're definitely going to marry Mabel, then?"

Archibald hesitated. After what had happened the night before, that required reflection, and the young man, still intoxicated by his success, had not had time to reflect.

Gorden looked at him, and seemed to read his thoughts. He continued: "The principal reason that made me renounce my courteous rivalry with you is that, for me, for a man in the situation I occupy here, Mabel Smith has none of the qualities necessary to a colonist and a man who wants to found a family. You, who have lived with the Smiths more than I have, might judge otherwise. Mabel has been, above all else, a socialite. Her father's immense fortune has been able to satisfy her most eccentric desires. Her beauty, in dazzling me, annihilated my reflection. The misfortune that overtook her, in forcing me to accompany you, permitted me, with time, to reconsider and to analyze a sentiment that was entirely impulsive. Mabel Smith is not the wife I need, so I renounced her."

"Which you don't think unfortunate for yourself, and excellent for me."

"If you weren't my friend, I might fear offending you, but between us, nothing needs to remain obscure. There's a great difference between the two of us. My life, since leaving England, has been nothing but a series of brutal adventures, and that suits my nature. You on the contrary, have remained, by habit and almost by profession, what is conventionally known as a man of the world. Furthermore, an intense liking for sports bring you even closer to Miss Smith, creating a perfectly natural bond between you. The events through which we've lived have been, for you, an anomaly; if they were to continue, it would displease you."

Archibald was on the point of confessing that the abnormal events were continuing, but a certain modesty prevented him from admitting to Gorden that Mabel had given to him that which, in his youthful fatuity, he attributed to love.

"You're right. Mabel is bored here. We'll get married as soon as possible and go back to America."

"Where I wish you all possible happiness, Wilson. For myself, I won't forget you, and will keep you up to date not just with our business affairs, but with my life. I hope that you'll do the same."

"Certainly—one doesn't forget a friendship born amid such perils."

"Perils that might be renewed, my dear Archibald, if you stay in the islands. Leave! Go as soon as possible. Remember what I told you about the great apes. If their leader isn't dead, I believe him to be dangerous."

Archibald felt a shiver run through him. It was not fear of the orangutan but fear for Mabel. For the first time it occurred to him that the previous night's scene might only have been, for Mabel, an exercise in comparison. He clenched his fists. Ah! Mabel would return to the ape. He would rather kill her."

Gorden noticed the gesture.

"When are you leaving.

"From here, tomorrow morning—and for the cave of gold and diamonds, as soon as we reach our vessel."

"We'll drink to your success this evening, then."

"And I to your marriage, my dear chap, and to your happiness."

Archibald went pale, but did not unclench his teeth.

"My dear Archibald," said Gorden, "you're hiding something from me. I won't insist, of course, on penetrating your secret—but remember, if you need me, that I can postpone our expedition for a few days."

"Thanks. You're not mistaken. Something has happened that I can't tell you about."

"Hey, you up there! We're going for a ride in the forest!"

The two men looked down into the courtyard. Mabel, her father and the doctor, already in the saddle, were waiting for them; two domestics were holding two horses for them. They went down rapidly, and a few minutes later, they were all galloping around the Temple's enclosing wall.

LXXIX. Combat Between a Tiger, a Woman
and an Orangutan

The weather in the period that follows the rainy season is delightful, and it remains the best time of the year. After ten days or so, when the earth has finished absorbing the mass of water accumulated in the vegetal humus that covers it and the atmosphere is rid of the mists caused by evaporation, the forest continues its intensive life, but the growth of the plants ceases to be abnormal and resumes a healthier and more even pace.

On Harry Smith's orders, a few paths had been traced around the habitation, which permitted excursions of several kilometers. Two parallel routes, departing from Riddle, extend into the heart of the forest, to a crossroads fabricated in the virgin forest, from which four other projected paths departed. The little troop set off at a trot along the left-hand path, eyes and ears alert, in the hope of encountering some game.

The first shot was fired by the billionaire; he brought down a superb pelican, which was also hunting on the edge of a lake. That exploit animated the entire band; instead of proceeding in a group they dispersed, questing through the forest anywhere that a horse was able to set foot.

Mabel had taken the lead. First, she galloped quite tranquilly; then, intoxicated by the ride, she launched her animal at top speed, and her companions were left behind.

"A rally! A rally!" Mabel shouted to them. "Catch me if you can..."

Within a few minutes, she had reached the crossroads, and recklessly launched herself at a gallop into a small track, summarily traced out to make the route of a future path—a track just large enough for a horse and rider, which had not yet been visited since the previous season. After a hundred strides, she found her route blocked by an enormous tree, whose roots, undermined by the water, had been unable to sustain it, and which had toppled across the track.

To jump over it was impossible. Its branches and the lianas with which it was laden made an inextricable tangle. Entirely given over to her game of tag, the young woman saw nothing in that sylvan accident but a means of giving the slip to her friends. Dismounting, she took her horse by the bridle and forced it into the undergrowth, in order to go around the obstacle. She got half way without any difficulty, but the ground on the other side, horribly broken up, rendered any passage impossible. Frustrated, she was about to turn round; she could already hear the horsemen calling; she was caught.

At that moment, she saw a gap in front of her. Still pulling her horse, she went into it, laughing in advance at the disappointment of the hunters confronted by the obstacle and her disappearance. She had no intention of going very far, though. Masked by the foliage, she heard her father and his friends stop at the fallen tree and call out to her, laughing at first, then becoming anxious. She was about to reply to them when her horse made a sudden bound, which knocked her over, and then fled, terrified, into the forest. Furious, Mabel launched herself in pursuit—but she soon had to stop, fearful of going astray.

She called out. No voice replied. She was about to call out again when a muffled growl made her turn round. Ten paces away, ready to pounce, was a tiger.

Mabel was brave, but at the sight of the monster, so close, she felt a chill of fear grip her heart.

With a terrible roar, the tiger launched itself forward. She only just had time to throw herself sideways, behind a tree that was fortunately right beside her. Carried by its momentum, the enormous beast went straight into a clump of thorn-bushes, where it struggled for a few moments before succeeding in getting free.

Mabel had recovered a degree of self-possession. She picked up her rifle, which had fallen to the ground, took aim at the animal, and fired. The bullet only grazed the tiger's skull, rendering it even more furious. It hurled itself upon its adversary. Swiveling around the tree, the young woman avoided it once again.

With one bound, the tiger was at the foot of the tree. Rearing up on its hind legs, it reached out an enormous paw, whose sharp claws brushed Mabel's face. She fired again, at point-blank range. The bullet went into the monster's breast, but only served to augment its rage. It came around the trunk. Mabel tried to do likewise, but her heel encountered a root and she fell.

This time, she was well and truly doomed. Then, however, there was a racket of broken branches. A hairy mass tumbled down: an enormous brown body, which fell directly on to the tiger's head, at the same time as a clamor tore through the silence of the woods:

"Ouha! Ouha! Ouha!"

Mabel stood up, and saw the two enormous animals at grips. The orangutan had seized the tiger by the neck, while his inferior arms clasped the sides and belly of his adversary. But he latter, suddenly rolling on the ground on top of Ouha, lying on his back, turned round with a thrust of its hips and raked the ape's body with its terrible curved claws.

Ouha was able to seize his enemy's muzzle, and, sticking his fingers into the fuming nostrils, forced it to retreat. Then, getting up, braced on his hind legs, he pushed it further, holding back the immense effort of wild beast and nailing it to the ground. The tiger snorted, making hoarse sounds; a frightful rictus uncovered Ouha's teeth.

The two adversaries remained thus, face to face, without the tiger or the ape venturing a gesture. Ouha sensed that at the slightest movement, the tiger would reach him again and lacerate his flesh. His hide was already stained with large patches of crimson blood, dripping on to the ground in heavy garnet drops. Muscles taut, they were both breathing heavily.

Suddenly, the tiger freed its head with a abrupt effort, and seized one of the orangutan's hands; he uttered a cry of agony. But neither body was displaced, so tightly were they gripping one another, each certain of falling as soon as the equilibrium in which they were held was broken.

With his free hand, however, Ouha seized the feline's upper jaw and with a magnificent effort, while his half-crushed fingers pressed down on the monster's teeth and gums, forced the terrible vice open. Bones cracked in a sinister fashion between the enormous hairy palms. From the tiger's gaping throat, the muzzle and maw of which were breaking almost lamentably, a whistling sound emerged, continuous and obsessive, mingling rage and complaint.

With a convulsive somersault, in a last effort of its entire body, the tiger found the strength and courage to attack Ouha again; with a supreme bound of savage energy it planted its claws on the shoulders and in the breast of the sovereign ape, tearing with feverish thrusts at his muscles, still powerful in spite of the atrocity of his wounds, through which all of its blood was spurting over the wild beast and the black stripes of its marvelously beautiful body.

Mabel dared not fire. The two adversaries were too close together, too confused with one another for her not to fear wounding Ouha while trying to help him. Before that combat, in the face of the superhuman devotion of her bestial lover, she remained a spectator, admiring as well as terrified.

For an instant, Ouha weakened. The tiger's claws struck at his entrails, his neck, his face—but he grabbed the monster's forepaws, drew them apart as far as they would go, and with a sudden thrust of his giant arms, tore his enemy's breast apart. The tiger fell, dying, with a muted death-rattle, a tattered cadaver, in the long grass, on to the soil wet with their mingled, fuming blood.

Mabel, emerging from her stupor, went to the wounded victor, panting, intoxicated by his strength, joy and unleashed desire. She spoke to him in a very soft vice, slowly and with coaxing gestures. She staunched Ouha's wounds, put compresses of fresh herbs on his cuts, which she bandaged as best she could with her handkerchief and her underwear, which she ripped into pieces.

Ouha, exhausted by the merciless struggle in which he had just engaged, let her do it, still utterly intoxicated by having found Mabel again. Suddenly, he pushed the young woman away and stood up, growling. Shouts resounded in the distance.

The hunters had heard the tiger's roars and the young woman's two gunshots. Guided by them, they had tied their horses to the fallen tree, and had come running. Rounding the uprooted tree, Harry Smith had fallen into the hole in the ground freshly opened up by the tree's fall, and his companions were obliged to pull him out before continuing their search. They were about to start off again when there was a noise of trampled and torn brushwood not far away, and they saw Mabel's horse surge out of the thicket. They caught it and tied it up with theirs.

Their anxiety was at its peak when Archibald discovered the gap into which Mabel had gone. At the same time, formidable roars made the forest tremble. In the blink of a eye, the four men understood, and with one movement launched themselves in the direction indicated by the wild beast's rage. A rifle-shot signified: "Be brave! We're coming!"

They ran forward, firing a second shot to reassure Mabel. *She's there!* they thought. *Will we arrive in time?*

A moment later, they stopped; they could no longer hear anything. They called out. Still nothing. The gap had come to an end in front of a thorn-bush.

The four men stamped their feet in rage. Where should they go? In which direction? The dense forest enveloped the with its foliage, its bushes and the trunks of its trees, all entangled with creepers and climbing brambles, tenacious in their grip and as resistant as coils of barbed wire.

Again they called out. Ten times, then twenty, their shouts were lost in the thousand sounds of the forest.

"Let's go back," said Gorden, "and try to pick up her trail at her departure-point; otherwise, we'll go further and further astray.

Having retraced their steps and found the hole from which they had started, they shouted again: "Mabel! Mabel! Mabel!"

"I'm here," she said, suddenly standing up ten meters from the hunters. Disheveled, her clothes in disorder, her hands and face scratched, but her features cheerful and radiant, the young woman advanced toward hem.

"My daughter!" cried Smith, holding out his arms.

Having embraced him effusively, she said: "Forgive me—I've made you all anxious again, but there's no great harm done as you see. Shall we go back to the house?"

"But what about the tiger?" Archibald demanded. "We heard terrible roars...."

"It wasn't me who made them. I haven't seen it."

"But the gunshots!" said the doctor.

"Oh, the gunshots! They were to guide you to me."

"Anyway, you're safe, that's the main thing," said Harry Smith. "Another time, though, don't be so foolish in this damned forest, until I've had it cleared."

"Bah! Then it would lose all its charm."

Having got back to the fallen tree, they mounted up again, and went back to Riddle-Temple without further incident.

LXXX. Lunch, Music, Sleep

What had just happened had, in sum, taken very little time, and an hour later the riders sat down at table for lunch, in the ancient chamber fitted out as a dining-room. After their appetites had been calmed, for all that anguish had made them very hungry, their tongues were loosened and the conversation naturally turned to the day's events.

"What animal can have disturbed that tiger?" said Gorden.

"It can't have happened far away from me," said Mabel, "for I, too, thought that those roars were addressed to me. I regret it; it would have made me another beautiful fur."

"Hmm! You have no suspicion—but I've hunted tigers several times, and I don't take such matters lightly."

"How many times, Mr. Gorden?"

"I've only killed one in Borneo, and three in India, but it's here that I've been in the greatest danger."[20]

"It seems to me, however, that a well-placed bullet..."

"Certainly—but the difficulty is conserving the necessary composure, and when a tiger looks at you, the bravest of men is affected..."

"Then..."

Mabel stopped abruptly. She had been about to say: "Then I have a right to be proud, for I didn't tremble much." But she remembered the lie she had told just in time.

"For myself," Archibald said, "I admit that this morning's roaring had an odd impression on me."

"But you've heard those of orangutans, which are no less terrible."

---

[20] The author seems to have forgotten Gorden's earlier claim to have killed many more, made after his tale of an encounter with a tiger that led him to declare eternal enmity on the species.

"Yes, but then I was coming to your rescue; I was indifferent to danger."

Mabel frowned; that reference to the past did not please her.

"You know, Miss Smith, that I'm leaving tomorrow morning," Gorden said. "Won't you give me the pleasure of a little music, in order that I can take the memory of your admirable voice away with me. Perhaps it will be the last time I hear it."

Mabel smiled in a singular fashion. "With pleasure, my dear friend. Let's go into the hall. I want to try out the organ."

When they were installed, Mabel made a sign to Archibald to sit down at the keyboard. Then, when her flirt had played a prelude, she sang "Yankee Doodle" at the top of her voice. Her voice had never been so extensive and so vibrant, had never seemed so vivacious, so exuberant with health and strength.

Gorden, who had reasons for thinking thus, looked at Archibald with a concerned expression. After the national song, Mabel sang a sentimental melody, and then a tango song to a furious rhythm; she seemed indefatigable. But the four men, overwhelmed by the morning's excitement and fatigue, combined with the heat of the beautiful afternoon, did not take long to feel the effects of a final lullaby and gave in to inclination, and nodded off. Archibald too felt the effect of his own chords and pressed the ivory keys with increasing softness.

"Come on, let's leave it there," said the young woman, pointing to the three sleepers. "I believe, my dear, that it won't be long before you're imitating them. For myself, with your permission, I'll go up to my room to do the same."

Archibald would have liked to retain her, politely, but he sensed that she wanted to get away from him. Scarcely had Mabel gone out than he too let himself slide into the amicable arms of Morpheus.

LXXXI. Juliet Prepares for Romeo's Coming

A few minutes went by, and then the door opened softly and the blonde head of the young American woman reappeared She looked at the four sleepers in turn, with an ironic smile on her lips. Soon, she was in the garden, heading for the palisade, toward the place where Ouha had once escaped, carrying off Dilou. An enormous boulder blocked the hole the anthropoid had dug. Mabel considered the huge stone for some time, and shook her head.

Nothing to be done, she thought.

Rapidly, she turned to face Riddle-Temple. At that hour of the day, all the domestic staff were having a siesta, like their masters. She went to the sheds in which all the tools and accessories used for repairs were stored, and had no difficulty finding several coils of rope. She took two of them, each about ten meters long, took one up to her bedroom and went back to the garden.

The location of the hole made by Ouha was behind a dense mimosa bush; it was rarely visited by the inhabitants of Riddle-Temple. Having got there, she attached the end of the rope to one of the stays supporting the palisade from inside and threw the rest of the rope over the barrier. Unless chance led one someone from the house to go along that section of the fence, it was impossible to see the rope.

She went back to the house, went up to her room, lay down on the bed and fell asleep, like everyone else, departing for the land of dreams and apes.

LXXXII. The Known Trail

The first of the four sleepers to wake up was Silven Gorden. Seeing his companions still plunged in a profound sleep, he went silently to the door and went downstairs. Wanting to leave at dawn the next day, he still had a few petty details to settle with the Malays. He headed for the door of the vast habitation. The part occupied by the Malays was a large building that must once have been a kind of pagoda prior to the construction of the great Temple.

Those pagodas, repaired and fitted out as modern pavilions, ere twelve in number, six to the right and six to the left of the immense paved courtyard, surrounded by colonnades after the fashion of European cloisters, thus forming a covered gallery around the interior courtyard in which there're were several doors opening to the sheds situated behind. As Gorden arrived at the pagoda, she saw Eg Merh and To Wang coming in from behind the gallery through one of those doors. The two Malays seemed to be conversing with a certain animation. On seeing the Englishman they hurried toward him.

"What is it?" Gorden demanded.

"Come," said To Wang, laconically.

The three men went back to the sheds. The two Malays led Gorden to one of the store-rooms. There, they pointed at the ground.

As we have said, the surplus materials and tools had been put away in the sheds. When the distribution had been made, several sacks of cement had split and their contents had spread out over the floor. In that fine dust, fresh footprints were distinctly visible.

Gorden did not have a moment's hesitation. "Miss Smith's feet," he said. "What the devil was she doing here?"

"Looking for ropes," said Eg Merh. "Look at the traces."

Indeed, the ropes removed by Mabel had left their imprints in the dust. They followed the trail of footprints around the galleries to the other wing, where the masters' apartments were located, but the trail grew fainter as it progressed, until it faded out completely.

Without hesitation, they went along the palisade to the bounder. There, they only had to look up to see the moored rope thrown over the enclosure.

To Wang wanted to pull the rope in.

"Leave it," said the Englishman, "and let's go back inside. We can talk about it there."

A few minutes later, they were in the pagoda. Eg Merh summoned his sister and told her what they had just seen.

"The free man has bewitched the mistress," said Rava. "He must be prowling around in the vicinity, and Miss Mabel wants to let him in."

"Has she spoken to you about it?" Gorden asked.

"Oh, no—but I can see clearly, and I tell you that the big free man is a sorcerer."

"Then you think that Miss Smith is forced to obey him, in spite of her own will?"

"Buddha has permitted it. In exchange for speech, he has given the orangutan terrible secrets; if Ouha wishes it, Miss Mabel will go with him."

"What about you?"

"Oh, the orang doesn't desire me—and Buddha protects me. I'm a Hindu, but pale faces don't interest him."

Gorden reflected. He remembered the morning's adventure, and Mabel's strange response on the subject of the roaring they had heard. Connecting the dots, he concluded that the American woman must have seen Ouha again, and that they had come to an agreement. Now, would the anthropoid come alone? Or would there be an organized attack on the Temple? He had seen the expedition leave. If the army of apes had conserved its numbers, resistance was almost impossible; in that case, there was only one thing to do: retreat to White House, where an army of resistance could be organized. If, on the other hand, Ouha was alone, it would be easy to kill him—for,

251

in order to take him prisoner, they would have to catch him, and conditions were no longer the same as before.

In any case, they still had a few hours ahead of them; they had only to watch the palisade. If Ouha was alone, let him in; if he was at the head of his army of apes, keep the horses ready and take flight for White House.

Gorden told the Malays his plan. They approved it, and undertook to set an ambush that night.

LXXXIII. The Alert at Riddle-Temple

That having been agreed, Gorden went to find Archibald, Smith and the doctor, who were still asleep in the hall. He woke the up and brought them up to date with the situation. Archibald and Harry Smith were consternated by Mabel's complicity. They all approved the plan of defense. In case of an attack by the orangutan army, Mabel would not be warned; she would be taken away by force. In that anticipation, Harry Smith had the tilbury hitched up; other horses, ready-saddled, would be mounted as soon as the alert was sounded. The women in the carriage and all the men on horseback would leave, until they could come back in force.

LXXXIV. A Comparison Unfavorable to Humans

During these preparations, Mabel was sleeping peacefully in her bedroom. She came down for the evening meal, fresh and rested. Her father and his friends could not see anything abnormal about her, except that she seemed a trifle impatient with the slowness of time.

Archibald was finally able to retain her in a corner of the hall, determined, this time, to obtain a definitive response. He began the conversation thus: "I've received a letter from John Singleton. His marriage to Bertha Bettmann has been arranged for the end of next month. Bertha wants to know whether she can count on you to be maid of honor. It's a precautionary request, before approaching you officially. What should I reply? You know that John is one of my best friends; it would be painful for me not to be there for the occasion."

"Well, who's preventing you from going?"

"I beg you, Mabel, don't laugh. Don't play this cruel game with me, after what has happened between us. Many things, even the most flattering for me, should make me reflect, but I don't want to argue with myself; I love you too much."

"Archibald, you know as well as I do that I can't be a 'maid of honor.' As for marrying you, I'm sure that we'd both be making a stupid mistake." She took his hand. "Understand this, Wilson. There are, in life, facts that can't be forgotten. If I were still worthy of being your wife, perhaps I'd accept—but that's still not certain, for Mabel Smith is an eccentric, in the true sense of the word, and I have, above all, a horror of being like everyone else. I can manage a house, like my father's, where I have only to abandon myself to every whim— provided that they're not banal, he's always approved of them—but to go back, especially now, to the social life I led before is beyond my strength and my will-power."

"It's not your reason that's talking now but your fantasy. Make an effort to suppress that need to be exceptional, to play to the gallery, and you'll become what every woman should be: a fiancée, a wife, a mother, following the routine course of your existence."

Mabel burst out laughing. "What, me—the founder of a family, consenting to live like everyone else, parading a fat belly around for months, becoming ugly and jaundiced, having morning-sickness, in order, afterwards, in conformity with the customs of the aristocracy, to confide my child to strangers, only seeing my son or daughter as a elegant doll designed to be admired by friends who attach no more importance to it than to some trinket. Do you remember your childhood, as I remember mine?"

"We couldn't arrive immediately at what we are today."

"Well, what are we today? You consider yourself to be emancipated because your studies are over, and you can play your role in the human comedy in your turn—a ridiculous role, forcing you to interest yourself in all sorts of turpitudes and domestic filth."

"If that profession displeases you I'll take up another."

Mabel stamped her foot angrily. "You're decidedly mad, my dear. What difference does your profession make to me? Whether you were a solicitor, or a scientist like Goldry, or anything whatsoever, wouldn't you, even so, be in contact with the humanity that I find repugnant in every way?"

"In that case," said Archibald, brutally, "You'll have to go back to the apes."

"Perhaps. In any case, you've taken a long time to realize it."

Archibald let himself fall into a chair and hid his face in his hands. Mabel considered him momentarily, and shrugged her shoulders. She was about to leave but, looking up, she saw that her friends, grouped on the other side of the hall, were watching her. She understood that Archibald had, in a sense, only served as their spokesman. Unable to suspect that her secret was known to everyone, she merely judged that it was merely one more attempt to lead her to a marriage they all desired.

She sat down facing the young advocate. "I've hurt you, Wilson, and I'm sorry. You know how wicked I am, don't you? But why pester me incessantly? I'm not asking you, or your friends, for anything except to be treated as a comrade, not to be watched like a precious object that it's necessary to protect from thieves."

Archibald raised his head and looked her in the face. "For me, you're more than a precious object—and I do indeed fear thieves. You seem to be forgetting that you gave yourself to me. You're mine, and I'll punish anyone who dares to steal you from me..."

"That's the tone you're taking? Well, I swear to you that I'll break any shackle. There are needs for sensation in me that you're incapable of satisfying. I've proved that, since it was necessary for you to set the evidence before my eyes. Don't be under the illusion that I gave myself to you. No, I took you, and since you're pressing me to the end, you were the loser in any comparison.

Archibald leapt to his feet, raising his fist. Mabel raised herself up to her full height. "Ah! You are wounded, you men, more than anywhere else, in your male vanity! Why don't you hit me, Archibald?"

Wilson stepped back, lowering his head.

"You have all kinds of false ideas, my poor boy. Now that I've opened your eyes, go and live your American life, and leave me to live mine as I wish."

She left him, and, without affectation, went over to her father and his guests.

"Do you know, gentlemen, that this seems to me to be a veritable ambush. I spotted it the moment your delegate came to kill me. So you're in great haste to get rid of me, my dear Papa?"

"You know that's not true, Mabel—but there's a limit to everything, and this flirting has gone on long enough."

"With Wilson? I don't say…Father, have you any intention of marrying again?"

"Oh! No, certainly not."

"Then let me live with you."

"But this country's dangerous for you/"

"The decision has obviously been made. I'm the ultimately precious object. Have one of the rooms in the Temple lined with steel and lock me in it, as if in a safe."

"Dinner is served, Mademoiselle," said a domestic, from the threshold of the dining-room.

"To the table gentlemen! You keep to keep your strength up to defend your golden fleece!"

With a mutinous gesture, Mabel unfastened her hair and, shaking her head, caused her splendid tresses to flow over her shoulders, covering her like a mantle of living gold. Taking her father's arm, she preceded her guests.

At that moment, To Wang and Eg Merh came in; as usual, they had come to sit down at the masters' table. They exchanged a glance with Gorden.

"He's here," said Eg Merh, rapidly.

"Alone?"

"Yes. My brothers are watching for him."

LXXXV. A Beautiful Tropical Evening

It was one of those splendid nights unique to the tropical zones. The ardent heat of the day was succeeded by a delightful coolness. From the sky, so richly sprinkled with stars that it was nothing but an immense scintillating luminous vault, light descended like diamond dust. The dark green trees took on, at a certain distance, the colorations of a magical effect passing through all the shades of dark blue, almost black velvet, to the most delightful violets. In places, a flamboyance made a bright or dark red stain within the mass, punctuated from time to time by yellow orange or bright pink streaks.

Crouched down in the tall grass, which hid them completely, Sing Mah and Mog Kih were watching with the patience particular to their race; they were waiting. For two hours, they had been certain of Ouha's entry into the Temple enclosure. He had been squatting beneath the palisade, unmoving, for some time. Evidently, he was waiting for a signal before heading for the habitation—unless Mabel was coming to join him.

It had been shortly before dinner-time, when the four Malays were together, watching the part of the palisade to which Mabel had attached the rope. In the midst of the great silence of the starry night, they had heard a slight rustling. The four men had crouched down even lower in the grass. The rope had been drawn taut, and then a mighty hand had gripped the top of the barrier, and Ouha's had had appeared. He remained attentive for a moment, and then, slowly, without making the slightest sound, he had appeared in his entirety, gripped the rope and let himself slide down inside. That had taken scarcely a minute.

Then with infinite precaution, To Wang and Eg Merh, crawling backwards, had withdrawn to the edge of the cloister. There they had been able to stand up, and, going around the immense courtyard, had reached the Temple, arriving in time to warn Silven Gorden and take part in the meal. They excused the absence of their brethren by a visit to the Muni-Wali residence—something that had happened frequently since their return from the land of the apes.

The meal was scarcely animated, except for Mabel. She was in full possession of her mocking and teasing spirit. This time, it was Goldry who had to suffer her sarcasm most of all.

"Tell me, Godfather, was it in the land of the Orangs that you acquired that meditative expression? Are you preparing an imminent lecture for us on the precursors of humankind on the terrestrial globe? I hope your work is making progress and that you can give us a glimpse of it this evening."

"It would go more quickly if you'd help me with it a little," the doctor replied. "You were better placed than I was to observe the habits and customs of the apes."

"Oh, I didn't get into their skin, as you did."

Involuntarily, Goldry thought, mockingly: *Ouha got into yours.* Benevolently, he said: "I'm not sorry to have lived those few months among the anthropoids, and it's certain that no naturalist know more about them than me—except you." He added the last remark maliciously.

"Oh! A stone in my secret garden! But I'm a good sport, and no longer have any regrets."

"Oh, Mabel!" exclaimed Mrs. Simyan. "How can you say such things!"

"Oh, Betty," the American woman replied, imitating the governess's gestures, "wouldn't you be curious to experience those sensations, during a sojourn of a few months among the Orangs?"

"What horror! I'd rather die!"

"Before, perhaps—but afterwards?"

"After what? After what?"

"Brrou!" said Mabel, shaking her head like a dog emerged from the water. "Help, Godfather Abraham! This ingénue is drowning!"

"A dangerous conversation, Daughter," said Harry Smith. "Let's go to bed."

"My word, you're right. I'm joking like this to keep myself awake, for I'm falling asleep."

"Nothing astonishing about that, after this morning's events," said Gorden.

"Then, gentlemen, I'll wish you good night. Until tomorrow!"

Mabel kissed her father and the doctor on the cheek, shook hands with the others, and retired to her room.

LXXXVI. By Moonlight

"It's up to us now!" said Gorden, deliberately taking command. "Sir Harry, I beg you, lock your daughter in her apartment, carefully." He turned toward the Malays. "Return to your companions and cut off the orang's retreat if he escapes us. And above all, don't hold back. We need him dead rather than alive. As for us, let's get good rifles and install ourselves in the gallery in front of Miss Smith's windows. If the whole army of apes arrives, everyone retreat toward the main gate. The horses and carriages are waiting for us there. All right!"

When the four men went into the gallery facing Mabel's bedroom, a faint light indicated that the young woman was still awake. Crouching down behind the thick balustrade, the night-watchmen took up their positions. Through the stone latticework they saw the young woman's window open. A lamp lit in the depths of the apartment illuminated the immense room confusedly. It was one of the defects of Riddle-Temple that all of it rooms had large dimensions scarcely in accord with modern furnishing.

The American woman leaned on the window-sill and imitated the call of a nocturnal bird that hunted fireflies. A muffled growl replied to her. The form of the gallery prevented the watchers from seeing the base of the monument, save for Mabel's windows. Suddenly, without them having heard the slightest noise, the colossal anthropoid appeared.

Going back into the apartment, the young woman had picked up the rope, already attached to the window-ledge, and had thrown the end down to Ouha. In less than ten seconds, the orang had grasped the rope, climbed up and leapt into the room. Mabel drew him in, the lamp clearly illuminating their kiss.

Archibald uttered a cry of rage. He aimed his rifle at the tightly-interlaced couple. An iron hand shoved the weapon down.

"Leave it," said Gorden. "It was necessary for you to see that. I've already seen much more; that's what cured my love for Mabel."

"What shame! What shame!" murmured the father.

As for Abraham, he said nothing, but scratched his head as energetically as his former pupil Ouha.

Wilson, doubtless rendered mad or imbecilic by the spectacle, recited Shakespeare: "'I have night's cloak to hide me from their eyes; and but thou love me, let them find me here. My life were better ended by their hate, than death prorogued wanting of thy love.' Thus thinks, no doubt, the simian Romeo at this moment. But of the two of us, Archibald will add the tragic denouement."

"My daughter, my daughter!" moaned Harry Smith. "My daughter loves an ape, an orangutan!"

"Loves? That remains to be determined. We're more likely in the presence of a special physiological phenomenon. It's impossible to love such a monster."

"What are we going to do?" Gorden demanded. "Are we going to lie in ambush for the ape or leave those grotesque lovers to their erotic capers?"

The four men looked at one another, indecisively.

"Let them live!" exclaimed Wilson, suddenly. "For myself, I can't survive such a spectacle. May my sin have its remorse and punishment!"

Before his friends had time to stop him, he ran along the terrace and, leaping over the stone rail, plunged on to the pavement of the courtyard, directly under Mabel's windows. A triple exclamation of horror escaped the throats of the witnesses to that tragic crisis of self-respect. Wilson dead! The poor idealist!

The three men raised their eyes. Ouha and Mabel together at the window, were looking alternately down at the broken body of the young American and across at the horrified faces of Harry Smith and his friends. The orang was growling at the three men with increasing fury, his eyes blazing—but a gap of more than ten meters prevented him from attacking them.

Mabel saw the rifle barrels gleaming, and understood the danger. "Go! Save yourself!" she cried, gesturing toward the forest.

The orang understood—but, seizing Mabel with one arm, he took hold of the rope with three powerful hands and let himself slide down.

"Fire!" cried Harry Smith. "Fire! Better that my daughter die then…!" Without finishing his sentence he discharged his weapon at the entwined couple.

There was a heart-rending cry from Mabel, struck by the bullet: "Father!"

The wild beast, seeing the blood of his wife flowing, turned toward the colonnade threateningly. Two shots, better aimed this time, hit him in the breast and shoulder.

Ouha understood that, thus visible, he was powerless. He beat a retreat, still hugging Mabel to his breast, and, hurling himself into the shadow of the building, he headed for the palisade. The three Europeans also moved back, in order to go through the apartments of the courtyard and the gardens. That gave the beast a ten-second start. He was no more than twenty meters from the enclosure when five menacing shadows stood up in front of him, rifles at the ready, and bowed to him.

Ouha sensed that he was doomed; he embraced Mabel recklessly, and stood up to his full height, uttering his war-cry—and thirty roaring voices repeated the formidable cry:

"Ouha! Ouha! Ouha!"

The Malays, taken by surprise, turned round. Grimacing heads and gripping hands appeared at the top of the palisade. One monster hoisted himself over and let himself fall inside. It was almost instantaneous; in no time at all thirty Orangs surrounded Ouha, repeating in chorus the terrible cry:

"Ouha! Ouha! Ouha!"

The king of the apes pointed at the five petrified Malays. The orangs launched themselves forward.

To Wang was the first to recover his self-possession. "Retreat!" he ordered. They discharged their weapons as they turned round, then fell back toward the Temple. They collided with two running Europeans. Harry Smith had fainted after the unfortunate rifle-shot that had hit his daughter.

"The army of apes is behind him!" Gorden shouted.

They all took flight, pursued by a hail of stones and tree-branches. The doctor tottered, his arm broken. Two of the Malays fell. Gorden grabbed hold of the doctor and dragged him away.

They reached the galleries. Swiftly, the Englishman closed the gate. They were safe.

"To the horses!" he shouted. "Everybody out!"

There was a mad stampede. The domestics, Betty and everyone else ran for the exit, and were soon all galloping toward White House.

Riddle-Temple was in the power of Ouha and the anthropoids.

LXXXVII. Of What Young Women Dream

Harry Smith was roused from unconsciousness by an infernal racket. The orangutans, in pursuit of the fugitives, were uttering ferocious howls and shaking the gates of the covered gallery. The American billionaire, dazed at first, did not take long to recall the recent events and the maladroit gunshot he had fired at Mabel and her abductor. His daughter's cry was still ringing in his ears, and the thought that had felled him also came back to his memory: *I've killed my daughter!*

Looking over the balustrade, he saw, vaguely, in the shadow of the house, a black mass and a motionless white form: Ouha and Mabel. Without thinking about the danger he was running, he went into the apartments of the Temple. First he took a medical kit from Goldry's room; then, going to Mabel's room, he stepped over the windowsill and let himself slide down the rope. He found himself in the presence of Archibald's body. A rapid examination told him that there was nothing more to be done for him. The poor sentimental boy had fallen head first; his skull was smashed.

Then he ran to his daughter. A dull growl from Ouha made him recoil at first, but his daughter—his daughter!—was lying there, inanimate. Without paying any heed to the peril, he marched toward them.

Ouha undoubtedly understood that it was help that was arriving; he ceased growing and let matters take their course.

The American carried Mabel into the illuminated part of the garden. The ape followed, dragging himself along, leaving a trail of blood behind him. The bullet had struck the young woman in the shoulder above the clavicle and had lodged beneath the left scapula. He could feel it with his finger. With the aid of a scalpel, he extracted it, and then swabbed the wound with alcohol. He applied a tampon of cotton-wool to the two wounds and bandaged the injury as best he could. The patient, relieved, eventually sighed and opened her eyes. The first thing her gaze encountered was her father.

"Father! I remember…a gunshot…yours! I'm hurt."

She sat up, examined herself, and said: "It's not serious"—but a hoarse sigh caused her to turn round. At a glance she saw that the great ape was seriously wounded.

"Father," she said, "help him!"

"Are you mad? Care for the ape that tried to carry you off!"

"He saved my life, and I love him. Listen, father! His companions—his subjects—are coming back. If you don't help me tend to him, so far as they're concerned, you're the enemy. They'll kill you. If, on the other hand, they see you with me, caring for their master, they'll spare you."

That argument convinced Smith. He went to Ouha and examined him. In addition to the wound in the shoulder, which had shattered it, the breast had been pierced right through—perhaps fortunately, for, if no essential organ had been hit, it would not be fatal. The orang had lost an enormous amount of blood, though; he was very weak. Allowing himself be handled, like a little child, he was moaning softly, gazing at Mabel with an expression of truly touching tenderness.

Harry Smith dressed the wounds, aided by his daughter, whose right arm was fortunately sound. The orangs had returned a few moments ago, but they kept their distance, attentively watching all the movements made by Mabel and her father.

When they had finished, the American turned to his daughter. "Shall we go inside?" he said.

"It's unlikely that they'll permit us to do that. Our situation demands reflection. Let me collect my thoughts."

"There's no need for much reflection. It's not possible to stay with these apes. Let's find a means of getting rid of them. It seems to me that the best thing is to go back inside, barricade ourselves in the servants' quarters, which seems to me to be best-placed to withstand a siege, and wait for help."

"And afterwards, we resume life as before?" said Mabel. "No, I've had enough—too-much—of that. When you came to Borneo to cure your neurasthenia, I was worse afflicted than you were. The life we were leading had become intolerable. You see, Father, beings like us are exceptional individuals—or, rather, life has made us such."

She stopped a gesture by her father. "Have you ever thought about what might be going on in my head? As a child, I was deprived of the care of a mother: your wife, by virtue of her worldly carelessness, was only interested me as an object of luxury, to keep need and well-decorated, for the amusement of the high society frequenting your house.

"I'll render you this justice: that at certain times, always too short for me, you came to embrace me and play with me—which my mother never did. Believe me, the increase of intelligence in small children is a curious process. Our mentality is formed very slowly, and when it isn't guided by an absolutely devoted superior intelligence, it turns inwards and soon makes judgments that are perhaps erroneous but which, in the mind of a child, take on an enormous importance.

"Thus, I can say that, since my earliest youth, I was left to my own devices and judged my entourage, perhaps with more severity than I should have done. Everything around me yielded to my slightest caprices, my mother by indifference and you because you thought that your immense fortune put you and your kin above the rest of humankind.

"What might have made someone else happy didn't have that effect on me. I exercised a despotic authority over everything—not that I was wicked, but everyone, thinking that giving me everything might bring them a large profit, encouraged my most eccentric caprices, and I had some bizarre ones.

"Later, as a young woman, after my mother's death, when I took the worldly direction of our house, the immoderate adulation and base platitudes of my over-interested admirers, only succeeded in filling my heart with nausea. Without your knowledge, I had strange, unhealthy fantasies, realized thanks to the complicity of domestics ready to satisfy all the turpitudes of the mind of an amoral virgin, for money. In brief, Father, I was, unknown to you, the best-informed of all the joyful virgins in New Jersey.

"That sensual excitation, in any case, had no other results for me but a sort of exaltation that relieved itself in all kinds of mockery and teasing of the masculine society that surrounded me. I was too well aware of the appetites of young men coveting the only daughter of a billionaire. Yes, I observed everyone around me, male and female, and perceived that the same instincts, the same needs, enslaved humankind. I once saw you, Father, on returning from your club, throwing down a maid in the antechamber, who submitted, not daring to resist the billionaire master. I imagine that you were generous to the poor child, but that doesn't alter the fact and doesn't destroy the impression it made on me.

"In brief, as neurasthenic as you, I had as much need as you did of solitude and distractions other than those of sickening worldly life. The hazard of an adventure has made me the mate of an orangutan. Well, Father, I find a bitter satisfaction in feeling myself estranged from that so-called civilization for which, before we came to this island, I had conceived a disgust. There are, to be sure, among these primitives, the same sexual needs, *less the hypocrisy*. Moreover, my lover seems to be progressing beyond his companions; under my influence, his intelligence has developed more rapidly. He was, for me, both an extraordinary male and a prodigious child.

"Then again, the free life, has gradually dissipated the unhealthy state of my mind, I've become interested in a thousand aspects of the evolutions of matter and force. I've felt a new philosophy born within me, devoid of egotism as of constraint. When you came with your friends to rescue you, I confess that I was not yet detached from my old habits, and I allowed myself to go. Also, the adventure seduced me: the unexpected marvels of that immense cavern, a cathedral of gold and precious stones; the pleasure, in spite of everything, of seeing old companions again; the thousand dangers of the return journey—all that dazed me enough to make me forget, temporarily, my ignoble and marvelous spouse, and my simian subjects...

"Since then, though, having returned to Riddle-Temple and being obliged to resume the old life, I've experienced once again all the emptiness of our civilization. I tried to react, though; I made heroic efforts; I tried, I don't say to love, but to esteem sufficiently the man you had designated as a fiancé for me. To be sure, Archibald was a good fellow, but he stunned me with banalities. Finally, as a last effort toward the norm, I gave myself to him, in order to see. Another disappointment!

"What, then, can I do? Return to the land of the apes? I've considered it seriously, and only the impossibility was holding me back when we went out yesterday. Playing tag, I lunged into the virgin forest and found myself face to face with a tiger. I was doomed. Ouha arrived, and killed it. Saved from the tiger and from progress, I made a rendezvous with Ouha so that he could spend the night with me. I had the romantic fantasy of making him play the role of Romeo—except that, at daybreak, I would go with him. You know the rest, Father."

Harry Smith had listened to that long confession—which was, for him, a kind of indictment—with his head bowed.

"I share your ideas to some extent," he said. "But where does that leave us? Although you can't leave your hairy lover, I'm not sufficiently misanthropic to live with the apes. In any case, they probably wouldn't tolerate me. And what will become of you if your Ouha dies of his wounds? Will you give him a successor of the same species? Whichever way we turn, it's an impasse. Devil take Abraham, who made us come here. Perhaps I should have committed suicide—then I wouldn't have these troubles today."

"There's still time," said Mabel.

The American started. "What! You think I should?"

"You're looking for a way out. That's one, for you as for me. Listen, Father—life wearies you, and me too. At the idea of resuming the old life, my heart revolts. One can find one

Wilson, but not two. As for the simian life, I don't think that's possible either. Look at Ouha—he's dying."

Indeed, during that long conversation, the orang had increasingly let himself go. His head was hanging down on his breast; his breathing was labored; bloody foam was oozing from his mouth.

Mabel contemplated him; she did not feel love for the monster, but an immense pity. *It's for me*, she thought, *for me, the egotist, the sensualist, that he's going to die, taking with him my last reason to live. I feel terrible weary. Why persist? The days will follow one another now, all alike.*

Suddenly, raising her head, her eyes shining, and a sardonic rictus creasing her lips, she said: "Let's get out of this stupid maze in an original fashion! Would you like that?"

LXXXVIII. *The Arrival of the Liberators*

Meanwhile, the doctor, Gorden and his companions were not idle. Scarcely had they arrived at White House than they send urgent appeals for help in every direction. The colonists, understanding the danger that everyone in the vicinity was running with the anthropoids so close, gathered their servants, armed them, and came in a crowd to respond to the alarm call, to put themselves at the disposal of the Englishman. The latter was recognized by everyone as the most capable of leading the little army to Riddle-Temple, to destroy the invaders and annihilate them forever.

By the end of the day, Gorden had fifty men, most of whom were used to combating the wild beasts of the great forest. Anxious about Smith, who had been forgotten in the confusion of the departure, he decided to set forth immediately.

Gorden's plan was quite simple: to occupy the Temple and his galleries, expelling the orangutans if they had installed themselves there, and shoot them all through the windows of the galleries, if they had the imprudence to remain in the great courtyard or the garden, in the open.

All the necessary horses were gathered, and at daybreak they were within sight of Riddle-Temple. Everyone dismounted, and, leaving the horse under the guard of a few men, the troop climbed the monumental stairway, making as little noise as possible. Having arrived at the top, they scattered into the apartments. The orders were to fall back and call out as soon as an orang was sighted.

The apartments were empty, and had been strangely pillaged. The floor was littered with all kinds of objects, and the wooden furniture had vanished. They all met up in the hall, without having seen a single ape.

"Either they've already gone, or they're in the gardens. Let's advance prudently through the galleries."

A bestial clamor rose up:

"Ouha! Ouha! Ouha!"

"They're in the gardens! Forward, my friends. We'll shoot them from the galleries..."

LXXXIX. The Apotheosis of Fire

They launched themselves under the arcades. A cry of astonishment and amazement escaped them.

In the middle of the immense courtyard was an enormous pyre, composed of all the furniture of the Temple, to which had been added all the wood from the stores. The whole was crowned by the immense table from the hall, on which a heap of cushions, carpets and curtains formed a kind of magnificent throne. On that heap of velvet and silken fabrics, Ouha, supported by Mabel, was dying, while the billionaire was emptying cans of gasoline, oil and alcohol—all the accelerants he could find—over the pile of furniture and wood.

"They're mad!" cried Goldry. "Smith, Smith, stop, you fool! What are you doing?"

The misanthropic billionaire turned round, stared at his friend, and then, pointing at the immense pyre, said: "This is what I should have done in the beginning; my life no longer interests me. Goodbye, Abraham! I give you Riddle-Temple— make better use of it than I did."

He struck a few matches, and threw them on the pyre. The flames sprang up immediately. Then, hurling himself forwards, he climbed the heap, and disappeared into the flame and smoke.

A moment later, they saw him emerge on to the platform, next to Mabel and the anthropoid. Supported from both sides by Mabel and her father, Ouha stood up to his full height.

What was passing through the mind of the great ape? Was he conscious of the grandeur of that suicide of civilization, or was it only the last convulsion of his agony?

It seemed to him that his brain, enlarged under the influence of death, suddenly embraced an immense horizon. Where does animality begin and end?

At the supreme moment there is, for some individuals, an instant when a gleam of great mystery comes to illuminate the profound darkness. At that moment, the entire life of a man sometimes passes through his thoughts with the velocity of a dream, a dying appeal to his consciousness: all the mistakes, the sins and the crimes accomplished in the brief evolution that is a life. But those words, which only have meaning with regard to human thought, can have none with respect to an animal; for him, there are only sensations without judgment, or nearly so.

In that last instant, at the tragic denouement of his love, Ouha was very close to humanity, for, although he could not translate his thought into words, a flood of vague imaginations, fetuses of ideas, desires and regrets filled his brain.

He had, then, the intuition of an apotheosis, in which his brutality was more artificial than real; he suspected that his mentality was scarcely inferior, leaving aside the education he had received, to that of the wife that he had adored as a divinity, and who had descended to his level.

For that idol, he was about to die—and his vague, misted gaze embraced, even so, the last ray of sunlight that he was to see. In the east, the sky was tinted with a delicate mauve, as tender as a flower or a precious stone. The colossal mass of the Temple was profiled there, with the thousand details of its monstrous sculptures, its tiara- and miter-embellished gods with innumerable arms, bearers of lotus-blossoms and emblems, its monsters, its dragons, its serpents, its elephants, its horses and its tigers, bizarrely contorted amid the dancing-girls and the goddesses. All that architecture covered sections of wall three hundred feet long, whose height was lost in the azure, with its pillars, its columns and capitals, cut out like lace. The Temple, still half-veiled by the shadows of the night, was hollowed out here and there by violently blue shadows, although the summits and reliefs were already gilded with a prodigiously ardent red.

Then, on the opposite side, there was the forest: the forest whose dense foliage was nuanced with all imaginable shades, from the dazzling green of emerald to the most varied decompositions of yellow and blue. All those colors merged with the brighter hues of the lianas and flowers, which, melted by distance, formed an infinite and vague continuum. The virgin forest was shining, awakening in the distance—his domain! The forest in which his four hands found purchase and support on all sides, where he could roam, half-human and half-avian. The forest, his shelter, his refuge, his horn of plenty, his life. The forest, and his superb excursions through the branches, the lianas, where he found both his nourishment and his repose, hammocks of flowers and leaves in which he could lull his idleness, having all the fruits, berries and coconuts within arm's reach: magnificent comfort for the terrible hairy athletes, kings of that wilderness of verdure, that exuberant vegetation.

Everything, at present, acquired an aspect of infinite calm and tenderness. The trees of his forests appeared to him in images different from before, in silhouettes that they had never known, with colors that faded into one another, becoming nothing but a sequence of fantastic reflections. The mountains took on the contours and graces of recumbent women. The torrents still ran impetuously, but fluidly, as if immaterial. All of it became as transparent and limpid as the sky overlooking it.

But the magnificent orangutan, the king of the apes, redirected his gaze at Mabel, the strange and marvelous beauty who had allowed herself to be vanquished by his formidable ugliness.

Then, an immense expansion overwhelmed his being, in spite of his weakness. He stood up to his full height, and, against the ruddy background of the gigantic pyre, he displayed his silhouette, a savage and mighty giant—and, seizing his wife, he lifted her up above him, offering her to the rising sun, presenting her to the Master of the Universe, like a tribute of his expiring strength to the Eternal Torch.

And in order to express these confused ideas in his head—as an emerald scarcely disengaged from its matrix might evoke the verdant Ocean with its innumerable waves—the monster uttered, for the last time, his resounding cry:

"Ouha! Ouha! Ouha!"

Gently, he set Mabel down beside him, and, crossing his hairy arms, sat down again upon the pyre. Like a supreme caress of the Father of Life, the first rays of the of the sun came, in the midst of the swirling flames of the blaze, to halo the great anthropoid's tragic, humanized mask with a surge of light. A thick cloud of smoke, driven by the morning breeze, massed behind him, making a somber screen on which the gigantic flaming heap stood out like a pedestal of honor and victory. A hero of simian strength in advance of humankind, he died triumphantly, thanks to the eternal lust that propagates life.

He died, suppressing on that pyre the inequality of animals and humans, of woman and ape, demonstrating by his adventure—without knowing it—the inanity of the Himalayas of fortune and civilization, both impotent before reciprocal desire.

And he repeated his war-cry, more hoarsely each time:

"Ouha! ...Ouha! ......Ouha!"

Formidable voices in chorus, echoed that wild cry, causing the guttural anthropoid howl to resound. And the orangs, habituated by the sight of their chief no longer to fear fire, began an infernal dance around the blaze.

Ouha's fading pupils, contemplating the infinite nourishing forest, directed what one might have taken for a reproachful glance toward the treetops, to the mysterious Sylvan, Pan, the unknown god that had betrayed him—and he cried, for the last time, amid the clamors of the other apes, in a resonant and painful exhalation:

"Ouha! Ouha! Ouha!"

That was the simian monarch's final effort. He sank, slowly at first, into Mabel's arms, and then collapsed, and did not move again. The young woman had followed him in his fall; and suddenly, there was a greater collapse, and a sheaf of flame and sparks shot up. Then there was the crackle of fireworks, amid the smoke, blazing particles, and the sizzling of burning flesh—and in the red swirls, larger and higher, the rumble of the conflagration became louder.

The apes, frightened, took flight, pursued by rifle fire.

The tale of Beauty and the Beast had ended.

SF & FANTASY

Henri Allorge. *The Great Cataclysm*
Guy d'Armen. *Doc Ardan: The City of Gold and Lepers*
G.-J. Arnaud. *The Ice Company*
Charles Asselineau. *The Double Life*
Cyprien Bérard. *The Vampire Lord Ruthwen*
Aloysius Bertrand. *Gaspard de la Nuit*
Richard Bessière. *The Gardens of the Apocalypse*
Albert Bleunard. *Ever Smaller*
Félix Bodin. *The Novel of the Future*
Alphonse Brown. *City of Glass*
André Caroff. *The Terror of Madame Atomos; Miss Atomos; The Return of Madame Atomos; The Mistake of Madame Atomos; The Monsters of Madame Atomos*
Félicien Champsaur. *The Human Arrow; Ouha*
Didier de Chousy. *Ignis*
Captain Danrit. *Undersea Odyssey*
C. I. Defontenay. *Star (Psi Cassiopeia)*
Charles Derennes. *The People of the Pole*
Georges Dodds (anthologist). *The Missing Link*
Harry Dickson. *The Heir of Dracula*
Jules Dornay. *Lord Ruthven Begins*
Alfred Driou. *The Adventures of a Parisian Aeronaut*
Sâr Dubnotal *vs. Jack the Ripper*
Alexandre Dumas. *The Return of Lord Ruthven*
Renée Dunan. *Baal*
J.-C. Dunyach. *The Night Orchid; The Thieves of Silence*
Henri Duvernois. *The Man Who Found Himself*
Achille Eyraud. *Voyage to Venus*
Henri Falk. *The Age of Lead*
Paul Féval. *Anne of the Isles; Knightshade; Revenants; Vampire City; The Vampire Countess; The Wandering Jew's Daughter*
Paul Féval, *fils. Felifax, the Tiger-Man*
Charles de Fieux. *Lamékis*
Arnould Galopin. *Doctor Omega; Doctor Omega & The Shadowmen*
G.L. Gick. *Harry Dickson and the Werewolf of Rutherford Grange*
Edmond Haraucourt. *Illusions of Immortality*
Nathalie Henneberg. *The Green Gods*
V. Hugo, P. Foucher & P. Meurice. *The Hunchback of Notre-Dame*
Michel Jeury. *Chronolysis*

Gustave Kahn. *The Tale of Gold and Silence*
Gérard Klein. *The Mote in Time's Eye*
Jean de La Hire. *Enter the Nyctalope; The Nyctalope on Mars; The Nyctalope vs. Lucifer; The Nyctalope Steps In; Night of the Nyctalope*
Etienne-Léon de Lamothe-Langon. *The Virgin Vampire*
André Laurie. *Spiridon*
Gabriel de Lautrec. *The Vengeance of the Oval Portrait*
Alain le Drimeur. *The Future City*
Georges Le Faure & Henri de Graffigny. *The Extraordinary Adventures of a Russian Scientist Across the Solar System* (2 vols.)
Gustave Le Rouge. *The Vampires of Mars The Dominion of the World* (w/Gustave Guitton) (4 vols.)
Jules Lermina. *Mysteryville; Panic in Paris; To-Ho and the Gold Destroyers; The Secret of Zippelius*
Jean-Marc & Randy Lofficier. *Edgar Allan Poe on Mars; The Katrina Protocol; Pacifica; Robonocchio; Tales of the Shadowmen 1-8*
Xavier Mauméjean. *The League of Heroes*
Joseph Méry. *The Tower of Destiny*
Hippolyte Mettais. *The Year 5865*
José Moselli. *Illa's End*
John-Antoine Nau. *Enemy Force*
Marie Nizet. *Captain Vampire*
C. Nodier, A. Beraud & Toussaint-Merle. *Frankenstein*
Henri de Parville. *An Inhabitant of the Planet Mars*
Gaston de Pawlowski. *Journey to the Land of the 4th Dimension*
Georges Pellerin. *The World in 2000 Years*
Pierre Pelot. *The Child Who Walked on the Sky*
J. Polidori, C. Nodier, E. Scribe. *Lord Ruthven the Vampire*
P.-A. Ponson du Terrail. *The Vampire and the Devil's Son*
Henri de Régnier. *A Surfeit of Mirrors*
Maurice Renard. *The Blue Peril; Doctor Lerne; The Doctored Man; A Man Among the Microbes; The Master of Light*
Jean Richepin. *The Wing*
Albert Robida. *The Adventures of Saturnin Farandoul; The Clock of the Centuries; Chalet in the Sky*
J.-H. Rosny Aîné. *Helgvor of the Blue River; The Givreuse Enigma; The Mysterious Force; The Navigators of Space; Vamireh; The World of the Variants; The Young Vampire*
Marcel Rouff. *Journey to the Inverted World*
Han Ryner. *The Superhumans*

Brian Stableford. *The New Faust at the Tragicomique;The Empire of the Necromancers (The Shadow of Frankenstein; Frankenstein and the Vampire Countess; Frankenstein in London); Sherlock Holmes & The Vampires of Eternity; The Stones of Camelot; The Wayward Muse.* (anthologist) *The Germans on Venus; News from the Moon; The Supreme Progress; The World Above the World; Nemoville; Investigations of the Future*
Jacques Spitz. *The Eye of Purgatory*
Kurt Steiner. *Ortog*
Eugène Thébault. *Radio-Terror*
C.-F. Tiphaigne de La Roche. *Amilec*
Théo Varlet. *The Xenobiotic Invasion; Timeslip Troopers* (w/André Blandin); *The Martian Epic* (w/Octave Joncquel)
Paul Vibert. *The Mysterious Fluid*
Villiers de l'Isle-Adam. *The Scaffold; The Vampire Soul*
Philippe Ward. *Artahe*
Philippe Ward & Sylvie Miller. *The Song of Montségur*

MYSTERIES & THRILLERS

M. Allain & P. Souvestre. *The Daughter of Fantômas*
A. Anicet-Bourgeois, Lucien Dabril. *Rocambole*
A. Bernède. *Belphegor; Judex* (w/Louis Feuillade)
A. Bisson & G. Livet. *Nick Carter vs. Fantômas*
V. Darlay & H. de Gorsse. *Lupin vs. Holmes: The Stage Play*
Paul Féval. *Gentlemen of the Night; John Devil; The Black Coats ('Salem Street; The Invisible Weapon; The Parisian Jungle; The Companions of the Treasure; Heart of Steel; The Cadet Gang; The Sword-Swallower)*
Emile Gaboriau. *Monsieur Lecoq*
Steve Leadley. *Sherlock Holmes: The Circle of Blood*
Maurice Leblanc. *Arsène Lupin vs. Countess Cagliostro; Lupin vs. Holmes (The Blonde Phantom; The Hollow Needle); The Many Faces of Arsène Lupin*
Gaston Leroux. *Chéri-Bibi; The Phantom of the Opera; Rouletabille & the Mystery of the Yellow Room*
Richard Marsh. *The Complete Adventures of Judith Lee*
William Patrick Maynard. *The Terror of Fu Manchu; The Destiny of Fu Manchu*
Frank J. Morlock. *Sherlock Holmes: The Grand Horizontals; Sherlock Holmes vs Jack the Ripper*

Antonin Reschal. *The Adventures of Miss Boston*
P. de Wattyne & Y. Walter. *Sherlock Holmes vs. Fantômas*
David White. *Fantômas in America*

SCREENPLAYS

Mike Baron. *The Iron Triangle*
Emma Bull & Will Shetterly. *Nightspeeder; War for the Oaks*
Gerry Conway & Roy Thomas. *Doc Dynamo*
Steve Englehart. *Majorca*
James Hudnall. *The Devastator*
Jean-Marc & Randy Lofficier. *Royal Flush*
J.-M. & R. Lofficier & Marc Agapit. *Despair*
J.-M. & R. Lofficier & Joël Houssin. *City*
Andrew Paquette. *Peripheral Vision*
R. Thomas, J. Hendler & L. Sprague de Camp. *Rivers of Time*

NON-FICTION

Stephen R. Bissette. *Blur 1-5. Green Mountain Cinema 1; Teen Angels*
Win Scott Eckert. *Crossovers* (2 vols.)
Jean-Marc & Randy Lofficier. *Shadowmen* (2 vols.)
Randy Lofficier. *Over Here*

HEXAGON COMICS

Franco Frescura & Luciano Bernasconi. *Wampus*
Franco Frescura & Giorgio Trevisan. *CLASH*
L. Bernasconi, J.-M. Lofficier & Juan Roncagliolo Berger. *Phenix*
Claude Legrand, J.-M. Lofficier & L. Bernasconi. *Kabur*
Franco Oneta. *Zembla*
L. Buffolente, Lofficier & J.-J. Dzialowski. *Strangers: Homicron*
Danilo Grossi. *Strangers: Jaydee*
Claude Legrand & Luciano Bernasconi. *Strangers: Starlock*

ART BOOKS

Jean-Pierre Normand. *Science Fiction Illustrations*
Raven Okeefe. *Raven's L'il Critters*
Randy Lofficier & Raven OKeefe. *If Your Possum Go Daylight...*
Daniele Serra. *Illusions*